"*Mesdames et Messieurs*
Ladies and G[...]
said the an[...]
"prepare to b[...]
None of what you are about
to see is an illusion!"

"Le Cafe Noir," he continued, "is now proud to present one of the world's most gifted thespian adepts, the one, the only, the incomparable . . . Jacques Pascal!"

There was a dramatic stab of organ music, a flash of lightning, and a crash of thunder as a jagged bolt shot down from the ceiling and struck one of the graves, sending up a shower of earth and rock. Stiffly, like a vampire rising from the grave, Jacques Pascal rose straight up from a lying position, wrapped in a flowing black cape, hands crossed against his chest. The public applauded.

Wyrdrune grimaced. "Cheap theatrics," he said. "Nothing a first-year student couldn't do."

"Never mind," Modred said, leaning forward intently. "Don't you *feel* it?"

Even as he spoke, Wyrdrune became aware of a sudden, burning sensation in his forehead. Kira gasped and clutched her hand. She opened her palm. Her sapphire runestone was glowing brightly.

"They're here!" she said.

"It's him," said Wyrdrune. "Pascal! He's the Dark One!"

ALSO BY
SIMON HAWKE

The Wizard of 4th Street
The Wizard of Whitechapel
The Wizard of Sunset Strip

Published by
POPULAR LIBRARY

THE WIZARD OF RUE MORGUE

SIMON HAWKE

POPULAR LIBRARY

An Imprint of Warner Books, Inc.

A Warner Communications Company

POPULAR LIBRARY EDITION

Copyright © 1990 by Simon Hawke
All rights reserved.

Popular Library®, the fanciful P design, and Questar® are
registered trademarks of Warner Books, Inc.

Cover design by Don Puckey
Cover illustration by Dave Mattingly

Popular Library books are published by
Warner Books, Inc.
666 Fifth Avenue
New York, N.Y. 10103

 A Warner Communications Company

Printed in the United States of America

First Printing: September 1990

10 9 8 7 6 5 4 3 2 1

For Marge Sjoden

Prologue

By day, Jacques Pascal scuttled through the darkness of the Paris sewers with nothing but rats and water bugs for company. He paddled through the tunnels in an old boat left over from the days when guides had taken tourists on short excursions beneath the city streets. The complex network of sewer tunnels was like an underground city beneath the streets of Paris. That they had once been a tourist attraction was something of a mystery. They were only sewers, after all, and there was not that much to see, but the public curiosity about the Paris sewers began centuries ago with the publication of Victor Hugo's *Les Miserables*. The image of Hugo's romantic fugitive, Jean Valjean, sloshing through the slimy tunnels had captured the imagination of the public and after that, the sewers beneath the Paris streets became the setting for all sorts of strange and nefarious goings-on, at least in fiction.

In the days prior to the Collapse, guides had taken tourists on short fifteen-minute boat rides through the principal tunnels, beginning on the Left Bank at Pont de l'Alma, explaining to the visitors how the sewage was chemically treated for use as fertilizer in the fields outside the city. They had pointed out the telephone lines and the old system of pneumatic tubes once used for sending letters across Paris. They had shown tourists how the streets above were clearly labeled in the tunnels and how the branch pipes were all numbered, corresponding to the buildings above. They had often pointed out the ones leading to some of the more famous establishments of Paris. Now, no one came down to the sewers anymore. At least, no one in their right mind.

The Paris sewers had long since ceased being a tourist attraction. Sewage was no longer treated chemically. At the outlet points, it passed through thaumaturgic treatment plants, where it was magically processed. But under the streets, the dark and musty sewers stank and no one remembered who Jean Valjean was anymore. No one came down to see where he had fled from the relentless policeman who pursued him. Only the desperate and the crazed ever ventured down into the sewers now and Jacques Pascal was both.

By night, he crept through the back alleyways and side streets of Montmartre, searching through the garbage, sustaining himself on scraps thrown out from restaurants and nightclubs, dressing himself in rags. He wore battered, lace-up army boots; threadbare woolen pants and sweater; a moth-eaten coat he had fished out of a trash bin and regardless of the weather, he kept his face swaddled in a frayed and dirty muffler, his long gray hair sticking out from beneath a shapeless old fedora. He looked like an old, decrepit derelict, which was exactly what he was.

Once, many years ago, Jacques Pascal had been a featured performer in the nightclubs whose garbage he now picked through in the dead of night. He had been a handsome young man, tall, muscular and graceful, and he had set many a chorus girl's heart to fluttering with his acrobatic feats and carnival stunts. But after trained adepts had started entering the entertainment business, Jacques found himself unable to compete. His acrobatics, his fire-eating stunts, his feats of strength and miraculous escapes seemed trivial compared to the illusions that adepts could conjure up. No one cared about the skill involved and no one was impressed that he could do those things without the aid of magic. What could be done *with* the aid of magic was a great deal more spectacular. Jacques Pascal's career was ruined.

Having no other skills, he was reduced to working menial jobs, performing unskilled labor and competing in an already overburdened job market with much younger men and women. He had never saved up any money, so he fell farther and farther behind, eventually losing his apartment and most of his possessions. He wound up on the street, one of the city's homeless, and with no regular address, he was unable to find work. His pride had succumbed to mortal wounds and his spirit had been bludgeoned to the ground. Somewhere deep inside, the essential part of Jacques Pascal expired. He became one of the walking dead. He did not survive so much as he merely managed to exist.

The sewers were his home now, his place of sanctuary. He had found little nooks and crannies here and there where he could curl up and sleep and if occasionally he did encounter another lost soul like himself down in the tunnels, they usually fled from him, being just as frightened as he was. His reason had not fled entirely, it had simply become thoroughly numbed. He was filthy, scrofulous, tubercular and the moisture of the sewers had seeped into his arthritic, eighty-year-old bones. He was old and sick and his mind had long since retreated from the horrible reality that his existence had become. Life had been reduced to a hopeless and deadening routine, scraping through the city's garbage by night, like an emaciated alley cat, and shambling through the sewer tunnels by day, ceaselessly exploring his underground domain. And nothing ever happened to change this soul-deadening routine until the day he discovered the new tunnel.

It was not, actually, a new tunnel at all, but an extremely old one that had been exposed when one of the old sewer walls collapsed. Taking one of the crude torches he used to light his way along the dark tunnels, he climbed through into the passageway that had been exposed. It was very narrow, with just enough room for him to pass if he stooped slightly, which had long since become his normal posture. Like a hunchback, he shuffled down the musty corridor until it opened out into a larger chamber, with several other tunnels branching off from it. Strewn all around this chamber were ancient bones, dark brown with age, some simply scattered, others stacked in piles, some laid out in bizarre arrangements.

He had found an old tunnel that led into the ancient Catacombs, originally formed out of Roman quarries dating back to ancient times. Over the years, the Catacombs had been expanded, scooped out to provide building materials for the city and a place to dump the bones of millions of dead bodies transported from overcrowded cemeteries and graveyards such as Les Innocents, which had given way to urban development. During the Reign of Terror, the bodies of those claimed by the guillotine were brought down into the Catacombs by cartloads, which saved the time and expense of proper burial. Like the sewers, the corridors of the Catacombs honeycombed the ground beneath the city. No one alive had ever explored them fully. They were like a vast underground maze, a dark and foreboding final resting place for millions of dead souls. It would be easy to become lost in them forever.

Jacques Pascal did not think about any of those things as he shuffled through the subterranean corridors, the light from his torch throwing garish shadows on the rock walls and mounds of ancient bones. He did not think to mark his way, nor did it occur to him that he might never find his way back to the more familiar sewer tunnels once again. Something drew him onward through the dark and ancient passageways. It was like walking through the halls of Hades, exploring the city of the dead. After he had walked for what seemed like hours, he perceived a dim light at the end of a long corridor ahead of him. He quickened his step, moving toward it like a moth attracted to a flame.

He came out into a large, rectangular chamber hollowed out from solid rock. Here, there were niches carved into the walls, some containing piled-up skulls, others holding entire skeletons propped up like grisly statues. The light came from burning braziers placed around the perimeter of the chamber. Spiderwebs covered the ancient skeletons like transparent shrouds and rats nosed among the heaped-up bones. The air was thick with a peculiar smell, a cloying, pungent odor that came from the burning braziers, filling the chamber with a smoky mist.

"Come in, Jacques," said a deep, mellifluent voice. "We have been waiting for you."

He spun around with a startled gasp.

At the far end of the chamber, standing on a rock ledge slightly raised above the floor, were three black-robed, hooded figures that had not been there a moment earlier. It was as if they had simply appeared suddenly out of nowhere. The torch fell from his hand and he started to back away, but one of the hooded figures raised an arm and Jacques found that he could not take another step.

"Come closer, Jacques," the hooded figure said, beckoning. "Don't be afraid."

The old man was terrified, but he slowly started moving toward the hooded figures. He couldn't help himself. His heart hammered within his chest like a wild thing trying to escape, to claw its way out of his rib cage.

"Who . . . who are you?" he stammered fearfully.

"We are your life, Jacques Pascal," the hooded figure said. "We are your life and resurrection."

He stood before them, uncomprehending, trembling as he gazed up at their shadowed features. The one who spoke stepped closer to him and brought his hands up to pull back his hood. Jacques caught his breath. Long, flame red hair cascaded to his shoulders. It framed perfect, finely chiseled features. The youthfully smooth skin was of a slightly golden hue. The eyes that gazed at him were a bright, metallic green that seemed to glow with an inner light. The other two reached up and pulled their hoods back. One was a young man, as handsome as the first, and the other was a stunningly beautiful young woman, both with the same red hair and copper-hued skin. They looked like angels, but there was something frightening about them, something palpably malevolent.

"How . . . how do you know my name?" said Jacques hoarsely.

"We know everything about you, Jacques Pascal," the first one said. He reached out and Jacques flinched as the young man put his hands upon his shoulders. "We know how you have suffered. We know how unjustly life has treated you. We sensed you groping in the darkness and we have summoned you to us so that we could make amends."

Pascal looked around him wildly, seeking some means of escape. The thought crossed his mind that he had died back in the sewer tunnels and he was now in Hell, confronting demons. His mind recoiled from the idea, he did not want to accept it. It wasn't possible. He couldn't be dead. He did not remember dying. Surely, one would remember such a thing. Unless, perhaps, he had died in his sleep and it was his spirit that had come here, to remain beneath the earth, wandering tormented through the stygian corridors forever. No, he thought, no, it simply couldn't be. After all the misery that his life had encompassed, surely he was entitled to an afterlife in Paradise. Surely, he had not been such a sinner that he was now doomed to suffer in Hell for all eternity. But then, the hooded figure had spoken of redemption. Of life. He clung to that thought desperately. Perhaps this was no more than a dream. But the reality of his surroundings seemed unmistakable and the hands grasping his shoulders were strong and solid.

"What do you want with me?" cried Jacques, cringing fearfully. "Please, let me go! I meant no harm! I have done nothing!"

"There is no need to be afraid," the man said gently, still holding Pascal by his shoulders. "We are going to give you a great gift, Jacques. You are about to be reborn. Look at me, Jacques. Look into my eyes."

Jacques could not resist. As he met that intense, emerald green gaze, he began to tremble violently. He couldn't breathe. Those unsettling eyes seemed to glow brighter and the grip upon his shoulders tightened. He felt a strange, burning sensation as those awful eyes glowed brighter still and the whites around them disappeared entirely. Suddenly, two brilliant beams of green light shot forth from them and struck Jacques in the eyes, penetrating deep into his brain. He screamed as thaumaturgic fire exploded in his mind. He tore loose from the man's grasp and fell to the floor, writhing in agony and clutching his head with both hands. He was suffused with an incandescent, burning pain unlike anything he'd ever felt before. His flesh felt as if it were melting away from his bones.

He tore away the muffler covering the lower part of his face and gasped for air. He brought his hands up to his face. . . . and suddenly the pain was gone. He touched his face in amazement and wonder. It felt very different. He could hardly believe it. His face was smooth. Unlined. His scraggly beard was gone, as if it had been burned away. Slowly, he got up to his feet and found that he could stand up straight. His skin tingled. He could feel the blood coursing strongly through his veins and the dull, arthritic ache in his bones was gone.

"What . . . what have you done to me?" he said, and he was startled at the sound of his own voice. It was no longer hoarse. It sounded young and strong.

"We have given you back that which was lost," the man said. "Behold."

He made a pass with his hand and a full-length, gilt-framed mirror suddenly appeared in front of Jacques. He stared at his reflection with utter disbelief.

The years had magically dropped away from him. He was no longer an eighty-year-old man, but the same Jacques Pascal who had appeared in the nightclubs of Montmartre, young and strong and vibrant. His hair was no longer limp and gray, but black and lustrous. His jawline was firm, his teeth were no longer rotted, but sparkling white and even. He stared with disbelief at his youthful features, touching his face, feeling the power in his muscular arms and chest. He ran his hands over the rock hard abdominal muscles beneath his sweater. He had been magically given back his youth.

"I must be dreaming! How is this possible?" he said with awe.

"For us, anything is possible," the black-robed sorcerer said.

"No, it cannot be," said Jacques. "Not even sorcery can do this!"

"Oh, but it can, Jacques," said the woman, coming close to him and lightly touching his cheek. "Can you deny the evidence of your senses?"

She gently stroked his cheek and ran her hand around behind his neck, pulling his face close to her. She kissed him lightly on the lips. He felt her tongue slip into his mouth and suddenly he was kissing her hungrily, feeling the supple body underneath her robe as she pressed against him. He hadn't touched a woman in years. He felt a desperate longing building up within him, but she broke away from him, laughing. He looked up at her two companions and blushed with embarrassment.

"There will be time enough for that," she said, touching his cheek again. "That was but a hint of the pleasures you will be able to enjoy again. Merely a taste to whet your appetite. But you will have appetites for other things, as well."

Pascal was dazed and overwhelmed by what had happened to him. He couldn't think straight. Conflicting emotions raged within him, fear, confusion, joy and an overpowering desire for the incredible creature that stood before him.

"I. . . I don't understand," he said.

"You will," she said with a cunning smile. "You have lived for years in darkness and it has sheltered you. Now you will truly learn its power."

She put her lips to his once more and he clutched her to him, eagerly opening his mouth to receive her tongue. Instead, she exhaled into him. Her hot, burning breath hissed down his throat like a jet of steam, spreading through his entire body. He tried to break away, but she held him tightly, breathing her fire into him. She let him go suddenly and he staggered back, clutching at his chest and staring at her wildly.

And then the change began.

Chapter
ONE

Max Siegal hurled his paintbrush across the dingy, unkempt garret that was his studio on the Left Bank, near the old church of St.-Germain-des-Prés.

"*God damn it, you moved again!*" he shouted at his model, in French that was only slightly tinged with an American accent.

Joelle sighed and pouted at him, making a sad little girl face. "But Max, I'm tired!" she said plaintively. "I've been holding this pose for hours! Can't we rest now? I'm cold! Look at me! I have goose pimples all over!" She smiled and tossed her long, ash blond hair. "Why don't you bring some of that cognac over here to warm me up?"

She was completely nude and reclining on a sofa covered in black velvet. It was not, by any means, an uncomfortable position and the pose that Max had carefully arranged her in, while deliberately intended to be erotic, was not very difficult to hold. It was simply that Joelle was young and not very patient. The thrill of being asked to pose for the celebrated artist had worn a bit thin and Joelle was fidgeting impatiently. She had heard that Siegal often had torrid, passionate affairs with his models, but now she was starting to think that he was interested only in her body.

Siegal rolled his eyes up in exasperation and ran a hand through his thick, dark, curly hair. He poured her a small snifter of cognac. "How do you expect me to paint you if you won't *sit still*?" he snapped at her in frustration. "You're squirming about like a dog with fleas!"

"Why don't you come over here and squirm about with me?" she suggested coyly, arching her back and stretching out her lovely legs.

Siegal sighed as he handed her the snifter. "For God's sake, Joelle, I've got *paintbrushes* older than you are."

"You don't find me attractive?" she said, shifting around on the sofa, putting her legs up and swirling the cognac around in the snifter. She dipped a fingertip into the amber liquid and gently sucked it while gazing at him with a smoldering look.

"I find you very attractive, Joelle," he said, wearily. "That's why I wanted to *paint* you. You're a beautiful girl, but I didn't pay you to come here and have sex with me, for God's sake. In fact, I don't know why I'm paying you at all," he added in a surly tone. "As an artist's model, you're an absolute disaster!"

"Do you really think I'm beautiful?" she said, slowly moistening her lips with her tongue and taking a small sip from the snifter.

He made a low sound in his throat, halfway between a moan and a growl. It was just impossible. Lately, every time he found a model who possessed all the right physical qualities, a certain look he wanted to capture on canvas, the moment he got her to the studio, all she wanted was to make love with him. It was probably his own fault for having unrealistic expectations. He had thought that Joelle had a lovely, waiflike innocence about her, but it seemed there was no such thing as an innocent young girl in Paris. Even at sixteen, Joelle was already fully aware of her own lush sexuality.

"Max," she said softly, "what's the matter? Don't you want me?"

"Yes, Joelle, I want you," he said in a tired voice. "I want you to put your clothes on and go home. This isn't going to work. It's pointless."

"But Max—"

"Get dressed, Joelle," he said impatiently. He reached for his wallet. "I'll pay you for your time, though Lord knows, you've wasted mine."

She stared at him and he saw the anger flare up in her eyes. He knew what was coming and he braced himself for it with an air of resignation. The brandy snifter shattered as she hurled it to the floor and launched into a torrent of scathing verbal abuse, questioning his masculinity, his talent, calling him a tired old man . . . he'd heard it all before. He simply sat there quietly, waiting for her to run out of steam and make her dramatic exit. He had been through variations of this scene many times before and it no longer angered or even surprised him very much. It just left him feeling sullen and depressed.

Tomorrow, she would undoubtedly tell all her friends that the great "See-gál," as they pronounced his name in Paris, had asked her to pose for him and that the moment she got to his studio, the passion between them had been so over-whelming that they had made love with wild abandon all through the night and he had raised her to new heights of ecstasy. And the next time he asked someone to pose for him, chances were he'd run into the same damn problem. There was a time when he had thoroughly enjoyed it, but he was weary of it now. It happened over and over again, with monotonous regularity, and for the thousandth time, he wondered why he bothered painting nudes. Doing landscapes or bowls of fruit would have been infinitely less aggravating.

Unfortunately, he had already tried that, but there was simply no demand for him to do that sort of work. They wanted Siegal to paint women, preferably naked women or girls in various states of deshabille. He could sell a painting of a café street scene for a few hundred thousand francs because, after all, it was a "See-gál," but the nudes were what brought the big prices at the galleries. Such was his legend, the handsome, muscular, passionate and temperamental Italian Jew from Brooklyn who spoke French as well as any native-born Parisian, who could drink and swear and brawl with the best of them, and who could do amazing things with light and color on canvas, producing images of women that conveyed such a powerful, stimulating sensuality that he had become one of the most famous painters in a city that had produced such immortal talents as Picasso, Dali and Chagall.

It was a pathetic joke. Siegal knew perfectly well that he wasn't on the same level with such people. He knew what real talent was and he also knew he didn't have it. He was merely competent. He would sometimes gaze for hours on end at a Van Gogh and be moved to tears, knowing he could never hope to produce such work. He had never even planned to become a painter. He had come to Paris to study thaumaturgy at the Sorbonne, but despite all his efforts, it had not taken him long to realize the dismal truth. He simply had no talent for magic.

He could never be a wizard. At best, he could perhaps achieve the status of a lower-grade adept, learning a few simple and relatively undemanding spells such as levitation and impulsion, enabling him to get a license as a public transportation adept so he could pilot a barge down the Seine or operate a cab or bus. As for becoming a sorcerer, which had been his dream, it was simply out of the question. The only magic he was capable of performing was the illusion of making women look like wanton angels when he painted them. And it was a cheap trick, at that.

He winced as Joelle slammed the door behind her. He took a slug of cognac from the bottle and examined the aborted painting on the easel with disgust. He picked up the canvas and looked at it for a moment, then swore and smashed it down over the easel in a sudden fit of temper, tearing a gaping hole in it. He left it that way, impaled on the easel, picked up the bottle and settled down on the couch for yet another night of solitary drinking.

It had all come about by accident. He had always been able to draw, but he had never seriously pursued it beyond making caricatures of people for his own amusement. He started painting only after he had come to Paris, because Paris was awash in artists and many students liked to fancy themselves painters. It was a good way to meet attractive women. One day, while he was out walking with a date, they happened upon an artist painting a young woman at a sidewalk café.

There was a crowd of people watching. The painter was none other then Francois Benet, then the current rage of the Paris art world. Max had heard of him and seen some of his work. He thought the man was overrated. As they stopped to watch him paint, Max's date had teasingly asked him what Benet was doing wrong. Without thinking, because he was preoccupied with watching the man work, Max told her. Benet had overheard him.

He suggested wryly that if the young man thought he could do better, perhaps he should take the brush himself and show them all how it should be done. With an amused look, the painter handed him the brush and palette. Max stepped up to the easel, pursed his lips and closely examined what the artist had been doing, then carefully selected a few tubes of paint, made subtle changes in the pigment mixtures that Benet was using, and quietly began to paint. The artist moved up close behind him, watching intently over his shoulder as he worked. After a few moments, Max heard Benet swear softly and say, "Yes . . . yes . . . of course, *exactly*!"

He continued painting while Benet watched with growing enthusiasm. Soon the people in the crowd were asking who the young painter was. And that was how it started.

It wasn't long before the paintings of Max Siegal were appearing in the Paris art galleries, commanding prices Max wouldn't have dreamed possible. It was Benet who had started him on painting nudes and Max soon became famous for it.

Inevitably, women started coming to him, wanting him to paint them, and he soon had more models than he knew what to do with.

It all went to his head. He started frequenting chic night spots, drinking to excess and making a reputation for himself as a wild carouser. He became romantically involved with women who had posed for him, many of whom had lovers or even husbands, which led to the inevitable public confrontations, brawls, and lawsuits. The newspapers loved him because he was flamboyant copy and before long, his escapades were being exaggerated or even fabricated outright. He would come home to find naked women in his studio. People he didn't even know claimed intimacy with him. It all became too much for him and he started drinking even more. He was out of control and well on the way to self-destruction. And then he met Jacqueline.

They met at a party hosted by a wealthy collector who had bought many of Max's paintings, along with many nearly priceless works by the old masters. Max had been the center of attention, as usual, with all the women in the room fawning over him while the men smoldered with resentment. All the women except one.

He had noticed her immediately, a woman in her late thirties or early forties, with shoulder-length dark hair prematurely streaked with gray. She had been dressed in a neo-Edwardian black suit and boots, she chain-smoked unfiltered French cigarettes and spoke in a husky, whiskey baritone. There was something about her, quite aside from her striking beauty, that Max had found incredibly compelling. There was a certain knowingness about her, an utterly implacable self-assurance that was evident in her slightest gesture and expression. He was fascinated by the character in her face and he decided that he had to paint her. Only she had refused.

Her refusal had astonished him. He was besieged by women who wanted him to paint them and here was one not in the least bit interested. He kept after her, pressing his card on her, but it was no use. She wouldn't change her mind. This only made him want to paint her that much more. Eventually, the ebb and flow of the party took him away from her and he did not see her again that evening. He asked everyone who she was, but no one seemed to know her. And then, the next day, it was discovered that several of his host's most valuable paintings had disappeared. When Max found out about it, he was mildly insulted that none of his own paintings were among those that had been stolen. The police came to question him, not that he was a suspect, but they were anxious to learn who had been present at the party. They showed him several photographs. One of those they showed him was Jacqueline's.

He had not even known her name at that point and when the police had seen him hesitate on seeing her photograph, they asked him if he recognized her as someone he'd seen at the party. Without really knowing why, he told them no. As an artist, he said, he merely found her face quite fascinating. He asked them who she was. Her full name, they told Max, was Jacqueline Marie-Lisette de Charboneau Monet.

They told him that she was a witch, a talented adept with an extensive dossier at most of the police agencies of Europe, as well as at the Bureau of Thaumaturgy and the I.T.C., the International Thaumaturgical Commission. She had been arrested scores of times, under suspicion for crimes ranging from fraud to grand larceny, but she had never been convicted. She was, they told him, one of Europe's most successful and accomplished thieves, and it was rumored that she had a link with a man known only by the name of Morpheus, a deadly international assassin.

Max had been astounded. He had heard that such people existed, but he had never actually met anyone like that before. The police were certain that Jacqueline was responsible for the theft of the paintings, but they had only circumstantial evidence, merely the fact of her presence at the party. There was no proof. They thanked him for his assistance and departed, leaving Max wondering if he would ever run into her again. Then several days later, he came home to find her waiting in his studio.

If he still wanted to paint her, she had told him, she would be willing to sit for him, but only under several conditions. She would not pose nude and the painting would be only of her face. Furthermore, he was not to tell anyone that she had ever sat for him and he was to sell the painting to her the moment it was finished. It was not to be displayed. It was to be a present for a friend and he could name his price. Amused more than irritated by these demands, he had named a truly outrageous figure, even for an original Max Siegal. She had readily agreed to it.

It had been the beginning of what became a very close and intimate friendship. It was a relationship unlike any that Max had ever had before. They eventually became lovers, but it was months before that happened and when they finally did become physically intimate with each other, it was not the sort of grand, yet ephemeral passion that Max had experienced so many times before. They went to bed as friends, as a logical extension of their warm and affectionate feelings for each other. They loved each other, but they were not *in* love, a subtle distinction that, perhaps, only the French could fully appreciate.

Jacqueline loved someone else, but Max understood that it was an unrequited passion and he soon came to suspect who that other person might be, though they never spoke of him by name. As for Max, he was thoroughly burned out on passion. It had brought him nothing but pain, problems and frustration. He told her that if he had slept with even half the women who claimed that they'd been intimate with him, he would have been hospitalized long ago for sheer exhaustion. Jacqueline had laughed and told him that if she had committed only half the crimes she was accused of, she would be one of the richest women in the world. He always found an ease with her that he could not find with anybody else. He hadn't heard from her in months and he missed her terribly. He seemed more in control of things when Jacqueline was around.

As he drank morosely, he mused about what his life had become since that fateful day when he had met his mentor Francois Benet. He had become a famous man, a flamboyant personality often written about in the gossip columns. He knew that thousands of struggling artists in the city would kill to be in his position, and yet he could find little pleasure in the pinnacle of success he had achieved. Despite his popularity, he felt that he was only second-rate. He felt that he was stagnating, that his work was becoming derivative of itself, and for all his frenzied social life, he was a lonely man. It seemed to him that everything in his life had become repetitive and somehow automatic. He desperately longed for something different, something new.

He was wealthy now, but he continued to live simply, in a garret like a starving artist, spending his money on entertainment and assisting other artists less fortunate than himself. Conscience money, he called it. He had financed several galleries and restaurants, merely to help his friends and taking no profit for himself. His famous temper was still with him and he was arrested fairly regularly for brawling in one night spot or another; it was practically expected of him and the Paris police generally regarded his escapades with nothing more than mild amusement. They always treated him with courtesy. They were courteous when they came to see him the next morning, but they were not at all amused.

He had passed out on the sofa, fully dressed, and he awoke with a hangover, startled out of sleep by the relentless pounding on the door. He had no idea what time it was and his head felt as if it were being squeezed slowly in a vise. Each knock on the door was like a hammer blow directly to his skull. He swore and lurched up off the sofa, then swore again as he struck his shin on the coffee table.

"All right! All right! I'm coming!" he shouted, pressing his hands up to his temples at the pain caused by the sound of his own voice.

He opened the door to admit two police officers dressed in civilian clothing.

"Police, Monsieur Siegal," one of the men said, giving his name the French pronunciation and showing him his badge and identification. "We would like to ask you a few questions, please."

Max groaned. "What is it *now*?" he said in a surly tone. "Whom did I assault this time?"

The two men exchanged glances. "May we come in, monsieur?"

"Yes, yes, come in, come in," Max said, standing aside to let them enter. "Pardon the mess, but I was drunk last night."

They glanced at one another once again.

"You have been drinking heavily, monsieur?"

"Of course, I have been drinking heavily. I'm always drinking heavily. Don't you read the newspapers? What is it you want? If you're going to place me under arrest, get on with it, but kindly do it quietly. My head is simply killing me."

Another exchange of glances.

"Monsieur Siegal," said the other man, "are you familiar with a young woman by the name of Joelle Muset?"

"Joelle?" said Max. He grunted. "Ah, lovely Joelle. I should have known she would be trouble."

Another meaningful exchange of glances. "We understand that she was here last night," the first policeman said. "To model for one of your paintings."

"Yes, yes, she was here," said Max, slumping back down onto the sofa and putting his head in his hands. "The whole thing was a mistake," he said. "It was never meant to happen. I should have known that it would lead to trouble, the silly little bitch. . . ."

She had probably told the police he had assaulted her, to get even with him for not succumbing to her nubile charms. He'd been through this sort of thing before. There would be reporters and an investigation, possibly a trial; it would get very tiresome now, tiresome and sticky—

"Marcel. . ." said one of the policemen. "Have a look at this."

Max looked up. They were both standing by the easel, looking at the painting of Joelle that he'd smashed over the easel in a fit of pique.

"What happened here, monsieur?" the one named Marcel

said, pointing to the ruined painting, on which Joelle's face was still clearly visible. The easel impaled her image right through the chest. "You had an argument last night? A fight, no? The famous Siegal temper? She was, perhaps, not quite as obliging as you'd hoped?"

Max could see where this was leading, but he was simply too hung over to deal with it. He sighed. "Look, why don't you just arrest me and get it over with?" he said with resignation. "I simply can't take this now. Let my lawyer handle it. I haven't got the stomach for it anymore."

There was a brief moment of silence as the two policemen looked at one another, and then the one named Marcel said, "Monsieur Siegal, it is my duty to inform you that I am placing you under arrest for the murder of Joelle Muset."

Max's head jerked up. "*What?* Wait a minute—"

"Please come along quietly, monsieur."

"Wait! What the hell are you talking about?" He leaped up from the couch and swayed unsteadily, fighting a sudden surge of dizziness and nausea. "*Joelle's been murdered?*"

"Come along, monsieur—"

The policeman reached for his arm, but Max shook him off furiously. "Let go of me, damn you! I'm trying to tell you—"

It was the wrong response. He suddenly found himself thrown to the floor and handcuffed. Stunned, he tried to protest as they hauled him back up to his feet and quickly patted him down.

"Wait a minute! Wait! This is all wrong! There's been some sort of mistake!"

"Tell it to the inspector, monsieur," Marcel said. "Please come along peaceably. Resisting will only make it worse for you."

Stunned, Max allowed himself to be half marched, half carried outside. The bottom had dropped out of his stomach. He felt sick and he couldn't think clearly. This can't be happening, he thought, but it *was* happening and through the fog of his hangover, he suddenly realized that what he'd said to them made things look very bad, indeed. She'd been at his studio, modeling nude, and the painting . . . the painting! God, the way he'd smashed it down over the easel, they must think . . . they *did* think it! They thought he'd gotten drunk and killed her. And there was no way he could account for his whereabouts last night. He had been drunk, at home. Alone. As they escorted him to the waiting police car, he realized that there was no way he could prove his innocence.

"I didn't kill her," he said as they got into the car.

In a daze, he kept saying it over and over again as they drove down to police headquarters.

Chapter
TWO

Inspector Armand Renaud was having his morning coffee and croissant when Legault came bursting into his office without knocking, saying, "You'll never guess who's outside, asking for you."

Renaud sighed and put down his croissant. It seemed he couldn't even have his morning coffee without being interrupted. "All right, who?" he said wearily.

"Jacqueline Monet," Legault said.

Renaud stared at him. "You're joking. *The* Jacqueline Monet?"

"The very same."

"And she wants to speak with *me*?"

"She asked for you by name. She won't say what it's about."

Renaud quickly brushed the stray croissant crumbs off his desk with his crumpled-up paper napkin, then pushed his hair back with his fingertips and straightened his tie. He looked up to see Legault grinning at him.

"What are you grinning at? Send her in."

Still grinning, Legault left and a moment later, she came through the door. She was even more beautiful in the flesh than she was in her photographs. Jacqueline Monet was in her late forties. Her exact age was subject to some question, but she had the figure of a woman in her twenties. With a face and body like that, she could easily have landed a spot in the chorus of any Montmartre nightclub. Her legs were long and her waist was girlishly trim. She wore a well-tailored neo-Edwardian suit of dark crimson brocade, with white lace at the throat and cuffs. In her high-heeled boots, she was just under six feet tall and her long, thick, gray-streaked hair was a rich mahogany color. She wore it loose, down past her shoulders. He got to his feet as she came up to his desk.

"Mademoiselle Monet," he said, offering his hand. "I am Inspector Armand Renaud. To what do I owe this unexpected pleasure?"

She took his hand in a strong grip. "I seem to have interrupted your morning coffee, Inspector," she said in a deep and sexy voice. "I would like to speak with you in private concerning a matter of some importance. There is a small café across the street. Perhaps I could buy you an espresso?"

"Allow me the pleasure of buying you one," said Renaud. He picked up his jacket. "After you, mademoiselle."

Every eye in the station house followed them as they went outside and down the stairs. There wasn't a police officer in all of France who did not know who Jacqueline Monet was and the idea of her strolling casually into a police station as if she owned the place was typical of the brazen effrontery for which she had become famous. Infamous, perhaps, would have been a better word. In any other country except France, the sight of a notorious criminal walking into a police station with such an air of impunity would have elicted reactions of outrage and anger, but in France, and especially in Paris, the police had a somewhat different attitude when it came to certain types of criminals.

Those who committed violent crimes, such as rape or murder, armed robbery or assault, were hated just as much by the gendarmes as they would have been in any other city, but master thieves, especially those who never had injured anyone and carried on their trade with a flamboyant sense of style, could often command a certain admiration from the gendarmes who sought to catch them in the act. When it came to someone like Jacqueline Monet, it became a fascinating game between the criminal and the police, with mutual respect on both sides. It was not unlike the relationship between a big game hunter and his quarry. The hunter would stalk his prey relentlessly, but if it was a clever beast and managed to escape, the hunter was not angry. Rather, he felt respect and even an affection for the creature that had managed to elude him and he would look forward to stalking it another time. So it was with Jacqueline Monet and the Paris police.

Renaud accompanied her across the street to the café. The waiter greeted him by name and they took a small table in the corner. Renaud ordered two espressos and a couple of croissants. He tried to keep from looking anxious. The two of them had never met before. Jacqueline Monet's activities were generally considered the province of the French Bureau of Thaumaturgy and the I.T.C., though the police were often involved, as well. Renaud wondered what was on her mind.

He did not have to wonder long. She came right to the point. She took the newspaper she was carrying under her arm and spread it out before him. "Would you be so kind as to tell me what this is all about, Inspector?" she asked, pointing to the headline.

He glanced at the article. He had already seen it. It concerned the arrest of Max Siegal for the murder of Joelle Muset.

"I should think that it was self-explanatory," he said. "You have some interest in this matter, mademoiselle? Some information that is pertinent to the case?"

"Max Siegal is a close personal friend of mine," she said.

"Ah. I see."

"And he is not a killer."

She took out a cigarette and Renaud lit it for her. "With

all due respect, mademoiselle," he said, "the evidence indicates otherwise. Unless you have some information that would prove him innocent?"

"If I had such information, he would not be in custody right now," she said. "But I would stake my life upon his innocence."

Renaud shrugged. "Such loyalty is very commendable, mademoiselle, but of course you realize that I would require something a bit more tangible than just your word."

"I'm not a fool, Renaud. The newspaper says you are in charge of the case. I tell you that you have arrested the wrong man. If what you really want is justice, then I have certain connections that might be of help in your investigation. I could pursue avenues of inquiry that would be closed to the police. In helping Max, I would be helping you to catch the real killer."

"A most intriguing offer," said Renaud, "but you see, I believe that we already have the real killer."

"What evidence have you got against him?"

"Well, this is all somewhat irregular, mademoiselle," he said, "I am not in the habit of discussing police business with outsiders, especially criminals." He smiled. "Correction, 'suspected criminals.' However, since I am interested in seeing justice served and you have been kind enough to join me for breakfast, then speaking strictly off the record, I can tell you what I have already said to his attorney. It does not look very good for your friend. He engaged young Joelle Muset to model for him in the nude. Her friends have testified to this and there is no question but that she was in his studio on the night that she was murdered. He admitted it. The arresting officers found the canvas that Siegal was working on that night. It was unfinished, yet it was a painting of Mademoiselle Muset. Her face is clearly identifiable and the pose that she was in was quite, shall we say, provocative?"

"All of Max's nudes are highly provocative," said Jacqueline. "That in itself proves nothing."

"Perhaps," said Renaud, "but the painting was discovered impaled upon its easel. Siegal evidently smashed it over the easel in one of his famous fits of temper. He *is* known for being violent on occasion.''

"That still doesn't mean he killed her," said Jacqueline.

"Perhaps not, but it does indicate that there was some sort of violent argument," Renaud replied. "And aside from his famous temper, Max Siegal is also known for his romantic liaisons with many of his models and he has been accused of assault before. It would appear as though he had tried to pursue a sexual liaison with Mademoiselle Muset, but she protested and one thing unfortunately led to another. Siegal admitted to being very drunk that night. And some of the things he said to his arresting officers clearly indicate his guilt.''

"What sort of things?''

"He referred to the deceased as 'a little bitch' and said he knew that something like this would happen, that he should have known she would be trouble. While being interrogated, he asked to be arrested and to call his lawyer. He confessed that he could not take it anymore. That he hadn't the stomach for it.''

"But did he actually *confess* to having killed her?''

"Well, not in so many words," Renaud said. "By the time he realized what was happening, he had apparently regained enough of his sobriety to start denying it, but then they always do, don't they? And he resisted arrest, as well. Would an innocent man do that?''

"Max would," Jacqueline said wryly. "How was the girl killed?''

Renaud pursed his lips. "She was murdered in a particularly violent manner, mademoiselle," he said. "Her body was discovered in the apartment that she shared with two other young women in the Rue Morgue, just off the Rue St. Roch. One of them is her sister. They found the body when they came home from work at the Cafe Noir, where they are employed as dancers. She couldn't have been dead more than an hour or two. Siegal must have followed her home from his studio, gained entrance, found her alone and then attacked her. She was found nude, with her body badly mutilated.''

"Was there any blood on him when he was arrested?" Jacqueline said.

"No, but then he would have had ample time to wash it off," Renaud said.

"Was any bloody clothing found in his studio?"

"No, but then he could have easily disposed of it. We are still searching the vicinity of—"

"What sort of weapon was used?"

"Apparently a knife of some sort," said Renaud.

"Apparently? You mean you don't know for sure? Did you find the murder weapon?"

"No, but as I said, we are still searching—"

"So then you have no evidence tying Max in with the crime other than the purely circumstantial fact that the victim modeled for him on the night that she was killed and he destroyed the painting?"

Renaud patiently took a deep breath. "There is the sheer violence of the assault," he said, "and your friend's well-known propensity for violence. There is the fact that he was drunk and cannot account for his whereabouts on that night. He *says* that he was home alone, but there is no one who can corroborate that supposed fact. There is the fact that he destroyed the painting in an obvious fit of rage, the fact that he had once studied thaumaturgy at the Sorbonne—"

"Wait a moment," said Jacqueline, frowning. "What does thaumaturgy have to do with it?"

"Well, the symbols that had been carved into the body of the victim were—"

Jacqueline suddenly leaned forward and grabbed his hand across the table. "*What symbols?*" she said. "You said nothing about any symbols carved into the body!"

Renaud was a bit taken aback by her intense reaction. "I mentioned that the corpse was badly mutilated," he said. "The condition of the victim's body left little doubt but that the assault was perversely sexual in nature. She was slashed repeatedly and she had certain markings carved into her breasts and abdomen that were identified as runes, the sort of symbols that might be used in some sort of thaumaturgic ritual.''

"Give me a pen," Jacqueline said, her voice tense.

Puzzled, Renaud reached into his pocket and handed her a pen. She started to draw on one of the napkins.

"Did they look anything like this?" she said.

Renaud watched as she drew several obscene-looking symbols on the napkin. He frowned. "Yes, as a matter of fact, they looked exactly like . . ." His voice trailed off and he glanced up at her with new interest. "How did you know this? There was nothing about that in the papers."

"Listen to me, Renaud," she said urgently. "Max Siegal *didn't* kill that girl. He once studied thaumaturgy, that's true, but he never got very far in his studies. He had no talent for it. You can verify that for yourself if you contact the College of Thaumaturgy at the Sorbonne. These symbols are runes used in a very advanced thaumaturgic ritual, the kind that isn't taught in thaumaturgy schools. The killer was no ordinary adept and this was no ordinary murder. This girl was a victim of necromancy.''

"Necromancy! How do you know this?" said Renaud. "And how did you know about the runes?"

"There was a series of murders in California about a year ago in which the same pattern of runes appeared," she said. "Call the Los Angeles police department. Ask for Captain Rebecca Farrell and tell her how the girl was killed. Then call Scotland Yard and ask for Chief Inspector Michael Blood. Ask him about the so-called Ripper murders that occurred in Whitechapel about two years ago. And tell him about the murder of Joelle Muset.''

Renaud started quickly making notes. "May I ask what this is all about, mademoiselle?" he said. "How are you involved in this?''

"Never mind that for now," she said. "First I want you to be absolutely certain that I'm telling you the truth. We'll discuss it further after you've verified the information.''

"You may rest assured that I will do so, mademoiselle," he said. He glanced at her, puzzled. It occurred to him that she might have been involved in the crime somehow. "I assume that you will stand Max Siegal's bail?" he said, watching her for a reaction.

"No," she said. "Right now, jail is the best possible place for him."

"You believe that he is in some danger?" said Renaud.

"No, I don't think so, but I believe that this is only the beginning. There will be other killings of this sort, Renaud, I'm certain of it, and if Max is in jail when they occur, then you'll know he couldn't possibly have been responsible."

"You seem to know more about this than you're telling me, mademoiselle," Renaud said. "I really think it would be best if you—"

"I know you are suspicious of me, Renaud," she said, "and under the circumstances, I can hardly blame you. But you will soon think differently. I'll speak to you again after you've made those calls. Right now, I have to make some calls of my own. If I'm right, then what's happening here is too much for the police to handle alone."

"If what you're saying is true," Renaud said, "then it is my duty to call in the I.T.C."

She got up. "Do whatever you think you must," she said. "But at least speak to Blood and Farrell first, so you can satisfy yourself that I am telling you the truth. Then use your own best judgment. I can't tell you what to do. But I promise you that Max Siegal is completely innocent of this crime. I fear that this is only the beginning. It seems there is a necromancer loose in Paris."

He cried out as the sword bit deeply, cutting through his armor and slicing into his shoulder. He dropped his own sword, unable to hold on to it, and sank to his knees, raising his shield in a vain effort to ward off the punishing blows that kept raining down on him as Uthur smashed away relentlessly, chopping at his shield with repeated, powerful, two-handed strokes. He felt his strength draining away with his blood and he knew that he was finished. Merlin had cloaked Uthur in warding spells and with the fury of his attack, there was no opportunity to summon up an enchantment powerful enough to break through Uthur's magical protection. With a sinking feeling, he realized that he was going to die.

That it should end like this, that after all these years, he should die at the hands of a mere mortal, aided by the spells of his own abandoned son. . . . He thought briefly of his wife, Igraine, who would now be at Uthur's mercy, his to seize as chattel, his to use in whatever way he pleased. He thought of his three daughters, Elaine, Morganna and Morgause, whose fate would also be in Uther's hands, and he was filled with unutterable grief. He collapsed beneath the savage onslaught, his shield reduced to a battered lump of shapeless metal, and with the next stroke, his arm went numb and he could hold on to it no longer. There was one chance remaining, only one, but he did not know if he had the time or strength to take it. He concentrated with all the power left in him as Uther raised his sword for the killing stroke. His vision blurred and he felt the world receding from him as Uther screamed and brought the sword down at his head—

Billy Slade cried out and awoke, bathed in a cold sweat, his bedclothes twisted around him. He felt hands upon him and he struggled against their grip.

"It's all right, Billy, it's all right," said Modred, bending over him and holding on to his shoulders. "It was only a nightmare."

Billy stared at him wildly, then relaxed and sank back down onto the bed, shutting his eyes and breathing heavily.

"Gor, what a bloody awful dream. . ." he said in a thick cockney accent. He opened his eyes once more.

Kira and Wyrdrune were standing by his bed, looking down at him anxiously.

"I went an' woke everybody up again, didn't I?" he said. "I'm sorry. What time is it?"

"About four in the morning," Modred said.

"Bloody 'ell," said Billy wearily.

"Was it the same dream again?" asked Wyrdrune.

Billy nodded. "Yeah," he said in a tired voice. "Uther bloody Pendragon was cuttin' me to pieces, smashin' away at me with 'is sword. 'E was just about to finish me off when I woke up."

His facial expression suddenly changed, becoming grim, and when he spoke again, he sounded like a completely different person.

"It's Gorlois," he said. "He's doing it all for my benefit, blast him. He's making me experience his death, having me relive it over and over again because I was the one who helped bring it about."

The adult voice sounded incongruous coming from the slightly built fourteen-year-old. Billy sat up and ran his hands through his unusually styled hair, cut short at the sides and crested at the center, flowing down to the middle of his back like a horse's mane. But it wasn't Billy who was speaking. It was the entity that possessed him, the spirit of his ancestor, the archmage Merlin Ambrosius, court wizard to King Arthur Pendragon and father of the second thaumaturgic age.

"I simply can't get through to him," said Merlin. "He's there, he's part of us, but he's unreachable. Except when he takes over our dreams in order to torment us."

Billy looked at his hand, at the unusual ring he wore, a gleaming, fire opal in a heavy silver setting. The band of the ancient ring was engraved with tiny, intricate runes. The ring had once belonged to Gorlois, the last of the Old Ones, the sole surviving member of the Council of the White. He had given it to his daughter, and Morgan Le Fay had worn it throughout her life, never realizing that it was the source of much of her power, the repository of her inhuman father's spirit. She, in turn, had given it to the sorceror named Thanatos when they had married and he, too, had been unaware of its true nature until the moment when they had their confrontation with the Dark Ones and the spirit of Gorlois had manifested itself, taking him over to do battle with the necromancers. That struggle had cost Thanatos his life and when Billy Slade approached his body, the ring had fallen from his finger. Billy had picked it up and put it in his pocket. He did not remember putting the ring on, but now he couldn't get it off. Gorlois was now a part of him, as much as Merlin was. He was possessed by the spirits of two powerful archmages, the father and the son. And they hated one another.

"I wish the pair of 'em would just bugger off and leave me the 'ell alone," said Billy in his normal voice. "It was bad enough just 'avin Merlin muckin' about inside me 'ead, but now I've got 'is bleedin' dad to put up with. Between the two of 'em, I'm gonna lose me fuckin' mind!"

Kira sat down on the bed beside him. "I know, Billy. I know. I wish there was something we could do."

She took his hand in hers and he felt the hardness of the sapphire runestone embedded in her palm. Wyrdrune stood looking down at him with a worried expression, his long, curly blond hair falling over his face, partially obscuring the emerald runestone embedded in his forehead. Modred looked down at him with concern. His silk pajama shirt was open and the ruby runestone in his muscular chest gleamed darkly.

"I wonder if it's ever gonna stop," said Billy, wearily. "What does 'e want from me, anyway? I 'aven't done anything to 'im."

"It isn't you he's angry with, Billy," said Modred. "It's Merlin. Unfortunately, Merlin is a part of you. And Gorlois is still an unknown factor. There's really no way of knowing what he means to do with you. Or how Merlin will respond to it. Thanatos wore the ring for years and was never consciously aware of Gorlois. Morganna, too, although we don't know to what extent she was influenced by the ring."

"I've rubbed me finger raw tryin' to get the damn thing off," said Billy, "but it's just no use. No matter what I do, it simply won't come off."

"Do you people know what *time* it is?"

A broom came sweeping into the room on its straw bristles, a red nightcap perched atop its wooden handle. It looked like an ordinary, old-fashioned straw broom, except that it had two spindly, rubbery arms with three fingers on each hand.

"It's four o'clock in the morning, for crying out loud!" it

said. "*Gevalt!* What does a person need to do to get some sleep around here? It's not enough I have to work and scrub and cook all day, but then I have to put up with all this cáfe-klatching like a bunch of *yentas* in the middle of the night?"

Years ago, Wyrdrune had animated the broom to help his mother around the house while he was away at school. Now that his mother was gone, he had inherited the broom. Unfortunately, after years spent with his mother, the broom had taken on her personality. It stood with its arms on its hips—or at least on the spot where its hips might have been if it had hips—and though it had no mouth or anything even vaguely resembling a face, it spoke to them in an irritated, matronly tone.

"Doesn't anybody around here keep normal hours anymore? What is it with you people?"

"Billy had another nightmare," Kira said.

"Again?" said the broom, its tone softening. "Aw, poor *bubeleh*. I told you, you should drink some warm milk with honey before you go to bed at night."

"Thanks, but I'd sooner 'ave the bleedin' nightmares," Billy said, sourly.

"Well, then don't blame me if you won't take my advice," the broom said in a huffy tone. "Kids today! You talk and talk and talk, but will they ever listen?"

"Put on some coffee, Broom," said Wyrdrune.

"Sure, why not?" the broom said. "Just because no one else is sleeping, who am I to get a little rest?"

"Broom . . ."

"All right, all right, already, I'll put on some coffee. But you should have something to eat. Coffee on an empty stomach, you'll give yourself a heartburn. How about some nice French toast with cinammon and maple syrup?"

"No thanks," said Billy. "I'll just 'ave a beer."

"A beer? A *beer*? Four o'clock in the morning and he wants a *beer? Oy vey!* You'll have a nice hot chocolate and a little French toast to stick to your ribs. Honestly, drinking beer at your age! I never heard of such a thing!"

"Awright, awright," said Billy, reaching for his cigarettes

on the nightstand. "Christ, give it a bleedin' rest, Broom, willya?"

"Now there's gratitude for you," the broom said. It waved its spindly arms as Billy lit up the cigarette. "*Feh!* And now you're going to stink the whole place up with cigarette smoke! You shouldn't be smoking at your age, you'll stunt your growth."

"I'll stunt yer bloody—"

"Billy . . ." Wyrdrune said. Billy fell silent, scowling. "Coffee and some hot chocolate and French toast will be just fine, Broom. Thank you very much."

The broom sniffed, a peculiar thing to do since it had no nose, and waddled back out into the kitchen. Billy got out of bed and pulled his pants on over his undershorts. He went over to the sliding glass doors and opened them, stepping out onto the balcony of their apartment overlooking Central Park West. The others came up behind him. They stood for a moment in silence, looking out over the city.

"You okay, Billy?" Kira asked.

"Yeah, I guess so," Billy said, drawing deeply on his cigarette. Then he took it from his mouth, frowned at it, and flicked it over the side. "I don't know how he can stand smoking those damn things," said Merlin. He patted his pockets, then waggled his fingers and a moment later, a curved briar pipe and leather tobacco pouch came floating out onto the balcony. He plucked them out of the air and started filling the pipe.

By now, they had grown accustomed to the rapid changes in personality from Billy to Merlin and back again. Billy spoke with a thick cockney accent; Merlin spoke in a Celtic accent that sounded like a cross between Irish and Welsh. Billy smoked cigarettes; Merlin smoked a pipe and each detested the other's habit. Billy could not do magic; Merlin could.

"It's a hard thing for the lad," said Merlin, "being possessed on one hand and bound to a living runestone on the other. I feel partly responsible."

"You're entirely responsible," said Modred.

Merlin grunted and snapped his fingers. A flame jetted from his thumb and he puffed his pipe alight. He habitually smoked his own sorcerous blend of tobacco, with its ever-changing aroma. As he took his first puff, it smelled like toasted almonds, but an instant later, it had changed, giving off the smell of roasted chestnuts.

"I wish I could make it easier for him, somehow," he said. "I had never planned on any of this. After I died, I felt my spirit being inexorably drawn to Billy, but it wasn't until I took possession that I realized it was because he was descended from me. The same thing must have drawn the ring to him, as well." He glanced at the fire opal ring. "Gorlois must have used a spell much like the one the Council of the White cast when they fused their spirits with the runestones. His spirit fled his body and entered the ring the moment Uther killed him. I wanted my revenge on him for deserting my mother and now he's come back to haunt me. It's as if fate is punishing me for having misused my powers. And through no fault of his own, Billy's been caught up in it. So here we are, one not-so-happy family, trapped within one body. Strange how fate always has a way of screwing you."

Wyrdrune smiled. "You're starting to sound a bit like Billy," he said.

"Yes, there is something rather infectious about his personality," said Merlin wryly. "It's starting to rub off on me, much the way your mother's personality rubbed off on Broom. But if I start speaking with a cockney accent, slap me."

Modred chuckled. "There was a time, Ambrosius, when I would have dearly loved to do that."

"Yes, I know," said Merlin, blowing out a vanilla-scented smoke ring. "It's a funny thing. We've never talked much about the old days."

"The glorious days of Camelot, you mean?" said Modred sarcastically. "I thought that was something of a sore subject with you."

"It is, in many ways," Merlin admitted. "But you and I are the only ones left from that old time. Actually, since I'm dead, I suppose I don't really count. That leaves you as Camelot's last survivor.''

Wyrdrune and Kira listened silently, with interest. Merlin almost never spoke about those days and even after two thousand years, Modred still felt bitter about his past.

"When I was released from Morganna's spell," said Merlin, "I had only a vague idea how much time had actually passed. While I slept, I had only the dimmest perceptions of the world around me. I knew there had been wars, some truly terrible, and that mankind was accomplishing great things, things we never would have dreamed of in our day. Yet I sensed these things but dimly, as if trying to see through a thick fog. And then I awoke at the height of the Collapse, to see that all of mankind's efforts had led only to another dark age. Over two thousand years had passed and I awoke in the twenty-third century to find the world no better off than when I went to sleep. And I saw that there was still a need for me, a need for magic in the world. I can't begin to tell you how that made me feel. At Camelot, I had failed because I neglected to take into account the frailties of human nature. But here was a chance to start anew. I felt invigorated, imbued with a new sense of purpose.

He looked out over the lights of the city. It was a warm night and the city glowed beneath them like the dying embers of a giant campfire.

"I accomplished all of that," he said. "I brought back the light. But I brought the darkness back, as well. As the magic I taught spread throughout the world, the Dark Ones sensed it and began to stir. And now they're loose upon the world. I sometimes wonder if it wouldn't have been better if I hadn't come back at all.''

He glanced at Modred. "But you . . . you actually lived through all of it. You saw it all more clearly than I ever could. If anyone can judge me, Modred, it is you, who have suffered more than anybody else because of what I've done.''

"That almost sounds like an apology, Ambrosius," Modred said. "That's hardly like you." He sighed. "I'm not sure how to answer you. A long time ago, I might have judged you, but there seems little purpose in it now. You've always had a monstrous ego, but the truth is you didn't orchestrate events so much as you were merely a part of them.''

''Perhaps,'' said Merlin, ''but I can't help feeling that the fault is mine.''

''If the fault lies anywhere,'' said Modred, ''then I suppose it lies with Gorlois. It all began with him. But can we really blame him? He was the last of his kind. Here and there, sprinkled throughout the world, were people like you and me, half-breeds, descended from the mating of an Old One and a human, but there was no way he could know them and with each succeeding generation, the strain became more and more diluted. You and I were born immortal, or at least with a lifespan impossible to measure in strictly human terms. Wyrdrune and Kira, descended from my mother's sisters, but removed by many generations, will probably live out a lifespan much closer to the human norm. Gorlois was the last of the Old Ones. He knew his race was dying with him. And in a way, I think I can understand exactly how he must have felt.''

''Do you?'' Merlin said. ''Then perhaps you can explain it to me. If you truly love a woman, as he claimed to love my mother, then how can you desert her?''

Modred lit up a cigarette and inhaled deeply, gazing off into the distance. Somewhere in the night, a siren screamed.

''Sometimes, your love is the very thing that drives you away,'' he said. He paused a moment. ''I couldn't imagine living with a woman, loving her, and watching her wither and grow old while I remained the same. What love could stand a test like that? They say there's something fulfilling in growing old together, but for one person to grow old while the other remains youthful and eternally unchanged, no, there's a horror in that, a grotesque inequity that has to be impossible to bear. Year by year, you watch her grow away from you, dying by stages right before your eyes. I don't think that I could stand that. I'm not saying that Gorlois was right in doing what he did, but I think that I can understand it.

"As for your choosing to shoulder the burden of responsibility for everything that's come about merely because you wanted revenge," he continued, "I frankly think that's ludicrous. You might have convinced my father that he was an instrument of fate, but Arthur was always Uther's son and he had his father's lust for power. Guinevere had somewhat simpler lusts, though they were just as strong. And as for Lancelot, he was a mere child. Arthur might as well have put the two of them in bed together and tucked them in. I fail to see your role in that."

"Lancelot and Guinevere fell in love because I made Arthur a king first and a husband second," Merlin said. "But Arthur loved them both. Was that so difficult to understand?"

"No, not difficult to understand at all," said Modred. "But it wasn't their affair that bothered me so much as the grotesque hypocrisy surrounding it. Arthur and his high-flown code of chivalry. The Round Table was inviolate. We all knew that Lance and Guinevere were having at each other like a pair of randy goats, but so long as no one spoke about it, it wasn't really happening, because Arthur wanted all of us to live up to some ideal standard that was impossible for any normal human being to meet."

"Except for Galahad, perhaps," said Merlin.

"True," admitted Modred with a nod, "but Galahad was hardly normal, with his profound spiritual obsessions. To him, Arthur was a god. And Galahad wanted so desperately to believe in the vision Arthur painted. I envied him the touching simplicity of his faith, but I could never share it, even if I wanted to. I saw Arthur as he was, a man so obsessed with his own self-righteousness that he denied anything that seemed to threaten it. He was never able to really look me in the face. His eyes would always slide away from mine. He spoke to me when he had to, but we never really talked. I was a living reminder of his sin and he could not accept that."

"He was torn with guilt," said Merlin.

"Perhaps," said Modred, "but only because he did not live up to his own image of himself. Arthur, who was so pure of heart and spirit that only he could draw Excaliber from the stone—never mind that it was only because you had cast a spell on it so that no one else could do it—that paragon of chivalry and virtue had slept with his half sister and produced a bastard. He could not deny me, but he could not accept me, either. He certainly couldn't love me. And but for my mother poisoning my mind against him, I might have loved him. I really think I wanted to, despite everything Morganna did. But Arthur didn't want my love and so I gave him hate instead. He found that easier to live with. It fit in with his perverse sense of morality. In the end, I think he really wanted me to kill him, although he did his best to make sure that I died with him. That would have tied it all up neatly, I suppose."

"It was a sad thing," said Merlin. "A tragedy of human frailty and emotions."

Modred shook his head. "No, Ambrosius, the sad thing is that we all believed that we were caught up in some grand and tragic drama, and because all of us believed it, it came to be perceived that way. The fact is there was nothing grand about it. Nothing unique. Things like that happen all the time. We are all prisoners of our emotions in the end, which is why I've tried so hard to stifle mine."

"You seem to have succeeded," Merlin said.

"No, not really," Modred said wryly. "It only seems that way because I've had two thousand years of practice. I've often been accused of being cold and I've been called a cynic and to some extent, I must admit that's true. Oscar Wilde once told me that a cynic was someone who knew the price of everything and the value of nothing. I told him that the term cynic was rather imprecise. I preferred being called a 'post-romantic.' He found that quite amusing. But he was wrong in one respect. A cynic does know the value of at least one thing—truth. The reason he becomes a cynic is because he sees so little of it."

"I wonder if anyone ever really sees the truth?" said Merlin.

Modred smiled. "Strange that you should say that, of all

people. One of the more amusing aspects of the legend that our story has become is the myth that you were somehow living backward through time, that the future was your past and the past your future, so that you already knew everything to come. Unfortunately, you didn't know any better than the rest of us. You merely thought you did.''

"Nevertheless, it was I who gave Arthur the power,'' Merlin said.

"You merely gave him the opportunity,'' Modred replied. "He took the power for himself and seized it in a death grip. You were not the one who made him a king first and a husband second. Arthur did that all by himself. He set himself above the rest of us. Like you, he was obsessed with the idea of his sense of purpose. If he'd been more attentive to Guinevere, perhaps she wouldn't have turned to Lancelot. But it might have happened anyway. No one can predict such things. But by acting as he did, Arthur only made it easier. You were not the one who failed to take human frailty into account, Ambrosius. Arthur was. He created a code of conduct for us all that was totally inflexible. It did not allow for human fallibility. And it had no room for forgiveness. The ironic thing about it was that he was just as much a victim as Lancelot and Guinevere were. He could not forgive himself.''

"And what about you?'' said Merlin. "Have you room within you for forgiveness?''

"Whom should I forgive?'' said Modred. "Arthur? He's been dead for over two thousand years. My mother? I forgave her long ago, but she was unable to forgive herself and now she's gone, as well. You? What is there to forgive, Ambrosius? In spite of what you may think, you've never really done anything to me. My mother always blamed you because you helped Uther satisfy his lust for Igraine and then kill Gorlois. But she forgave you in the end, perhaps because she finally realized that what she had done was really no different from what you did. You were both motivated by revenge and you both paid the price. Both of you were victims. And if

Gorlois is listening, perhaps he'll understand that he's become a victim, too. There is an old saying: 'When you embark upon revenge, you must first construct two coffins.' One for your intended victim and one for yourself, as well. Revenge is like a chain reaction. There is no end to it. And sooner or later, it always comes full circle. It always comes back to you. Forgive yourself, Ambrosius. Because no one else can make things right by giving you forgiveness. Not even Gorlois. He must forgive himself as well. Because whenever revenge is the motivating factor, there will always be other victims. Like Morganna. Like myself, perhaps, though I don't truly feel myself to be a victim. Like Arthur, Guinevere and Lancelot. And, finally, like Billy.''

"Modred, look," said Kira.

She pointed at the ring on Billy's hand. The fire opal runestone was glowing softly.

The broom came out onto the balcony. "Breakfast is ready and there's a call for you," it said to Modred. "Person to person, from Paris, France, no less. I guess they don't believe in sleeping, either.''

"Broom, has it ever occurred to you that you don't *need* to sleep?" said Merlin.

"Oh, sure, I should just do housework around the clock, right?" said the broom. "I should stay up all night and catch the roaches when they all come out. Maybe I should take the opportunity of all the peace and quiet to scrub the kitchen floor? Or you want maybe I should give the whole apartment a brand new coat of paint? Baking, maybe? I should stay up all night and bake that tasteless Irish soda bread you like so much? Or maybe I can—''

"Never mind, Broom," Merlin said wearily. "If you want to sleep, then by all means sleep, however it is you manage to do it.''

"With you people staying up until all hours and phone calls from Paris in the middle of the night, I *don't* manage to do it," said the broom. "If you wanted to be useful, you'd make with the hocus-pocus and give me a soundproof broom closet. Maybe *then* I'll get some rest! Now are you coming in to breakfast or you want to wait until the toast gets cold and the maple syrup sets up?''

''We're coming in to breakfast, Broom,'' said Modred, coming back out onto the balcony. ''And then we've got to pack. We're going to Paris.''

''What, *now*?'' the broom said. ''In the middle of the night?''

''That was Jacqueline,'' said Modred. ''There's been a murder in the Rue Morgue. And the victim had necromantic runes carved into her body. The same pattern we've seen before, in Whitechapel and Los Angeles.''

''The Dark Ones,'' Wyrdrune said.

''It begins again,'' said Merlin.

Chapter
THREE

Suzanne Muset was in no mood to go to work. Fortunately, her employer at the Cafe Noir was an understanding man. He had read about the murder in the papers and before Suzanne had even asked, he told her to take as much time off as she felt was necessary and said that if there was anything that he could do, she had only to ask. He even offered to help with the funeral expenses. Suzanne's roommate, Gabrielle, had offered to remain with her, but Suzanne had insisted that she would be all right. After all, they both had bills to pay and she could not depend on their employer's charity. It was kind of him, but it simply wasn't right. She needed to return to work herself, but not just yet. She needed some time alone.

It had not been easy for Gabrielle, either. They had both found Joelle's body together. She would never forget that terrible sight. Joelle lying nude in a pool of her own blood, her young, innocent body horribly mutilated. They had both become hysterical and if it wasn't for Mr. Rienzi, who lived across the hall, Suzanne didn't know what they would have done. He had responded to their terrified screams and he immediately took control. He quickly ushered them both out of the room, into his apartment, and he had done his best to try to calm them down, talking to them and giving them strong brandy, before he summoned the police. He would not allow them to go back into their apartment, insisting that they stay overnight with him. He even gave them his bedroom while he slept on the couch.

Suzanne would be forever grateful to him. It was ironic. Until that night, they had never really known each other. They had said polite hellos when they passed each other in the hallway or met in the market, but they had never really talked. All she knew about Stefan Rienzi was that he was a struggling writer who lived by himself and kept late hours. He was working on a book. He was not a bad-looking man at all and she guessed that he was in his thirties, but he seemed very self-contained and shy. He was soft-spoken and hesitant in his manner and she and Gabrielle had often joked about him. Gabrielle had flirted with him outrageously and it always seemed to embarrass him. They wondered if perhaps he didn't like girls. He had seemed like one of those gray little men who went through life making as little noise as possible, taking pains to remain inconspicuous, like a mouse hiding in its hole. But after the night of Joelle's murder, Suzanne's opinion of Stefan Rienzi changed completely.

He had taken complete control of the situation, hovering over them while the policemen asked their questions, making sure they were all right. He had simply taken care of everything. After the body was removed and the police had gone away, he stayed up with them, trying to give them comfort. And when they finally dropped off to sleep, utterly exhausted and drained by their ordeal, he had gone out to an all-night market and bought groceries and toilet articles for the two of them. He knew that the apartment would be sealed for at least another day or two until the forensics investigators could complete their work. He had even offered to move out temporarily, so that they could use his apartment in privacy.

Gabrielle, always the more decisive of the two, had insisted that they couldn't put him out, that he had already done more than enough. Suzanne couldn't bear the thought of going back to their own apartment, not even for a moment. Gabrielle took it upon herself to find other lodgings for them. One of the girls at work knew of an inexpensive apartment for rent in the building where she lived and Gabrielle had gone to make the arrangements. Stefan offered to help them move as soon as the new apartment was ready. Suzanne felt guilty that she wasn't doing her part, but after the initial shock of Joelle's death wore off, she had simply become numb.

She blamed herself. She should have kept more careful watch over her sister. Joelle had always been too impulsive, too impatient, too anxious to grow up. She had wanted to be just like her older sister, a dancer in a chorus line, but Suzanne wanted something better for Joelle than dancing naked in a nightclub. Since their parents died when Joelle was only nine, Suzanne had raised her, but as Joelle got older, she grew more difficult. She became more willful and independent. Much like me, Suzanne thought. She had her own circle of friends and she had started going out with older men and there had been nothing that Suzanne could do to stop it. She had to work and she could not watch her all the time. And now she was dead.

At least they had caught the brute that did it. Max Siegal, the famous painter. Suzanne trembled when she thought of him. *Why?* Why had he done it? A man who could have any woman that he wished. He must have gone insane. No sane man could have done what he had done. When Joelle had told her that Siegal had asked her to model for him, Suzanne had been against it, but she had known that if she had forbidden her, Joelle would have done it just the same. Besides, Max Siegal was a very famous and well-respected man. He often came to the club and her boss had told her that most of the stories about Max Siegal were wildly exaggerated. He was an artist, temperamental and a bit eccentric, but he was not the sort of man to take undue advantage. He said that if Joelle posed for him, it could lead to bigger things, perhaps even a contract with a modeling agency. Maybe that was why her boss was going out of his way to try to help her now. He felt guilty for reassuring her about Max Siegal. But how could he have known? How could anyone have known? What could have possessed the man to do such an awful thing?

There was a knock at the door and she got up to answer it, thinking it was Stefan returning from the store. She opened it and came face-to-face with Max Siegal.

"Suzanne Muset?" he said.

She gasped and brought her hand up to her mouth, involuntarily taking two steps backward. "Oh, my God! *It's you!*"

"Please, I need to speak with you," said Max, coming into the apartment. "I just came to tell you how sorry I am about—"

"What are you doing here?" she cried. *"How did you get out of jail?"*

"Suzanne, let me explain. I didn't—"

She screamed. "*Get out!* Get out of here! *Murderer!* You killed my sister!"

"Please, you don't understand, I didn't—"

She screamed hysterically and ran into the kitchen, looking for a knife, something with which to defend herself. He followed her. She yanked open a drawer and pulled out a large carving knife, holding it before her.

"Get away from me! *Get away!*"

Max held up his hands. "Take it easy," he said. "I'm not going to hurt you. I understand how you must feel, but—"

Suzanne screamed and lunged at him with the knife. He caught her hand and they struggled, Suzanne screaming hysterically and kicking at him, but he managed to wrest the knife out of her grasp and shove her away. And then Stefan was there suddenly, spinning Max around and punching him. The knife fell from Max's hand as he tried to defend himself, but Stefan kept hitting him and Max had no choice but to fight back. His size was an advantage. He blocked the slightly built writer's blow and struck him in the mouth, then again in the stomach, winding him. He hit him once more in the face, dropping him to the floor.

Suzanne scrambled for the knife, grabbing it and crouching protectively over Stefan. "*Get out!*" she screamed, sobbing. "*Murderer! Get out!*"

Max backed away helplessly. "I'm sorry," he said, wiping the blood from his mouth. "I didn't mean. . . I'm sorry. . . ."

"*GET OUT!*"

He turned and ran out of the apartment. Suzanne dropped the knife and bent down over Stefan, sobbing. He groaned.

"Oh, Stefan, Stefan," she sobbed, kissing him. "Stefan, darling, are you all right?"

"Call the police," said Stefan.

To Merlin, the flight to Paris seemed much longer than it was because of the in-flight movie. While the plane winged its way silently across the Atlantic Ocean without benefit of engines, levitated and impelled by the sorcerer-pilots in the cockpit, the passengers were treated to a showing of the recent film, *Ambrosius*! Produced by Ron Rydell, who had made a fortune with his lurid series of *Necromancer* films, *Ambrosius*! was supposed to be Rydell's first effort at serious, big-budget moviemaking, based upon the life of "The Father of the Second Thaumaturgic Age, the Legendary Archmage, Merlin Ambrosius!" For Merlin, watching it was an excruciatingly painful experience.

The title role was played by that hammy, golden-throated British actor, Burton Clive, who never delivered a line so much as he declaimed it. He played Merlin in a broad, Shakespearian manner, all expressive eyebrows and elaborate gestures, with his eyes bulging and his nostrils flaring and his theatrical voice dramatically rising up and down the scale. It was like watching a man on the verge of an epileptic fit. Sex symbol Jessica Blaine simpered her way through the part of

Guinevere, dressed in outrageously revealing costumes and heaving her busoms with every breathy line. Lancelot was portrayed by action movie star Reese Richards, who took every opportunity to bare his chest and flexed even through the love scenes. The fact that the real Lancelot was rather homely and built like a fireplug didn't seem to matter in the least. Arthur was underplayed by veteran character actor Cleeve McCain, who mumbled all his lines and whose facial expressions seemed limited to a tic at the corner of his mouth and a squint. And Morgan Le Fay was played by Rydell's new discovery, a fashion model named Heather Hyatt, who was decked out for the occasion in skin-tight black leather and spike-heeled boots. And as if all that weren't bad enough, they'd made the film a musical, with the action stopping every fifteen minutes or so for someone to turn to the camera and break into song about "the shining glory, Camelot," or "the dreadful passion of our love."

Merlin suffered through the first half hour of the film, then decided to magically burn up the print in the projector, but Billy, who was enjoying the movie, prevented him and the two of them sat there, squirming, arguing like two movie critics trapped in the same body, much to the amusement of Modred and the others and the irritation of the nearby passengers.

"If he calls that ridiculous talking owl 'my faithful Archimedes' one more time, I'm going to blast that screen into oblivion!" said Merlin.

"You won't, either," Billy said. "I like the owl."

"I'm not surprised," said Merlin. "He's giving a better performance than anyone else in this disaster."

"'Ey, come on, it's not so bad," said Billy.

"Not so bad? It's a bloody horror!"

"It works for me," said Billy.

"That electronic cacophony you call music works for you," said Merlin. "You have the taste of a barbarian bogtrotter. I'm going to sue Rydell for defamation of character!"

"Now 'ow the 'ell can you sue someone when yer dead, eh?"

"He's got you there," said Modred, chuckling.

"I fail to see what you find so amusing," Merlin grumbled. "Look at the moron they've got playing you!"

The part of Modred had been reduced to a minor supporting role, played by the popular rock star, David Stone, complete with feathered, dyed blond hair and earring.

"I'll admit the earring is a bit much," said Modred, "but he does bring a certain feral energy to the part that's not entirely out of character, though personally, I could never hit such high notes. If I tried to sing like that, I'd hurt myself."

"I suppose you think it's funny," Merlin said.

"No more so than all the other books and films they've based upon us," Modred said. "At least Clive is merely overacting. Hyatt's playing my mother like some sort of lesbian stormtrooper. I particularly liked the bondage seduction scene where I was conceived. Under the circumstances, I'm amazed that Arthur could even get it up with her."

"That's disgusting," Merlin said.

"Oh, I don't know, I found it erotic, in a kinky sort of way," said Kira.

"You're all degenerates," said Merlin.

"Oh, sod off," said Billy.

The movie ended with the climactic confrontation between Arthur and Modred, in which both died, and in the final scene, the offscreen voice of Burton Clive talked his way through a song in the manner of stage actors who cannot really sing, intoning portentously about how "one day the magic will return, when souls cry out and cities burn" while the camera slowly zoomed in on a majestic tree growing up out of a rock promontory.

"I give it one and a half stars," said Wyrdrune.

"I hear they're already talking about a sequel," Kira said with a smirk. *"Ambrosius 2—The Second Coming."*

"Perhaps they should call it *Ambrosius, Out Of His Tree*," said Modred.

"That's it!" said Merlin. "I've had enough. I'm going to sleep. Wake me when we get to Paris."

Jacqueline met them when they landed at the Charles De Gaulle airport. As usual, they traveled light, with only one small suitcase for each of them. With Modred's vast resources, built up over the centuries, they could easily buy anything they needed and Modred always insisted on staying in the very best hotels. He had booked rooms for them at Le Ritz, on the Place Vendome, a luxury hotel dating back to the nineteenth century. In the pre-Collapse days, royalty and the cream of the upper crust had stayed at the Ritz, which boasted accommodations and service so refined that the word "ritzy" had become part of the language. The hotel was actually two town houses joined together, with courtyards and gardens on the grounds. The rooms were elegantly furnished with antique, bronze-trimmed chests, marble baths and crystal chandeliers. The lobby boasted Louis XVI antiques and tapestries. The hotel had undergone some damage during the street riots of the Collapse, but it had been extensively refurbished and as much of the original decor and furnishings as possible had been painstakingly restored.

They were delivered to the front entrance by a chauffeured limo. Jacqueline brought them up-to-date en route. They were conducted to their rooms and while they unpacked, Jacquline telephoned Inspector Renaud, to see if he'd made any progress with his inquiries. Unfortunately, he hadn't. Even worse, there had been a second murder and Max had been arrested once again, this time to be held without bail.

"What do you mean, he's been arrested *again*?" Jacqueline said while the others listened. "I thought he was in jail all this time!"

"Regrettably, mademoiselle, Max Siegal has many friends," Renaud replied wryly. "A collection was apparently taken up to meet his bail and he was released shortly after we last spoke. And he promptly committed another murder."

"No," said Jacqueline. "That's impossible. There must be some mistake."

"I am afraid not, mademoiselle," Renaud told her. "He returned to the scene of the crime and killed again."

"I don't believe it," Jacqueline said. "What proof do you have?"

"After he was released from jail," said Renaud, his tone very curt and official, "he made his way back to the Rue Morgue. He went back to the apartment where Joelle Muset had stayed with her sister, Suzanne, and her roommate, Gabrielle Longet. He found the apartment vacant, but the two girls were staying temporarily with a neighbor in the apartment across the hall. He apparently discovered that fact and forced his way in. We have witnesses this time. Stefan Rienzi, who was renting the apartment, came home to find Siegal assaulting Suzanne Muset with a knife. They fought and Rienzi managed to get the knife away from him, but he was injured in the struggle, sustaining a slight concussion and a broken nose. Suzanne Muset called the police, but by the time they arrived, Siegal had fled. A warrant was immediately issued for his arrest. However, before he could be apprehended, he returned to finish the job, while Rienzi was getting treatment at the hospital. Suzanne had accompanied Rienzi to the hospital, but Siegal found her roommate, Gabrielle Longet, alone at the apartment and he killed her. The method of the murder was identical to that of Joelle Muset."

"I simply can't believe it," Jacqueline said, stunned. "There must be some other explanation."

"I am afraid not, mademoiselle," Renaud said stiffly. "After our discussion, I was tempted to give your friend the benefit of the doubt, but now that is no longer possible. Another innocent girl has died and the newspapers are blaming us for releasing Siegal from custody. This time, he will remain in jail, where he belongs, until his trial and execution."

"Listen to me, Renaud," Jacqueline said, "I know you think that Max is guilty, but I assure you, he did *not* commit those murders, no matter what it looks like. You have to make those calls—"

"I am sorry, mademoiselle," Renaud cut her off, "but I have already listened to you long enough. I will not be a party to some scheme to get a demented killer back on the streets of Paris once again. Good day to you."

He hung up the phone.

Jacqueline stared at the dead receiver in her hand, then slowly replaced it in its cradle. "I can't believe it," she said. "The fool. *Why* did he go back there?"

"What happened?" Wyrdrune asked.

She told them what Renaud had said.

"Jacqueline," said Modred gently, "please don't take offense, but are you quite certain about this?"

She stared at him. "What are you saying? You think Max did it?"

"I don't know Max Siegal," Modred said. "I know only his work and what you've told me about him."

"And my word isn't good enough for you, is that it?" she said.

"No, that's not it at all. You should know better than that," said Modred. "But you yourself said that you hadn't seen Max Siegal in some time. It's possible that he might have had some sort of mental breakdown and—"

"Max Siegal is as sane as you and I," she said. "He's not a killer. And what about the runes?"

"There is that," said Kira. "You're sure they were the same?"

"I drew them for Renaud myself and he said they were identical to the marks found on the first victim's body," said Jacqueline. "Max couldn't possibly have known about them."

Modred nodded. "That's true," he said. "It seems Max Siegal made the mistake of being in the wrong place at the wrong time. Twice."

"I can't understand it," Jacqueline said. "Why on earth would he go back there? And threatening the girl with a knife, that simply doesn't sound like Max. He's temperamental, true, and he's been in fights before, but he's never hurt a woman. He isn't like that."

"If Max Siegal's innocent, then his only chance to prove

it is to remain in jail," Modred said. "He will be arraigned, but it will be a long time until his trial. If what we suspect is true, then the killer will surely strike again before then."

"So Max's only chance to gain his freedom is for someone else to die," Jacqueline said.

"It would seem so," said Modred, "at least for the moment. But even if the killer doesn't strike again—and if we're right, that's an extremely unlikely possibility—then there's still the fact that the evidence they have against Siegal is still purely circumstantial. Powerfully circumstantial, perhaps, but nevertheless not conclusive."

"I have to go and see him," Jacqueline said.

"They probably will not admit you," Modred said. "Let's not rush into anything. Do you know who his attorney is?"

"No," she said, "but I can easily find out."

"Do that. If he's reasonably competent, then perhaps we can work with him. If not, we'll get someone else to represent him."

"I'll get August Chautrand," Jacqueline said. "He's always represented me. He's the best criminal lawyer in France."

"Good. Give him a call. In the meantime, what can you tell me about this Inspector Renaud?"

"Not very much," Jacqueline said. "I've only met him once. Polite. Charming. He seemed like a reasonable man, but now he simply refuses to listen."

"Has he called in the I.T.C. or anyone from the French Bureau of Thaumaturgy?" Modred asked.

"I don't know," she said. "When we last spoke, he said that if what I told him was true, it was his duty to call in the I.T.C., but now it seems he's satisfied that no magic was involved."

"He may be determined to make the case himself, without having the I.T.C. or the Bureau take it away from him," said Wyrdrune. "In that event, he's going to wind up looking very foolish when the Dark Ones kill again."

"No, not the Dark Ones," Modred said. "At least, not personally. It would appear as if they're working through an accolyte. That would be their normal pattern. Send someone else out to do their killing and feed off the life energy released until they've accumulated sufficient power for mass slaughter. Until then, they will conserve their energies.''

"You think there may be more than one?" said Kira.

"I hope there's only one," said Modred, "but there may well be more. At this point, there's simply no way of knowing, so we might as well assume the worst. Have any of you had any reaction from your runestones?"

Kira shook her head. "Not me."

"Me neither," Wyrdrune said.

"Nor I," said Modred. "That means they can't be very close. Or their power isn't great enough yet, which would work in our favor."

"Have we landed yet?" said Merlin, as Billy yawned. "Where are we? Are we in our hotel already?"

"Good morning," Kira said.

"I thought I told you to wake me when we landed," Merlin said.

"What for?" said Billy. "So you could just start in bein' a bloody pain again?"

"Now you listen here, you young guttersnipe—"

"Not now, Ambrosius," Modred said. "It can wait. There have been new developments. We have to formulate a plan of action."

"What do you want me to do?" asked Merlin.

"'Ow's about keepin' quiet?" Billy said sourly.

"For the moment, nothing," Modred said. "I have to think. In a city like Paris, the Dark Ones could be almost anywhere. For the time being, I don't think we can expect any cooperation from the police."

"Maybe we should call Blood and have him get in touch with Renaud," said Wyrdrune.

"Let's hold off on that for now," said Modred. "If Renaud becomes convinced that necromancy is involved, as he inevitably will be, then we already know the first thing he's going to do is call in the I.T.C. and they're not liable to be very cooperative. There's also the fact that I'm wanted by them."

"But they don't know you're Morpheus," said Kira. "They don't even know what Morpheus looks like."

"Just the same, I'd rather not have them underfoot," said Modred. "Their sorcerer agents are very competent, but their bureaucracy gives them tunnel vision. The longer we have to operate unimpeded, the better our chances are."

"So what's our first move?" asked Wyrdrune.

"Well, since it doesn't seem as if we can expect any cooperation from the local authorities, we'll need more help," Modred said. "I'm going to call Makepeace and have him fly out as soon as possible. Then I'd like to have a look at the scene of the murders. There would have to be some thaumaturgic trace emanations on the site, even if they're very faint. Perhaps we can pick up something."

"That might be risky," Kira said.

Modred shrugged. "At the moment, we have nothing else to go on."

There was a sudden commotion in the hall outside their room. Wyrdrune went to the door and opened it. The broom was out in the hall, wrestling with a maid. They were both shouting at each other, Broom in English, the maid in a torrent of rapid French.

"Broom! What the hell are you doing?" Wyrdrune said. "Let go of that woman!"

"*Me* let go of *her*? She keeps grabbing me! Will someone for God's sake tell this person I'm not part of the cleaning equipment?" said the broom, appealing to them for help. "This crazy woman's stuck me in the closet four times already and each time I manage to get out, she yells and shoves me right back in again!"

"Pardon, madame," said Modred to the maid in flawless French, "but I believe that broom belongs to us."

The maid stared at him wide-eyed. "To *you*, monsieur?"

"Yes. It does not belong to the hotel. As you can see, it is a rather special broom. Could we have it, please?"

"I'm sorry, monsieur, but I thought it was one of the new cleaning tools. We have recently had our vaccum cleaners animated, you see, and I thought this was some sort of new attachment. . . ." Her voice trailed off as she looked from the broom to Modred, embarrassment plain on her face.

"A completely understandable mistake," said Modred. "Please think nothing of it. You see, my friend here is an adept and the broom is his familiar."

"Ah! *Mon Dieu!*" she said. "I did not know! You won't tell the management, monsieur? I will get in trouble!"

"We won't say another word about it," Modred said. "But perhaps you would be so kind as to inform the staff about our broom, in order to avoid any further misunderstandings of this nature."

"Yes, of course, monsieur! And please accept my apologies." She curtsied to him, then, after hesitating uncertainly, she curtsied to the broom, as well.

"What's she doing now?" the broom said suspiciously.

"Just say, *merci*, Broom."

"Merci," said the broom.

"*Oui, merci*," said the maid, and hurried off down the hall.

"Crazy woman," said the broom. "Couldn't she tell I wasn't just *any* broom, for God's sake?"

"Apparently not," said Modred. "It seems they have animated cleaning appliances in this hotel. She thought you were some sort of vacuum cleaner attachment."

"*Vacuum cleaner attachment*?" said the broom with disbelief. "They have animated vaccum cleaners?"

"Apparently so," said Modred.

"*Feh!*" the broom said. "What's this world coming to, I ask you? You mean to tell me I'm going to have to put up with some talking canister coming in here to make up the room? *Gevalt!* I never heard of such a thing! You just tell them to keep out of here, that's all. Animated vacuum cleaners, my *tuchis!*"

"Just stay in the room and you'll be fine, Broom," Wyrdrune said with a chuckle. "Watch some TV or something."

"Oh, swell," the broom said. "I finally get a trip to Paris

and he says stay in the room and watch TV! I could have done *that* at home! Besides, I don't speak a word of French. How am I supposed to understand the programs?''

"Maybe we can get a bilingual vacuum cleaner in here to interpret for you," Wyrdrune said with a grin.

"No, thank you very much," the broom said with a sniff. "Never mind me. You just go on about your business. I'll find some way to occupy my time. After all, it's only Paris. The Eiffel Tower is just a bunch of girders, the Champs-Elysees is just a street, the Louvre is only a museum. We've got musuems back home in New York. It doesn't matter. I'll be fine. I'll find something to do. Don't worry about me."

Wyrdrune rolled his eyes. "Mother," he said, "you've got a lot to answer for."

Modred chuckled. "Don't worry, Broom. We'll find something for you to do. Perhaps we'll hire a guide to take you on a tour. Would you like that?"

"You don't have to go to any trouble on my account," the broom said.

"It's no trouble at all."

"No, that's all right. I'll just stay here. I'll do some knitting. You just go have a good time. Never mind about me, I'll be fine."

"Broom . . ." said Wyrdrune. "Stop it."

"Well, all right, if you insist, I'll go on a tour. But you're sure it won't be too expensive? Maybe just a *little* tour?"

"We'll work something out," said Modred. "In the meantime, I suggest we have some dinner. The cuisine in this hotel is excellent. We are in Paris, after all. Then, afterward, we'll take a short trip to the Rue Morgue."

"You've done very well, Jacques," the Dark One said. "Very well, indeed. I see that we were right to choose you."

Jacques sat on the couch in the luxurious apartment, staring at the floor. "She was so young, so pretty. . . ."

"And so strong," she said, coming up to stand before him. "The young ones are fresh," she said. "Their life energy is the most vibrant. Their blood courses powerfully through their veins.''

"Blood,'' said Jacques, still staring at the floor. "There was so much blood. . . .''

"You will grow used to it,'' she said, dropping her hand to rest on the back of his neck. "It was not so hard, was it? The second one was easier than the first. And the third one will be easier still. And after awhile, it will trouble you no longer. You will even learn to take pleasure in the kill.''

"I *did* take pleasure in it, God help me,'' said Jacques. He stared at his hands. "I keep washing my hands, but I can still feel the blood upon them.'' He shivered. "It frightens me. I know it's wrong, terribly wrong, and yet, I find myself enjoying it. The way I enjoy making love with you. I cannot think straight, I cannot eat, I cannot sleep. I keep thinking about those poor young girls. I did not want to do it, but I couldn't help myself. . . .''

She sat down on the couch, next to him, and put her arm around him. "Would you rather go back to the way you were?'' she said. "Is that what you want? To be old and decrepit once again, diseased and lice-ridden, crawling through the sewer tunnels like a rat? Is that what you want?''

"No,'' he said with a shudder. "But perhaps I would be better off.''

"Better off in the filthy, stinking sewers than in this beautiful apartment?'' she said. "Better off dying down there like some vermin-ridden animal instead of living like a handsome young gentleman of means? This is only the beginning, Jacques. You can have your old life back again and more. You will be better than you ever were before, better than you could have dreamed! We are not ungrateful. We reward those who are loyal to us. Tonight you will be back upon the stage once more. You will be the star of the Paris entertainment world! You will be wealthy, sought after and admired. Isn't that what you really want?''

"Yes. No. I don't know,'' said Jacques. "I don't know what I want anymore.''

"You still want me, Jacques, don't you?" she said, pulling him close and kissing his cheek, lightly flicking his earlobe with her tongue.

He felt the irresistible, overpowering desire for her flow through him once again and he threw his arms around her, pulling her close, kissing her passionately.

"God help me," he said. "Oh, Leila, what have you done to me?"

"Not a fraction of what I'm going to do, my love," she said softly, kissing him deeply and pushing him down upon the couch.

Chapter
FOUR

Michel Fremont had accumulated more stored-up hatred in his seventeen years than most people experience in an entire lifetime. He had grown up in a sick, abusive atmosphere, with an emotionally deadened mother who sold her body on the streets to support her drug habit and a father who was a sadistic alcoholic. He had never experienced affection. He had never known what it meant to feel wanted. He knew only anger and resentment because that was all he ever got and he gave it back in spades.

When Michel's father came staggering home after the bars had closed, the shouting and the screaming would commence, with his father demanding money and his mother refusing to give him any, afraid that she wouldn't have enough to pay the rent and buy her drugs—never mind the food, of which there was never enough. His father would start beating her and she would put up token resistance, suffering the treatment long enough to make him think that he had pummeled her into submission, whereupon she would part with a portion of the money she had earned, hoarding the rest in various hiding places around the house. Michel's father would then pocket the money and start looking for Michel, to thrash him for good measure before he went to sleep.

Michel would hide, under a bed, inside a closet, behind a chair, and occasionally his father would fail to find him before he passed out on the couch, or on the bed, or often on the floor, and for at least one night, Michel would escape a beating. But it was a very small apartment and there were few places to hide. More often than not, Michel was pulled out from his place of sanctuary and "taught a lesson." Violence was the only lesson he had ever learned and he had learned it very well.

At school, he was surly and rebellious, indifferent to his lessons and meaner than a junkyard dog. All the other children were mortally afraid of him and, as he grew older, a good number of his teachers learned to fear him, too. They were secretly relieved when one day he failed to show up for school and never came back again. No one even bothered to report him for being truant. Nor did he bother to go back home. His father had beat him once too often and Michel had waited until he passed out on the floor, then he had stuck a knife between his ribs and stopped his snoring permanently. He had then gone to finish off his mother, but she had already saved him the trouble. He found her dead in her bedroom, of an overdose.

Michel never felt the least bit of remorse. For a while, he was afraid that the police would catch him, but it never came to that. It was not the sort of crime that received a great deal of priority. A prostitute dead of an overdose and a convicted felon stabbed to death. Perhaps one of her johns had done it. Perhaps she had killed him and then drugged herself into oblivion. Either way, nobody much cared. They were the sort of people who would not be missed. The neighbors had said something about a boy, and he was listed as being missing, but there were more runaways living on the streets of

Paris than the police could ever hope to find and so they didn't bother looking very hard. Michel was simply another casualty of a squalid family life.

He survived by stealing. He tried picking pockets, as many of the young street urchins did, but he found it far easier simply to select vulnerable victims, knock them down, kick them until they stopped struggling and then relieve them of their valuables. He had soon organized a small street gang of young hellions, keeping them in line with his father's time-honored methods. He taught them how to gang up on their targets, how to hit and run so they were never caught. The young runaway girls who gravitated to his gang were taught his mother's old profession, with a twist. They enticed the customers with their youth, luring them with promises of cheap, illicit sex to a place where the boys could stomp them into the ground and take their money. Occasionally, some of these girls would strike out on their own, finding it more profitable to actually deliver the goods and keep all the money for themselves. To keep that from happening too often, Michel made a habit of knocking them around every now and then, just as his father had done with his mother, until they coughed up some money. Most of them soon found it prudent to have some money on them to surrender, just in case Michel demanded an accounting. He was cold and vicious, without an ounce of compassion in his twisted soul, and he was afraid of nothing.

Until he met the Dark Ones.

The two old gentlemen were shuffling down the street, walking arm in arm. They looked like a couple of old queens, out for an evening's promenade. They were well dressed, which meant they probably had money. They should have known better than to be out at night in such a neighborhood, but perhaps they were out cruising, looking for some young flesh to fulfill their twisted appetites. Perhaps they thought that being together would provide them with some measure of protection. Well, thought Michel, the old fools would soon find out how wrong they were.

He beckoned his young headbreakers forward, silently directing three of them to cut around the block and get ahead of the two old men. Then, after giving them several moments to get into position, he gave the signal to the other three and they quickly began to close the distance. The two old men heard the sound of boot heels behind them and fearfully glanced over their shoulders, quickening their pace, but Michel and his young friends were already only yards behind them and closing fast. Then, suddenly, three more street punks stepped out of an alleyway ahead of them and the two old men found themselves boxed in. Like a well-trained assault unit, Michel and his gang, four boys and two tough-as-nails teenaged girls, hit the old men from both sides, forcing them into the alleyway where they could throw them to the ground and kick them into submission and that's where things started going wrong.

Suddenly, inexplicably, there was no sign of the two old men. One moment, they were shoving them into the alleyway, the next, they were simply gone. And they were no longer in the alley.

Stunned, Michel and his friends looked around them at the torches blazing on the rock walls, at the smoking braziers and the bones piled up in niches all around them.

"What the hell?" Michel said, gazing all around him wildly, looking for someone to pulverize.

"What happened?" one of the girls cried in a frightened voice. "Where are we?"

Involuntarily, they started to huddle together in a tight little group around Michel.

"Get away from me!" he said, shoving them away.

"*Adepts*!" one of the other boys said. "Those two old geezers must've been adepts! We tried to mug a pair of sorcerers! Oh, Christ, we've had it now!"

"Shut up!" Michel said.

"Michel, I'm frightened!" the second girl wailed.

Michel gave her a stinging slap across the face. "Shut up, I said! I'll give you something to be frightened of!"

"What *is* this place?" one of the other boys said.

"The Catacombs," another boy replied, his voice trembling slightly. "They must've sent us to the Catacombs. You could get lost in here forever! We'll never find our way out! We're dead!"

Michel grabbed him by the throat. "*Shut up!* We'll find our way out. Somebody found their way in, didn't they? Someone had to light these torches. We'll find 'em and *make* 'em show us the way out!"

"*Michel! Look!*" one of the girls said, pointing.

Two hooded, black-robed figures stood at the far end of the chamber, watching them.

"Get 'em!" snarled Michel, running at the figures.

Purely out of instinct, three of the boys went with him, but the others hesitated. One of the hooded figures casually raised an arm and Michel and the three boys suddenly found themselves being hurled back fifteen feet across the chamber. One of the girls screamed, the other threw her hands up to her mouth, speechless with fear. The boys who had hesitated began to back away slowly, their eyes wide. Two of the boys who had charged the robed figures lay stunned on the floor of the chamber. The third pulled himself up to his hands and knees, but prudently chose to remain right where he was. Things had escalated far beyond the point where any of them were willing to go on with this. Any of them except Michel, who immediately jumped to his feet and, with a scream of rage, launched himself at the necromancers, knife in hand.

The necromancer calmly raised his arm once more, palm out facing Michel, and it was as if Michel had run into a stone wall. He bounced hard off something that wasn't even there, ran at it again, only to encounter the same invisible obstruction. Snarling, he rained blows and kicks upon the unseen wall.

"Magnificent, isn't he, Azreal?" one of the necromancers said, his resonant, deep voice filling the chamber.

"A wild little beast," the other said. "Such rage and such intensity! Such deliciously delightful evil!"

"Yes, I think he will do very nicely."

Furious, Michel spun around to face his friends. "*Come

on!'' he screamed at them. ''Don't just fucking *stand* there! We can all smash through together!''

But his friends weren't having any of it. In his rage, Michel wasn't thinking beyond the fact that there was an obstacle of some sort between him and his quarry. All he wanted was to break through, but his companions all realized by now that they were facing sorcerers and they wanted no part of it. They turned and fled toward the tunnel they had seen behind them, but suddenly, it simply wasn't there. There was no exit from the chamber. The were completely enclosed by solid walls of rock.

They panicked. They ran to where the tunnel had been scant moments earlier, pressing their hands against the wall, refusing to believe it wasn't there. One of the girls backed away from the wall, whimpering, and tripped, falling into a heap of bones. She screamed hysterically as rats scampered away from the pile.

Michel spun around again and started stabbing repeatedly at the invisible obstruction. It gave way before his blade and sprang right back. He screamed with frustration and threw himself against it and suddenly he plunged through. He fell hard to the stone floor of the chamber. He could no longer hear the screams of his friends. He turned and looked back through the invisible wall, watching them scramble madly around the chamber, seeking an avenue of escape which wasn't there. It was like watching some sort of surrealistic silent movie. He saw their mouths opening and closing, but he couldn't hear a sound. He turned and looked up at the two necromancers, who stood motionless before him, and his face twisted into a grimace of bestial rage. He bent and picked up his knife.

''Listen to me, Michel Fremont,'' said one of them, pulling back his hood. Michel found himself staring not at an old man, but at a strikingly handsome young face framed by flaming red hair that cascaded down onto his shoulders. ''You have a great deal of potential. We can help you to realize it.''

"Realize *this*!" Michel said, and hurled the knife unerringly toward the necromancer.

The necromancer didn't move, but the knife came to a dead stop, hanging in midair only inches from his chest. He stared at it and it dropped to the floor.

"He truly is an animal," the other necromancer said.

"Then let him become one," his companion replied. He gestured at Michel.

Michel screamed in pain and doubled over as a searing heat suddenly washed over him. He sank to the floor, wreathed in a pulsating blue aura. He thrashed and clawed at himself, tearing off his clothes. It felt as if thousands upon thousands of microscopic insects were crawling all over him, biting and stinging furiously. Blood gushed from his gums as his teeth sprouted into fangs. His hands became twisted and gnarled, throbbing with agony as they metamorphosed into paws. His back felt as if it were breaking as it arched high, his spine writhing like a snake beneath his skin. His eyes changed color, becoming a bright, glowing, golden yellow. His jaw began to stretch as his lower face extended into a snarling, drooling snout. Black fur sprouted from his face and body and his screams became a bestial howling.

Behind the invisible wall, his friends stood huddled together, frozen with terror as they watched Michel being transformed into a huge and powerful wolf, only much larger than any normal wolf could ever be. It snapped its jaws and pawed at the ground, shaking its huge head back and forth, filling the underground chamber with the echo of its gruesome howls. And then, as the creature that had been Michel came toward them, they realized that the invisible wall was gone and the monster was moving with a slow, deliberate, stalking gait, its yellow eyes fixed upon them hungrily. They broke and ran, screaming, but there was nowhere for them to run.

The beast leaped and brought down one of the girls. She screamed hysterically as its right forepaw swept across her chest, tearing away her blouse, and then twin yellow beams stabbed down from the creature's eyes, burning strange and grotesque symbols into her young breasts. Her piercing screams filled the chamber as smoke curled up from her charred skin and then the creature brought its massive head down, snapping its powerful jaws at her throat, and blood gushed up in a fountain as her screams ended in a horrendous gurgle.

The two necromancers stood utterly motionless, their eyes closed as if in ecstasy, their chests swelling slightly as they absorbed the power of her life force. And then the creature snarled and leaped again.

They had no difficulty getting into the apartment. Wyrdrune had been about to cast a spell to release the lock, but Kira told him not to bother. She merely reached inside her jacket pocket and removed a slim little case of stainless steel tools, which she used to pick the lock open. It took her no more than a few seconds.

"Well, now what's the fun of that?" said Wyrdrune.

"It isn't about fun, it's about being quietly efficient," Kira said. "Anyway, knowing you, you'd have overdone it and blown open the entire door and half the wall, besides."

"I appreciate the vote of confidence," said Wyrdrune sourly.

They went in and shut the door behind them. There were only the four of them. Jacqueline had stayed behind at the hotel to make her calls to Max Siegal's lawyer and to her own attorney. They walked slowly around the apartment; two bedrooms, a small sitting room, a bathroom and a kitchenette.

The furniture was old and conformed to no particular style. There was a cheap, imitation Persian rug on the floor, stained and bunched up in several places. An old sofa with a garish floral print stood against the wall. It was spattered with blood, as was the wall behind it. Opposite it, a small television set had stood on a badly scratched coffee table, but the table had been knocked over and the television set lay broken on the floor. A battered end table beside the sofa had been knocked over, as well. The ashtray on it had been overflowing with cigarette butts, which were strewn across the floor, the filter tips stained with bright red lipstick. The surface of the end table was covered with cigarette burns. There were a dozen or more potted plants badly in need of watering placed around the sitting room in little groups, many of them knocked over, and a fake fireplace with a nonfunctional grate in which a stuffed dog with one eye missing had been placed on a ratty old cushion, a cherished toy from childhood, amusingly displayed.

Two posters hung on the wall above the sofa, one a framed advertisement for the Cafe Noir, done in a poor imitation of Lautrec's style, the other a photographic print of the skyline of Manhattan, with ''New York'' boldly lettered in white across it. The New York poster was hanging crookedly and there was a large smudge on the wall beside it, with a chip in the paster. Beneath it, a broken clay pot lay on the carpet, the plant and soil spilling out of it. It seemed as if the victim had hurled the pot at the killer in a vain attempt at self-defense. A battered, cloth upholstered reading chair stood in one corner, the standing lamp beside it leaning at a crazy angle against the wall. The mantelpiece was cluttered with all sorts of bric-a-brac; framed photographs, a few miniature figurines of unicorns and dragons, some of which had been knocked over and broken, a hair brush, an open pack of cigarettes, a brandy snifter containing matchbooks from various restaurants and night spots.

The kitchen was a mess. There was hardly anything in the refrigerator. One moldy container of strawberry yogurt. One withered head of lettuce. An open bottle of white wine. Several left-over cartons of Chinese take-out. And not much else. Unwashed cups and dishes were stacked in the sink. The countertop was sprinkled with spilled coffee grounds. There were shattered fragments of cups and dishes on the floor, as well as a few pots and pans. The kitchen chairs had been knocked over and the table had been shoved aside. Part of the struggle had taken place in here. The garbage stank.

In the bathroom, there was a veritable explosion of cosmetics, underthings and toiletries. Lipsticks, eye shadows, blushers, eyeliners, makeup base, panties hanging on the

shower rod and spigots, cold cream, moisturizers, acne med-
ications, lacy bras in black and various pastel shades, per-
fumes, curling sets, blow dryers, shampoos, creme rinses and
conditioners, silky slips, oil treatments, depilatory foams,
sanitary napkins, nail polish in almost every imaginable
shade, dirty towels, mascara, bunched-up stockings . . . it
looked as if someone had thrown a hand grenade in there and
closed the door to contain the holocaust. However, this was
apparently the result of the normal housekeeping or rather
the lack of it, not the struggle with the killer. The bedrooms
were not much neater. Clothes left wherever they were
dropped. High-heeled shoes spilling out of the closets.
Modred stopped in the doorway of the second bedroom,
where two of the girls had slept.

"They were here," he said, looking all around the room.

Kira glanced at Wyrdrune. The emerald runestone was
nearly hidden by his hair, but she could see a faint, telltale
green glow. She glanced down at her palm to see that her
sapphire runestone was also glowing dimly.

"They stood right here, in this bedroom," Modred said,
entering the room briefly, then going back out into the sitting
room. There was a large, dark stain in the center of the carpet.
He glanced back toward the bedroom. "They stood right there
and watched through the open doorway while he killed her,
then they absorbed her life energy."

"You said *they*," said Merlin.

Modred looked at him and frowned. "Yes, I did, didn't
I?"

"Don't any of you move," said a voice from behind them.
"Turn around, slowly, and keep your hands where I can see
them."

They did as the voice instructed. Standing behind them,
in the open doorway of the apartment, was a slim, dark-
haired young man holding a small semiautomatic pistol. He
looked nervous and his hand was shaking slightly.

"You heard them say that in the movies, didn't you?"
said Modred, smiling in a friendly manner.

"Just stay right where you are," the young man said. He moistened his lips. "Who are you people? What are you doing in here?"

"Stefan Rienzi?" Modred said.

"How do you know my name? Are you with the police? I'd like to see some identification."

"We're not with the police, Mr. Rienzi," Modred said, "but we are investigating the murder."

"Are you with the I.T.C.?"

"No," said Modred. "It's a rather complicated situation, Mr. Rienzi, and I'm afraid I haven't the time to explain it to you."

"I think I'd better call the police," Rienzi said.

The gun suddenly flew out of Rienzi's grasp and sailed across the room, landing in Billy's outstretched hand. "Never did like these damned things," said Merlin, handing the pistol to Modred. Rienzi bolted, but Wyrdrune gestured at the apartment door and it slammed shut. Rienzi grasped the doorknob and twisted it frantically, but the door refused to open. He turned around, his back against the door, staring at them fearfully.

"Who are you?" he said. "What do you want?"

"Calm yourself, Mr. Rienzi," Wyrdrune said. "We mean you no harm."

Modred glanced at the small-caliber pistol. It was of fairly recent manufacture, very small and made from inexpensive polymers and alloy. It had no knock-down power and was not a terribly threatening weapon unless one hit a vital spot. In the hands of someone who could hit that vital spot consistently, it would certainly do the job, although Rienzi was probably not that sort of man. Modred, on the other hand, was.

"In the future, before you point a weapon at someone, you might want to take the safety off," he said. He released the magazine, thumbed the bullets out onto the floor, checked to see that there was no round left in the chamber, reinserted the magazine and tossed the pistol back to Rienzi.

"I demand to know who you are and what you're doing here," Rienzi said, summoning up his courage and looking straight at him.

Modred held his gaze. "But we were never here," he said.

Rienzi blinked several times, but did not look away. He couldn't.

"You . . . you were never here," he said, his gaze becoming unfocused.

"You have never seen us," Modred said, staring at him intensely.

"I have never seen you," said Rienzi, his tone mechanical.

"If anyone asks, you couldn't possibly describe us, because you never saw us. There was no one here."

"Stefan!" A young woman's voice came from out in the corridor. She sounded alarmed. The doorknob rattled. "Stefan, are you all right? Is anybody there? What's happening?"

"There is no one here," he said mechanically.

"Stefan, I've called the police, they're on their way!"

"That must be Suzanne," said Kira. "You think she saw us?"

"I doubt it," Modred said. "Otherwise, she would not have asked if anyone was here. They must have heard us out in the corridor or moving around in here. In any case, if the police are on their way, I don't think we should remain. I think we've discovered all there is to learn here."

"Stefan! Stefan, I hear voices!"

"There is no one here," said Rienzi.

"Stefan, let me in!"

Modred glanced at Billy. "Ambrosius, will you do the honors?"

"My pleasure," Merlin said. He mumbled a quick spell under his breath and quickly brought his arms up over his head. They all disappeared, leaving Rienzi standing alone in the apartment.

"Stefan! Stefan, why won't you answer? What's wrong? Stefan?"

Rienzi blinked several times, then turned the doorknob. It

opened easily and Suzanne came rushing in. She had a large carving knife in her hand. She looked around, clearly frightened, but there wasn't anybody there.

"Stefan! I was frightened half out of my mind! I thought perhaps he had come back! Why didn't you answer me?"

"I told you there was no one here," he said calmly.

"But I heard voices."

"It must have been only your imagination."

"But I heard them, I tell you! Why was the door locked?"

"It wasn't. It was open."

"But I tried it!" she protested. "It was locked from the inside!"

"Nonsense. You're merely overwrought. As you can clearly see, there's no one here. Come, you shouldn't be in here. It's too much of a strain for you. We will be moving you soon. I will collect everything you need. Coming back in here will only upset you."

"I've called the police."

"Then we shall have to apologize to them for having wasted their time. I will explain to them. Under the circumstances, I'm sure they'll understand. Now come on, let's finish packing. The sooner you're out of here, the better off you'll be."

He gently turned her around and led her out of the apartment. He turned back to shut the door and his gaze fell on the bullets lying on the floor. He frowned and stared at them for a moment, then quickly went back inside, picked them up and put them in his pocket. Then he left the apartment and shut the door behind him.

They reappeared back inside their suite at the Ritz, giving Jacqueline a start. She had been on her way out of the bedroom, where she had changed, and had been about to call for room service when they all suddenly appeared out of nowhere right in front of her. She almost ran right into Wyrdrune. Startled, she cried out. Another step, and she would have been standing right on the spot where he'd materialized.

"That was a little close for comfort," she said.

"Yes, let's try to keep the middle of the room clear," said Modred, "just to avoid any potential accidents."

"That was a neat trick you did back there with Rienzi," Wyrdrune said. "You'll have to show me how it's done sometime. I didn't even hear you speak a spell of compulsion."

"That's because I didn't use one," Modred said. "And, regrettably, it's not the sort of trick that one can teach."

"Then what did you do?" asked Kira.

"He simply overwhelmed Rienzi's will with his own," said Merlin.

"How?" asked Wyrdrune, frowning.

"As I said, it's not the sort of trick that one can teach," said Modred. "I simply willed him to believe what I wanted him to believe. It isn't a technique so much as a talent. I discovered that I could do it about a thousand years ago and I've gotten somewhat better at it since. It takes a good deal of concentration. It doesn't work with everyone, but it's come in handy on occasion. I can't really explain it."

"It's an ability inherited from the Old Ones," Merlin said.

"You mean you can do it, too?" asked Wyrdrune.

"I could at one time," Merlin replied. "However, I've discovered that my inborn abilities are considerably diminished in Billy's body. As Modred said, it's a latent talent, one that develops with time, and it doesn't work with everyone, though I've found that it works fairly dependably with animals."

"I imagine it's where the myth about vampires bending people to their will came from," Modred said. "People descended from the Old Ones inherited many of their talents, such as extrasensory perception and, in certain rare cases, even telepathy, but I've noticed that those abilities tend to diminish with each succeeding generation unless both parents possessed the talent, in which case the child may have it stronger."

"You know, it's entirely possible that you may have it, too," said Merlin. "You may have acquired it through the spirits of the runestones."

"It's possible," said Modred. "I find it easier to do now that the runestone is a part of me. But it's not enough merely to inherit the talent. One must practice to develop it."

"I wonder if it would work on Broom," mused Wyrdrune. "Maybe if I really concentrated. . . ."

"To really concentrate, you first have to have a mind," the broom said, coming in from the back bedroom. "But I'm telling you right now, if you start staring at me and coming on like Dracula, I'll laugh so hard I'll *plotz*. Anyway, I've got all your things laid out. Is there anything else you want I should do or can I go back to watching television programs I can't even understand?"

"You won't have to suffer the frustration of watching French TV, Broom," Jacqueline said. "You're going out tonight."

"I'm going out?" the broom said. *"Me?"*

"Yes, it has all been arranged through the hotel," Jacqueline said. "I've engaged a guide who speaks English to take you out tonight and show you some of the Paris nightlife. He should be arriving any moment."

"I'm going *out*?" the broom said. "I'm actually going out? *Oy vey*, I can't believe it! I'm actually going to get to *do* something for a change?"

There was a knock at the door and Jacqueline went to answer it. She opened it to admit a very handsome and urbane-looking young man, dressed in the height of fashion. He took one look at Jacqueline and smiled broadly.

"Ah, *c'est magnifique*! Delightful! My name is Pierre Bouchet. I am the tour guide you engaged. Mademoiselle is ready to go out?" he said.

"No, not me," Jacqueline said, in French. She turned and pointed at the broom.

the tour guide's jaw dropped and his eyebrows shot up. *"That*?" he said. He stared at her with disbelief. "Mademoiselle is joking!"

"Mademoiselle is *not* joking," said Jacqueline, still in French.

"But . . . but mademoiselle . . . you cannot be serious! You mean you wish me to take that . . . that . . ."

"That broom," Jacqueline said.

"But I will be a laughingstock, mademoiselle! You cannot seriously expect me to escort a . . . a *broom* to the finest nightclubs and restaurants of Paris!"

"You will be paid three times your usual rate," Jacqueline said, "with a substantial bonus if the broom has a good time. You will treat it no differently than you would a wealthy socialite. You will be courteous and polite, and as attentive as if you were escorting me, is that understood?"

The man sighed with resignation. "*Oui*, mademoiselle. If that is your wish."

"That is my wish," Jacqueline said. "I might add that the broom is this gentleman's cherished familiar," she said, indicating Wyrdrune, "and he is most solicitous of its welfare. It had served his departed mother faithfully while he was completing his thaumaturgical training and it is the only thing he has left to remind him of her. He would take it very badly if it were treated with anything less than the utmost respect."

"Ah, *oui*, mademoiselle, I understand," the guide said, glancing at Wyrdrune nervously. "Please explain to the gentleman that I will take very special care of it. I would never wish to offend an adept under any circumstances."

"Good. See that you do not," Jacqueline said. She turned and switched to English. "Well, Broom, all the arrangements have been made. You'll be in capable hands. Go out and enjoy Paris."

"I can hardly believe it," said the broom. "Where are we going to go? Where shall we start?"

"I was thinking that perhaps we could start with a late dinner, perhaps, or a light snack at . . ." The guide's voice trailed off. He swallowed nervously and cleared his throat, glancing at Jacqueline. "Excuse me, mademoiselle, but . . . does it *eat*?"

"No," Jacqueline said, "but you could dine and I'm sure that Broom would appreciate the atmosphere of a fine restaurant, just the same."

"If you say so, mademoiselle," Bouchet said dubiously. With some trepidation, he offered the broom his arm and they left together, the broom sweeping down the hall with him.

"Don't stay out too late!" Wyrdrune called after it, then turned and shook his head. "What am I saying?"

"Perhaps we should go out, as well," said Modred. "I think I'd like to make some inquiries at the Cafe Noir."

Chapter
FIVE

The Cafe Noir was located in the basement of a brownstone on the Rue de Seine, in the district of St.-Germain-des-Prés. Unlike many of the chic, touristy nightclubs that surrounded it, its entrance was nondescript, with only a small sign over the stairway spelling out the club's name in blue neon letters. Inside, however, it was a different story. The moment they came through the heavy black lacquered front door, they were assailed by a throbbing wall of sound that filled the large, dimly lit, basement nightclub. They paid the cover charge and entered the large room, which was packed with people.

The decor was black, befitting the establishment's name. The floors, the walls, the ceiling, the banquettes, the chairs and tables, all were black with silver accents. The bar ran the length of the entire room along the left side of the club, with a long stage behind it. Scantily clad chorus girls danced onstage, not merely doing the bump and grind of strippers, but moving in precise, skillfully choreographed routines. The main stage was at the far end of the club, where another group of chorus girls dressed in flashy, revealing costumes was performing an elaborate dance number. The stage had several levels, consisting of scenery and dance platforms, rivaling anything seen in Las Vegas or Monte Carlo, with miniature waterfalls and flashing lighting effects orchestrated by the club adept. Crackling globes of ball lightning spun in arabesques around the dancing girls, discharging bolts of energy into the air in precise time to the music. Paragriffins with glittering, metallic wings darted among the artificial trees set up on the stage and swooped down over the patrons, whistling like skyrockets as they came gliding overhead. Some of the girls danced with enchanted instruments that played themselves and sang. It was a spectacular show.

An attractive waitress in a scanty black costume led them to a table and took their orders as the dance number reached its climax, with the miniature waterfalls flowing in a riot of glowing colors and the globes of ball lightning splitting up into smaller globes, circling around and around, discharging jagged bolts of energy that sparkled in the darkness as the number reached its dramatic conclusion. Then all the lights went out and the audience burst into applause as the voice of the announcer came on over the public address system, speaking first in French, then in English.

"*Le Danse Noir*, ladies and gentlemen! Let's hear it for the girls!"

He paused to allow the applause to die down, then the lights slowly came up over the stage again, revealing that the set had been changed. The multilevel stage had now become a stylized graveyard, illuminated in dark violet as a smoky mist undulated along its floor. On the various platforms of the stage stood tombstones, crosses and stone monuments of saints and angels. The full moon rose high and dark clouds scudded across the cyclorama. Bats cried out as they winged their way across the stage. Dirgelike organ music filled the air, slow, majestic and foreboding.

"*Mesdames et messieurs*, ladies and gentlemen," said the announcer, "Prepare to be astounded! None of what you are about to see is an illusion! It is all absolutely, one hundred percent real! Le Cafe Noir, in an exclusive engagement, is now proud to present for your entertainment pleasure one of the world's most gifted thespian adepts, the one, the only, the incomparable . . . Jacques Pascal!''

There was a dramatic stab of organ music, a flash of lightning and a crash of thunder as a jagged bolt shot down from the ceiling and struck one of the graves, sending up a shower of earth and rock. Stiffly, like a vampire rising from the grave, Jacques Pascal rose straight up from a lying position, wrapped in a flowing black cape, hands crossed against his chest. The public applauded.

Wyrdrune grimaced. "Cheap theatrics," he said. "Nothing a first-year student couldn't do."

The music changed tempo, with a rapid, steady, staccato dance beat underlying the organ music as Pascal stepped forward, spread his cape dramatically and bowed. Wyrdrune frowned at the strange familiarity of the music, then he realized what it was.

"'Danse Macabre,' " he said, naming the piece. "Only they've jazzed it up so much it's barely recognizable. Saint-Saens must be spinning in his grave, if you'll excuse the pun."

"Never mind the music," Modred said, leaning forward intently. "Don't you *feel* it?"

Even as he spoke, Wyrdrune became aware of a sudden, burning sensation in his forehead. Kira gasped and clutched her hand. She opened her palm. Her sapphire runestone was glowing brightly. Wyrdrune quickly slipped a headband on over his forehead, covering the stone before anyone could notice its telltale glow from beneath his hair. Modred's runestone was invisible beneath his shirt, but they both knew that the ruby was glowing just as brightly. Kira reached into the pocket of her leather jacket and took out a thin, black leather glove. She put it on, hiding the runestone's glow.

"They're here!" she said.

"It's him," said Wyrdrune. "Pascal! He's the Dark One!"

"No," said Modred, as Jacques Pascal began his act.

"But the feeling is so strong!" said Kira. "Are you sure?"

"I sense the presence," Modred said. "But the Dark One is not here."

"What do you mean?" asked Jacqueline.

"I don't know," said Modred, frowning. "I feel the presence, but it isn't the same somehow. As if the Dark One is here, and yet not here. There is a sense of distance, somehow. . . ."

"Astral possession," Merlin said. They all turned to look at Billy, who was sitting watching the stage intently. The fire opal stone in his ring was gleaming brightly. "Pascal is not the Dark One, but one of the Dark Ones is working through him."

"You mean like you possess Billy?" Kira said.

"Not exactly," Merlin said. "Billy and I share consciousness. We share the same body. But the man up on the stage is not the repository of the Dark One's spirit. Only of the power."

"You mean the necromancer is controlling him, from somewhere else?" said Wyrdrune.

"Undoubtedly," Merlin replied. "It is an old spell, one that only the most powerful mages are capable of casting. Their physical selves can remain elsewhere, partly conscious, aware of everything that is going on around them, but they can send a portion of their consciousness, like a remote part of themselves, to control another person. They can then use that person as their agent, while they remain in safety, where they cannot be harmed."

"That would explain the feeling of the presence being here and yet not here," said Modred. "Pascal is acting as the vehicle for the necromancer's power. I didn't know that they could do that."

"It takes an enormous amount of energy and concentration," Merlin said. "This necromancer must be a very strong one."

"But why?" asked Wyrdrune. "Why expend so much energy just to stage a magic act?"

"I don't know," said Merlin. "Perhaps it was part of their

bargain with the acolyte, the price the Dark One had to pay to obtain his cooperation. Or perhaps because it amuses the necromancer and provides a focus for his concentration, much like a musician might do finger exercises to strengthen his technique. It will be interesting to watch what this man does. It will help us to judge the necromancer's power.''

"You think the Dark One knows we're here?'' asked Wyrdrune.

"It's possible, but astral possession takes a great deal of focused concentration," Merlin said. "The Dark One may not be able to sense the power of the runestones at a distance while working the spell."

"But you don't know for sure?" said Kira.

"No. I don't know for sure," Merlin replied. "In either case, we'll find out soon enough."

Jacques Pascal had started his act. As the music increased in tempo, he began to make dramatic passes with his hands and skeletons rose from the graves and began to dance upon the stage. Pascal choreographed their movements with expansive gestures, weaving among the dancing bones, bringing more of them out of the graves until the entire stage was filled with them, whirling about and dancing with a wild, jerky abandon. Several more skeletons drifted in from offstage, dragging a girl, one of the dancers, dressed in a long, filmy white nightgown. She cried out and struggled against them, but she couldn't get away. They brought her up to Pascal and he made several passes in front of her face. She went into a trance. As the skeletons danced around them, he slowly levitated her.

As she rose, a wind plucked at her gauzy nightdress, blowing her hair so that it streamed out behind her. She rose higher and higher, then began to turn, whirling around faster and faster. Her nightgown burst into blue flame and burned away from her, leaving her naked, yet unharmed. She turned in the air until she was horizontal, supported only by Pascal's magic powers. A stone altar rose up out of the stage and slowly, she descended to it as Pascal moved to stand behind the altar, guiding her down while the skeletons increased the frenzy of their dance. A long, gleaming knife appeared in Pascal's hand and he held it over her, making passes with it over her nude body.

"You don't think he's really going to . . ." Kira's voice trailed off.

"It's only an act," Wyrdrune said. "I hope."

Pascal plunged the knife down. The girl screamed and there was a blinding white flash and a puff of smoke and she was gone, vanished into thin air. A white dove fluttered up from the altar where she had lain. The audience applauded.

Suddenly, a group of dancers dressed as peasants came running out from the wings, carrying torches and weapons. Some of them had swords and clubs, others had pitchforks. They joined in the dance, fighting with the animated skeletons. A club swung and a skeleton's bones flew apart, only to reassemble once again and continue fighting, but the peasants kept on striking at the skeletons until bones were spinning through the air all over the stage, reassembling themselves into various strange configurations, flying apart again and coming back together to form new and more surreal shapes. And then a priest came out onto the stage and started sprinkling holy water. The bones began to smoke. The peasants retreated behind the priest as he continued to dash holy water all around him and the skeletons dissolved away until there were none left standing. Then it was only the priest, with the peasants behind him, facing Jacques Pascal. He held up a cross. Pascal shied away from it, holding his cloak up to protect his face, then he turned and twin beams of bright green thaumaturgic energy shot out from his eyes, striking the stone statues on the monuments. They began to move.

Slowly, ponderously, they came down off their pedestals and started moving toward the priest. The peasants shrieked and fled the stage. The priest dashed holy water on the statues and they began to smoke as well, but they kept on coming at him, surrounding him until he was hidden from view. Their massive limbs rose and fell and the priest could be heard screaming. Then, one by one, the stone statues began to crack and crumble. They all collapsed into a heap of shattered stone and the priest's arm could be seen rising from the pile, fingers twitching spasmodically. Pascal walked over to the pile, grasped the twitching hand and pulled, but instead of the priest, the girl who had been the sacrificial victim came flying up from the pile of rock. She sailed up into the air and slowly floated down to stand beside Pascal. He wrapped his cloak around her, hiding her from view, and when he opened up his cloak again, she had disappeared. As the music reached its crescendo and the first gray light of dawn showed against the cyclorama, Pascal spread his cloak wide and its bottom edges burst into green flame, rapidly burning upward as Pascal seemed to melt and flow into another shape. He ran forward toward the edge of the stage, leaped up into the air and turned into a giant bat with leathery wings. He flew out over the audience, shrieking loudly, and when he had reached the middle of the room, there was a bright green flash and he was gone. The audience erupted into wild applause.

"The incomparable Jacques Pascal, ladies and gentlemen!" cried the announcer.

There was another flash of bright green light, accompanied by a puff of smoke, and Pascal was standing center stage, taking his bows. He gestured to the wings and the sacrificial victim, the priest and the peasant dancers came out to take their bows with him.

"It's gone now," Modred said.

Wyrdrune and Kira could feel it, as well. The sensation of the Dark One's presence was no longer there. Kira took off her leather glove and looked at her palm. The stone was still glowing, but only dimly now, reacting to the presence of Pascal, the acolyte, one who'd been touched by the power of the Dark Ones.

"What did you make of it, Ambrosius?" Modred asked, turning to Billy.

"Taken individually, there was nothing terribly demanding about any of those spells," said Merlin. "Except for the shapechanging, which might have been real or merely an illusion. But when you take all of them together, many of them cast simultaneously at a distance through the medium of astral possession, which in itself requires considerable energy, it was really quite impressive. A display of thaumaturgical ability and control worthy of an archmage.''

''That good, huh?'' Wyrdrune said glumly.

''Much more than merely good,'' said Merlin. ''With a display like that, Pascal cannot avoid attracting the attention of the B.O.T. If he's a registered adept, they'll want to know how he suddenly came by the abilities of a full-fledged archmage. There are only four registered archmages in the entire world and he isn't one of them. The Bureau will be extremely curious about that, as will the I.T.C.''

''And you think that was the purpose?'' Wyrdrune said.

''The general public will not realize the true significance of what they have just seen,'' said Merlin, ''but a member of the Bureau or the I.T.C. would be sufficiently advanced to recognize the full extent of the abilities Pascal has demonstrated. They'll check their files and find out one of two things; either that Pascal is a registered adept who has demonstrated powers far beyond his level, or that he isn't registered at all, in which case they'll be even more curious about him. Either way, they'll want to bring him in for questioning.''

''And it would be a way for the Dark Ones to get close to someone in the Bureau or the I.T.C.,'' said Modred. ''If they could gain control of people in the Bureau or the I.T.C., it would give them a great deal more power. And at the same time, make things that much more difficult for us. The runestones are the single greatest threat to their existence. It would be to their obvious advantage to use the Bureau and the I.T.C. against us.''

''Then we'll have to make certain that they don't get that opportunity,'' said Wyrdrune. ''But taking out Pascal won't solve our problem. The Dark Ones can easily get themselves another acolyte, if they haven't got others already, and by moving against Pascal, we'd only be announcing our presence to them.''

''Assuming they don't already know we're here,'' said Kira.

"So what's the answer?" asked Jacqueline.

"It seems there are no easy answers," Modred said. "It will be hard enough trying to defeat the Dark Ones without the Bureau or the I.T.C. getting in the way. Yet if we follow Pascal and prevent him from claiming yet another victim, the necromancers will be alerted to our presence and Max Siegal will remain in jail."

"But we can't stand by and do nothing while Pascal kills someone else," said Wyrdrune.

"We may not have a choice," Modred said.

"No," said Wyrdrune, shaking his head. "We can't. We've got to stop him, even if it means alerting the Dark Ones to our presence."

Modred nodded. "I suppose you're right. But it does reduce our options."

"What's the name of that cop who's in charge of Siegal's case?" asked Wyrdrune.

"Armand Renaud," Jacqueline said.

"Maybe we can talk to him," said Wyrdrune. "The police have resources we don't have access to. Blood helped us in Whitechapel and Rebecca Farrell made things a lot easier for us in L.A. If we could convince Renaud to speak with them, we might be able to get him to cooperate with us."

"It's worth a try," said Kira.

"Perhaps," said Modred, "but it still doesn't solve our immediate problem. What do we do about Pascal?"

"We can't let him kill again," said Wyrdrune.

"Then there's only one way we're going to stop him," Modred said. "And there's only one of us who can get close to him without the Dark Ones sensing the power of the runestones."

He looked pointedly at Jacqueline.

Renaud stood in the alleyway, looking down at the corpse lying at his feet. He reached into his pocket and took out a pack of cigarettes. He shook one out and lit it. He noticed that his hand was steady. His mind was in a turmoil, but his emotions were under control. He had seen a great deal of violence in his years on the police force, and he had never grown immune to its effects. He always experienced the feelings of outrage, the anger and the sense of loss, but it had lost its ability to shock. His stomach no longer contracted, not even at a sight as grisly as this, and he no longer felt physically sick. His reactions to it were those of a moral man affronted by the animal nature of the baser members of his species, but these were essentially cerebral reactions, under control. Cold and logical.

He still remembered what it had been like when he had seen his first murder victim. No police officer ever forgot. The first one was always the worst. The sight of all the blood, the spectacle of a ruined human being, had a visceral, elemental effect upon the soul. The body reacted with revulsion, the stomach heaved, nausea became overwhelming, as if the physical act of vomiting could somehow regurgitate the horrible reality, expel it from the gut. No officer could ever predict how he would react until the first time he confronted it. Some became ill and vomited upon the spot. Others became numb with shock, staring helplessly with frozen fascination at the dead body of a fellow human being. Still others couldn't face it, recoiling from the sight, weeping uncontrollably. Invariably, they all became embarrassed by their reactions, but there wasn't a single experienced cop anywhere in the world who would ever hold that against them, who wouldn't understand. No matter how tough any of them thought they were, nobody was that tough.

Occasionally, though it happened rarely, they would run across a cop who would confront the sight of his first murder victim and not react at all. Then, if that cop had never before been in situations where he had been exposed to such things, if he had never been a soldier or experienced some kind of street violence in his youth, if it was the first time he had ever witnessed such a thing and it still failed to move him, his fellow officers would always be uneasy around him from then on. It would mean that something inside of him was missing, something very important. And it didn't matter that at some point in their experience, they all became accustomed to seeing death. It was something that they had in common with people like doctors and morticians. Eventually, they all developed a certain callousness, an ability to look at the ravaged remains of what had once been a human being without breaking down emotionally, because if they did not develop that ability, they could never continue doing what they did. Yet there was always that precious memory of the first time, precious because it was something they could cling to that reassured them of their own humanity, that kept them from thinking that they had become unfeeling brutes, no matter how accustomed to it they became. They could take refuge in the fact that they had learned to handle it only because they'd seen it so many times before, but that the first time, it had really gotten to them. That memory was precious to them because it was what made them different from the animals that were capable of doing such things.

Renaud thought about that now especially, because the first officer on the scene had been a rookie and this had been his first dead body. His first murder victim. It was a hell of a way to lose your police virginity, he thought. The corpse was that of a pretty young prostitute. Her short skirt was hiked up, revealing her thighs, and there were long, bloody scratches on her legs. Her bare arms were wet with her own blood. So much blood. Her throat had been torn out and her wide, sightless eyes stared up at the sky. Her blouse had been torn open to her waist and the area around her breasts and abdomen was mutilated with the same bloody symbols that Renaud had seen on the bodies of Joelle Muset and Gabrielle Longet. The same peculiar thaumaturgic runes that Jacqueline Monet had drawn for him on a paper napkin in the café across the street from the police station.

"The same as in the other killings," said Legault, standing beside him. "Only the symbols appear to have been burned in. Siegal couldn't have done this one."

"Obviously not," Renaud said. "Only in the other victims, the throats were not torn out."

"True," said Legault. "Still, there are the markings. . . ."

"Yes," said Renaud, "there are the markings." He glanced back to where the first officer on the scene stood leaning against the wall a short distance down the alleyway, which had been roped off. "Let's go have a talk with him," he said.

"First one?" said Legault.

Renaud nodded. "Can't you tell?"

"You can always tell," Legault said.

They approached the young officer, who immediately straightened up when he saw them coming and made an effort to compose himself.

"I'm sorry, sir," he said sheepishly. "I . . . I'm afraid I became ill." He looked away from them. "I couldn't help it. I just . . . didn't know. . . ."

"It's all right," Renaud said understandingly. "We've all been through it, every one of us. The first time was just the same for me. It's nothing to be ashamed of. The first time you must confront the body of a murder victim or the first time you have to kill someone in the line of duty—let's hope you will be spared that—it always hits you right in the gut. There's no way you can be prepared for it, no matter how many times you think about it. It's never like what you think it will be."

The young officer nodded. "No. It was nothing like what I expected. It . . . it just hit me, before I could do anything about it."

"You'll get over it," Renaud said. "And the next time, it won't affect you quite as badly. And the time after that, less still. But there will always be the feelings, even if you do learn how to control them. And thank God for that. What's your name?"

"Officer Jean Cassel."

"What have you got for me, Officer Cassel?"

"We responded to the call shortly after midnight," he said. "It was an anonymous report to the station of a woman screaming. We found the victim as you see her. She couldn't have been dead for long. I . . . I became ill when I saw her. My partner told me to wait down here and secure the area, then went to question the neighbors. That's all I know. I'm sorry I couldn't have done better, but . . ." his voice trailed off.

"That's quite all right, I understand," Renaud said. "Where is your partner?"

Cassel turned. "Here she comes now," he said.

Renaud and Legault saw a young uniformed policewoman moving purposefully toward them. She wasn't much older than her partner.

"Inspector," she said with a curt nod at Renaud. "Sergeant," she added, greeting Legault.

Renaud knew her and struggled to recall her name. "Officer DuFay, isn't it?"

"Yes, sir." She glanced at her partner and drew them off to one side. "It's his first time," she said.

"Yes, I know," Renaud replied.

"He's embarrassed, especially because of me," she said. "Being a woman, I mean. His breaking down like that and my remaining in control. He's a good cop, but he's new and, well . . ."

"Yes," said Renaud, "I understand. Don't try to make him talk about it now. Just leave it be. Afterward, when you've gone off duty, go have a few drinks together. That often makes it easier."

She nodded. "I wasn't much better my first time," she said. "I couldn't stop crying." She sighed. "It gets easier, but it never goes away completely, does it?"

"No, it never does. Did you come up with anything?"

"Not really," she said. "A number of people heard the victim screaming, but no one will admit to having seen anything. At least a few of them called the police. That's something, I suppose."

"Yes, at least that's something," said Renaud, knowing that there were others who had heard the victim's screams and done nothing whatsoever, except perhaps to pull their windows down.

"The medical examiner says she couldn't have been dead more than half an hour or so," Officer DuFay continued, checking her notepad. "She was still warm when we found her. The victim's name was Catherine Tourney. She was a prostitute. We don't know much more about her at this point. I assume she had a record of arrests, but there's been no time to check yet. The motive was apparently not robbery; we found her purse near the body and there were about a hundred and fifty francs still in it and some change. No jewelry was taken, though what she's wearing can't be worth much. We found no murder weapon. At first, I thought some animal must have attacked her, because of the scratches on her legs and the way her throat's been torn out. A rabid dog, perhaps. But then there are those marks burned into her chest and stomach. . . ." She hesitated. "Similar to that case that you were working on, Inspector."

Renaud grimaced. Word of the mutilations might not have leaked out to the press yet, but it had obviously gotten around the department. Which meant that it was soon bound to get out to the press.

"Yes," said Renaud without elaborating.

"Didn't you have a suspect in custody?" she said.

"Yes," he said again. "Have your written report ready for me first thing in the morning." He turned to Legault. "I want the Bureau called in on this one right away. Have them check for thaumaturgical trace emanations. Tell them I have reason to suspect the possibility of necromancy. If they find anything, they can decide whether or not to bring in the I.T.C. And I want a warrant issued immediately for Jacqueline Monet, wanted for questioning as a material witness."

"What about Max Siegal?" asked Legault.

Renaud pursed his lips. "I'm not taking any chances. Let his lawyers spring him. We have only circumstantial evidence against him and after this, they may be able to get him released, but that's a decision I'd rather not make. He could still be guilty. Except for the mutilations, the murders are not similar. There could be several killers. Monet knows much more than she's told me. I intend to find out what else she knows. See to it that she's found and brought in at once."

He turned and started to walk away.

"Where are you going?" said Legault.

"I'm going to have a drink. Most likely, more than one. And then I intend to make several telephone calls," Renaud said. "One to Scotland Yard and one to the Los Angeles Police Department."

Jacqueline sat in the small dressing room of Jacques Pascal, watching as he sat before a mirror, removing his stage makeup. He had changed into a green and purple paisley silk robe and ascot scarf. Jacqueline did not have any trouble getting in to see him. Even if she weren't confident that the waiter she'd sent the note with would tell Pascal that she was extremely attractive, she had known that the expensive bottle of champagne would do the trick. And it had.

He had greeted her warmly and charmingly, thanked her effusively for the champagne and insisted that she share it with him. They made small talk while he removed his stage makeup and Jacqueline proceeded to come on like a starstruck woman on the make.

"I've never seen anything like it," she said in an excited voice. "You were simply wonderful!"

"I'm pleased that you enjoyed the show," Pascal said, wiping off his face with a towel.

"It was positively thrilling!" Jacqueline gushed. "And it was so much more than just the sort of tricks that most adepts perform on the stage. There were so many things happening at once! And there was so much *style* to it, such an exciting element of . . . of sensuality. When you wrapped your cape around that girl and she disappeared, it was as if . . . as if she'd been *absorbed* by you! And when you shapechanged at the end . . . it was incredible! It was the most brilliant illusion I've ever seen!"

He glanced at her. "What makes you think that it was an illusion?" he said.

"You mean it *wasn't*?" she said, making her eyes wide.

"What do *you* think?" he said with a smile.

"I honestly don't know *what* to think!" she said. "I was simply overwhelmed by it! I decided I just had to meet you."

"And now that you've met me?"

"Well, I'm certainly not disappointed," Jacqueline said with a sultry smile.

"I'm so glad," said Jacques. "And did your friends enjoy the show as much as you did?"

"Oh, I came alone," Jacqueline said.

"A woman as attractive as you are?" said Jacques, raising his eyebrows.

"Well, at the moment, I'm sort of between relationships," she said.

"Indeed? Well, in that case, if it's not too late for you, I know a quiet place not far from here. Perhaps you'd care to join me for a drink?"

"I'd love to," Jacqueline said.

"I'll call a cab," said Pascal.

"Oh, no, let's walk," Jacqueline said. "It's such a lovely night."

"All right," Pascal said, removing his robe and putting on his jacket.

Jacqueline tried to hide her anxiety as they left the club together and started walking down the Rue de Seine, heading away from the Boulevard Saint-Germain and moving toward the river. She felt the comfortable weight of the 10-mm semi-automatic in the shoulder holster underneath her jacket, but she felt safer knowing that the others were following somewhere close behind. But not too close. The display that Pascal had put on back at the club had required a considerable expenditure of energy on the part of the Dark One who had possessed him and it was possible that the necromancer had not been able to detect the presence of the runestones close at hand. But she had little doubt that the necromancer would not resist the opportunity to feed on her life energy and that was what all of them were counting on. She tried to keep up a steady stream of idle conversation, peppered with sexual innuendo, to keep Pascal distracted. She wondered how long it would take for him to make his move. She did not have to wonder long.

They were walking arm in arm and no sooner had they left

the bright lights of the St. Germain entertainment district than Pascal gave her arm a sudden, powerful jerk, spinning her around in front of him and shoving her hard into a dark alleyway. She stumbled, quickly reaching for the automatic at the same time, fell forward and rolled onto her side, using her body to hide the pistol from him. She held it close to her waist, on the side facing away from him, ready to bring it up in an instant. He started moving toward her quickly and she saw his features shift, changing into something hideous and bestial. Something bright gleamed in his hand. She brought the automatic up and fired three rapid shots into his chest. He jerked and was thrown backward by the impact of the bullets and she heard the sound of running footsteps. At the same time, she felt something, a presence close behind her and she rolled over, facing back into the alley, bringing up her gun. For a moment, she couldn't see anything but the darkness in the alley, and then her eyes discerned a deeper darkness, a vague form as black as pitch, dimly outlined by a faintly glowing aura, and it was moving toward her rapidly. She fired.

The muzzle flash lit up the alley as she emptied the entire clip into the dark shape that was rushing at her, but the bullets seemed to go right through it. And then, suddenly, it stopped and she saw the outline of a shadowy arm flung out and a bolt of bright green thaumaturgic energy lanced out over her head and, behind her, she heard Modred yell, "*Look out!*"

She heard the energy bolt explode against the building wall behind her, filling the alleyway with smoke and flying chips of brick and mortar, and she scuttled back out of the way, but before the others could strike back, the shadowy form seemed to fold in upon itself and disappear. But before it vanished, Jacqueline felt a searing blast of hatred and fury wash over her mind and she cried out, bringing her hands up to her head. In another moment, Modred was kneeling at her side while Wyrdrune, Kira and Billy stood grouped around her alertly, searching the alleyway for any signs of movement.

"Are you all right?" asked Modred anxiously.

Jacqueline nodded, still overcome by the shock of the experience and the speed with which it happened. They heard the sound of a police siren approaching.

"Damn!" said Wyrdrune. "We weren't fast enough. He got away."

"*She* got away," Jacqueline said.

"She?" said Kira.

"It was a female," said Jacqueline, still holding her head. It was throbbing with pain. "Just before she disappeared, I felt her . . . in my mind. . . ." She shook her head. "I've never felt anything like that before. Such rage . . . such utter loathing. . . . God, it was awful!"

"What happened to Pascal?" said Wyrdrune. "We heard shooting. . . ."

"I shot him," Jacqueline said. "He had a knife. I think I killed him."

"Then where is he?" Wyrdrune asked, looking all around.

"Over'ere," said Billy.

Modred helped Jacqueline up to her feet and they all went to join Billy, who stood a short distance away, farther down the alley. He held up his arm and blue fire crackled around his outstretched fingers, illuminating the area around them.

"Look," said Merlin.

The blue glow showed a dark trail of blood leading farther back into the alley. They followed it to an open manhole cover.

"He's gone down into the sewers," Merlin said.

"With all the blood he's losing, he can't last much longer," Wyrdrune said.

"I intend to make sure," said Modred. He started to lower himself down through the opening. "Come on."

"Down *there*?" said Wyrdrune. But Modred had already disappeared down the metal ladder.

Kira started climbing down after Modred. Wyrdrune made a grimace of distaste as he watched her disappear down the ladder.

"The sewers," Wyrdrune said. "There's rats down there. I *hate* rats."

"Let's go, warlock!" Kira called up to him. "Get down here!"

Wyrdrune sighed with resignation. "Let's hear it for the glamor of Paris," he said, and started down the ladder after them.

"Hold it right there!" a voice cried out behind them.

Billy and Jacqueline turned to see several policemen standing at the entrance to the alley, their weapons drawn.

"Hold on to my arm," said Merlin. "I'll get us out of here."

"No," said Jacqueline. "We need to buy them time. Close the manhole cover."

Billy stared down at the heavy iron cover. It rose up slightly and floated over the opening, then dropped down into place with a scraping, chinking sound.

They were hit by the strong beam of a searchlight mounted on one of the police vehicles.

"Come out of there, slowly, with your hands up over your heads! Don't try anything or we'll shoot!"

Slowly, they raised their hands up and clasped them atop their heads, then started walking toward the entrance to the alley.

Chapter
SIX

Inspector Renaud entered the interrogation room together with Sergeant Legault. "Leave us," he said to the two other officers in the room and they silently walked out. Billy and Jacqueline were seated at the table, their hands cuffed in front of them. Legault leaned back against the door while Renaud came around in front of them. He took out a package of cigarettes, shook one out and lit it.

"Mademoiselle Monet," he said. "It seems that every time we meet, there has been a murder recently committed." He glanced at Billy. "Your young friend was not carrying any identification. Might I inquire as to his name?"

Jacqueline glanced at Billy. "He wants to know your name," she said.

"Slade," he replied. "Billy Slade."

"You're British," said Renaud, switching to English.

"'Gor, perceptive, ain't 'e?" Billy said to Jacqueline.

Renaud grimaced wryly. "How old are you?"

"Fourteen."

Renaud reached into his jacket pocket and pulled out Billy's knife. He pressed the release button and the blade sprang out. "You're a bit young to be playing around with one of these, aren't you?"

"I dunno. 'Ow old d'ya 'ave to be?"

Renaud shook his head. He closed the knife and put it down on the table.

"Where are your parents?"

"Dead."

"I'm sorry."

Billy shrugged.

"Who is your legal guardian?" Renaud said.

"Don't 'ave one," Billy said. "I can take care of meself."

"I'm sure you can," Renaud said, "but a minor needs a legal guardian in order to be issued a passport. How did you get into France?"

"On an airplane," said Billy.

Renaud tried to stare him down, without success. "What is your relationship with Mademoiselle Monet?"

"We're not 'avin' a relationship," said Billy. "We're just good friends, y'know."

Renaud took a deep breath and let it out slowly. "Young man, I advise you not to try my patience. This is a very serious matter. I'll get back to you in a moment. In the meantime, I strongly suggest that you reconsider your flippant attitude. Legault. . . ."

Legault took out Jacqueline's pistol and placed it on the table in front of her. The magazine had been removed.

Jacqueline said nothing.

"A ten-millimeter semiautomatic, spellwarded against detection," Renaud said. "The signature weapon of a certain gentleman known as Morpheus. Or perhaps Morpheus is not a gentleman at all, eh? Perhaps Morpheus is actually a woman."

"You think *I'm* Morpheus?" said Jacqueline. She gave a small snort. "You can't be serious."

"Can't I? It has long been rumored that you have connections with this individual and now we find this gun in your possession, exactly the sort of weapon that Morpheus is known to use. We've already examined it for fingerprints and yours were on it," said Renaud. "It has been fired. A trail of blood was discovered in the alley, leading to a sewer entrance. It would appear as if someone was shot in that alleyway and then the body was thrown down into the sewers. It was undoubtedly washed away, but before long, it's bound to reach one of the outlet points and be discovered. And then, mademoiselle, we will have you on a charge of murder. In the meantime, we have more than enough to hold you."

"If I'm being charged, then I have a right to call my attorney," said Jacqueline.

"As you wish," Renaud said. "But before you exercise your right to legal counsel, I thought that we might have a little talk. You have the right to refuse to respond to what I have to say, but you might find it interesting, just the same. Earlier tonight, the body of a young prostitute was discovered in an alley off the Rue Saint Honoré. She appeared to have been attacked by some sort of animal. There were claw marks on her body and her throat had been torn out. But her breasts and abdomen were mutilated in the same fashion as in the murders of Joelle Muset and Gabrielle Longet. The same thaumaturgic runes were carved into the flesh."

"I warned you that would happen," said Jacqueline. "And since Max Siegal was in police custody, he obviously could not have done it. You should have listened to me in the first place."

"Yes, perhaps I should have," said Renaud. "It might interest you to know that a short while ago, I placed a call to Chief Inspector Michael Blood of Scotland Yard. He would not answer any of my questions until he became satisfied that I was who I said I was, and even then, he was extremely guarded. He did not tell me a great deal, other than the fact that you and your associates, whom he was careful not to name, were instrumental in solving a series of grisly murders in Whitechapel and that Scotland Yard owed you a great debt of gratitude. He vouched for you unequivocally and urged me to give you my complete cooperation. He hinted at some sort of criminal conspiracy that was international in scope. When I asked him if necromancy was involved and if the I.T.C. was pursuing the investigation, he told me that he was unable to discuss the matter further, due to security considerations. He suggested that I should take my lead from you. I asked him if you were some sort of government agent or an operative of the I.T.C. and once again, he said that he was not at liberty to tell me, but urged me to cooperate with you to the fullest extent of my authority, and even beyond, if necessary. It was altogether a fascinating conversation, redolent of mystery and intrigue.

"After I got off the phone with him," Renaud continued, "I called the Los Angeles Police Department and spoke with Captain Rebecca Farrell, with equally fascinating results. Once again, I had to wait until she had verified my identity, and then I was told that you had been of invaluable assistance to the Los Angeles police in clearing up a series of brutal murders in which the same pattern I described to her had appeared. Captain Farrell was just as cryptic as Chief Inspector Blood, but she also vouched for you unequivocally and urged me to give you my complete cooperation. It was interesting to note that both of them were very careful not to volunteer any names or information, responding only to the facts I gave them, leaving me with the impression that I'd become involved in some sort of highly classified investigation. In all my years of police work, I have never encountered anything quite like this situation.''

He glanced from Billy to Jacqueline.

''I find it difficult to believe that you are connected with any government agency or with the I.T.C.,'' he said, ''and yet somehow you seem to have obtained the cooperation and the unqualified endorsement of senior officials in both Scotland Yard and the Los Angeles Police Department. How could someone like you manage such a thing? The possibility of bribery occurred to me, but that would seem unlikely. And then it occurred to me that you are a witch, a student of the thaumaturgic arts, and Inspector Blood and Captain Farrell might have been thaumaturgically coerced, through the means of a compulsion spell.''

''If that was the case,'' Jacqueline said, ''then aren't you worried that I could do the same to you?''

''That possibility occurred to me,'' Renaud admitted. ''Which is why Sergeant Legault has orders to shoot you if you so much as mumble or make a sudden gesture toward me.''

Jacqueline glanced over her shoulder and saw that Legault was holding a pistol at his side.

''If that was my intention,'' she said with a smile, ''then I could easily have done it when we were alone in that café together. Why didn't I do it then?''

''I don't know,'' said Renaud, frowning. ''There is altogether too much that I don't know and that disturbs me very much. I do not like being disturbed. You may call your attorney, if you wish, but we have more than enough grounds to keep you both in custody until I have some answers. And if I cannot compel you to speak, then perhaps a team of interrogators from the I.T.C. can.''

''You've called in the I.T.C.?'' Jacqueline said.

''The Bureau has. They detected trace emanations at the murder scene. I'm expecting the I.T.C. agents at any moment,'' said Renaud. ''You can speak with me or you can speak with them, but I think that you will find it easier to speak with me. I understand that their methods of interrogating uncooperative suspects can be quite unpleasant and severe.''

''I wish you hadn't brought in the Bureau,'' said Jacqueline.

''Under the circumstances, I didn't have much choice,'' Renaud said. ''Now what is it to be?''

But before they could reply, there was a knock at the door of the interrogation room. Legault opened it to admit two people, a man and a woman. The man was in his late thirties or early forties, of medium build, clean-shaven, with light brown hair worn in the sorcerer's style, down to his shoulders, dark eyes and angular features. He was expensively dressed in a conservative, dark blue neo-Edwardian suit. The woman looked about the same age. She was a big, large-breasted, Rubenesque woman with long, thick, wavy black hair. She was wearing the traditional robes of a sorceress, made of black velvet with intricate gold and silver embroidery, and she wore a profusion of rings and bracelets. Her face was round and cherubic, with a small nose, a wide, sensual mouth and a high forehead.

''Agent Raven, I.T.C.,'' she said, showing her credentials and giving her magename in French, with an American accent. ''And this is my partner, Agent Piccard.''

The man, evidently, did not choose to use a magename, following the practice of many of the younger sorcerers, who did not adhere to the traditional forms, though most of them still wore their hair long.

''These are the suspects?'' she said, glancing at Jacqueline and Billy.

'''Allo, Kimberly,'' said Billy. ''Still makin' your own clothes, eh? You always did like a bit o' flash, but then it suits you.''

Her eyes widened and she came around to stand in front of the table where Billy and Jacqueline sat. She stared at Billy intently. ''Who are you?'' she said in English. ''How do you know me? And how did you know my truename?''

"I always remember my students," Merlin said in his own voice. "You've hardly changed at all, Kim. However, I can hardly blame you for not recognizing *me*. You might say that I've become a completely different person."

Her eyes grew wider still and her mouth fell open. Piccard was beside her instantly. His lips moved silently and he brought his right hand up in a magical gesture.

"Tell your partner not to bother with his spell of compulsion," Merlin said. "I'm afraid that it won't work on me."

"No, it *can't* be!" said Raven, shaking her head.

"Don't you recognize my voice?" said Merlin.

Raven shook her head. "You sound just like. . . . But that's impossible. He's dead," she said.

Renaud and Legault both watched them, frowning, becoming more and more confused.

"Remember when we discussed astral projection in class?" said Merlin. "You asked if it was possible for something to happen to the sorcerer's body while in a state of astral projection, so that his physical self would die, while his astral self survived. You wanted to know if that couldn't be the explanation for ghosts. I said that it could, indeed, but that it was also possible for a disembodied astral spirit to settle in another person's body, which could also account for cases of possession or for people's belief in the idea of reincarnation. Well, ironically, that was exactly what happened to me and young Billy, here."

"It's a trick," Piccard said to his partner. "He is a natural. He's taking information from your mind. Concentrate. Shut him out."

"What the devil is going on here?" asked Renaud.

"Use your common sense, Piccard," said Merlin. "Do you really think it's possible for someone as young as I appear to be to possess enough skill to resist your spell or see into another's thoughts? Even given phenomenal natural ability, it would take years of study and training to fully develop such talents. If you had been one of my own students, you would have known to disregard deceptive appearances and use your sensitivity to guide you.''

Piccard moistened his lips. He put his hands up to his head, fingertips pressing lightly against the temples, and shut his eyes. Furrows appeared between his eyebrows as he concentrated.

"What's going on?" Renaud said anxiously. "Will someone *please* tell me what's happening here?''

Piccard put his hands down and swallowed hard. "We are in the presence of an extremely powerful adept,'' he said. "It hardly seems possible, but I know of only one mage who could have such power. The late Merlin Ambrosius.''

"Bravo, Piccard,'' said Merlin. "Full marks.''

"Just a moment,'' said Renaud. "Are you seriously suggesting that this *boy* is the legendary Merlin Ambrosius, reincarnated?''

"Not reincarnated, Renaud,'' said Merlin. "At the moment of my death, I flung my astral spirit from my body, so that only my physical self died. My spirit survived, floating free, until it was drawn to young Billy Slade and settled into him. You see, Billy is descended from me by way of a De Dannan witch named Nimue, from the time of Camelot. Our life energies are spiritually compatible, even if our personalities sometimes are not.''

"And you expect me to believe this nonsense?" said Renaud.

"What would you require as proof?'' asked Merlin. And as he spoke, Billy reached up with his right hand and stretched his collar. "Gettin' a bit warm in 'ere,'' he said. With his left hand, he held up the handcuffs. "These yours?'' he said.

Legault immediately brought up his pistol, but without even turning around, Merlin made it come flying out of his grasp. Legault cried out with alarm as it sailed across the room and landed in Billy's outstretched hand. As he held it up, the magazine detached itself and floated free. One by one, the bullets sprang out of the clip and came down to stand in a neat little row on the table in front of him.

"Jacqueline, luv, 'ave ya got a fag?" said Billy.

Jacqueline, her hands suddenly free, handed him a pack of cigarettes. As Billy shook one out and lit it with a jet of flame from his thumb, Legault cried out once again. He was suddenly handcuffed with the same bracelets that Jacqueline had been restrained with seconds earlier.

"Y'see, Inspector," Billy said, "we've been cooperatin' with you all along. We could 'ave easily popped off anytime we wanted to. Like this, see?"

Billy took Jacqueline's hand and snapped his fingers. They both suddenly vanished. A moment later, they came walking through the door of the interrogation room, past an astonished Legault.

"'Scuse me," said Billy, coming back to the table with Jacqueline and sitting down. "Can we 'ave done with the tricks now and get down to business?"

"Professor," said Raven, "it really *is* you!"

"I think perhaps I'd better sit down," Renaud said shakily.

Legault stood by the door, his hands still cuffed in front of him. He cleared his throat uneasily.

"Oh. Sorry," Merlin said, and the cuffs sprang apart and fell to the floor. Sheepishly, Legault bent down to pick them up.

"This is incredible," said Raven. "Why have you been arrested? Does anyone else know you're still alive?"

"And why are you with this woman?" asked Piccard. "I recognize her now." He turned to his partner. "Her name is Jacqueline Monet. She is a notorious criminal."

"Yes, of course," said Raven. "I thought she looked familiar. What is this all about, Renaud?"

"In all honesty, I have no idea, mademoiselle," Renaud said, shaking his head with resignation. "I was intending to hold them on suspicion of murder until I could find out more, but now . . . I must admit that I am totally confused."

"Perhaps I can enlighten you," said Merlin, "but it is a long and rather complicated story. But before I begin, let me give you all fair warning. If, at the end, I am not absolutely convinced that I can depend upon your full cooperation and

discretion in this matter, then Jacqueline and I will disappear
and no one present in this room will have any memory of
ever having seen us."

Renaud glanced at Raven. "He could actually do that?"

Raven nodded, her expression very serious. "Easily," she
said. "He may be in the body of a boy, but if he wanted to,
he could blast us all into oblivion in the blink of an eye."

"Comforting thought," Renaud said wryly. "If I've said
anything to offend you, Professor Ambrosius—"

"Merlin will do."

"Uh, yes," said Renaud uneasily. "Well . . . Merlin . . .
please accept my apologies."

"And mine, too," Legault added hastily.

"No need to apologize," said Merlin. "You were only
trying to do your duty. However, first things first. Max Siegal
is completely innocent. There is no reason for you to hold
him any longer."

"I will see to his release immediately," said Renaud.

"After we have had our conversation will be soon
enough," said Merlin. "In the meantime, let me first answer
your questions." He turned to Raven. "As to why we have
been arrested, Inspector Renaud was fully justified in his
suspicions. There *has* been a murder, or rather, a shooting
in self-defense. As to whether or not the perpetrator actually
died, we do not yet know that. As to whether or not anyone
else knows about what's happened to me, it is a closely
guarded secret. A small and very select group of people know,
among them Chief Inspector Michael Blood of Scotland Yard;
Captain Rebecca Farrell of the Los Angeles police force; Ben
Slater, a Los Angeles reporter; and Dr. Sebastian Makepeace,
of New York University. Two others who also knew are dead
now. I.T.C. agents Faye Morgan and Thanatos."

"The ones who disappeared," Piccard said. "*You* were
responsible for that?"

"No, don't be absurd," said Merlin. "They both died in
the line of duty, slain by necromancers."

"Necromancers!" Raven said. "Then the rumors are true!
There *is* some sort of conspiracy of necromancers!"

"Yes," said Merlin, "only it's far worse than you think. However, I'm getting ahead of myself. There are still many things you do not know. Such as the fact, for example, that the I.T.C. agent you knew as Faye Morgan was, in reality, a two-thousand-year-old sorceress named Morgan Le Fay."

Raven stared at Merlin with disbelief. "*The* Morgan Le Fay?" she said.

"The very same," said Merlin. "My very first pupil."

"But how could anyone possibly survive for two thousand years?" Renaud asked in astonishment. "Had she been in an enchanted sleep, like you?"

"No," said Merlin, "she was awake for all those years. She survived for so long for the same reason that I would have survived, had she not placed a spell upon me, partially suspending my life functions. We are both immortal. As is one other who knows about me, the last survivor of the days of Camelot. Arthur's son, Modred."

They stared at him, stunned. "*Modred is still alive*?" said Raven. "But according to history, he and Arthur killed each other!"

"If he had been mortal, as Arthur was, then he surely would have died," said Merlin. "But although everyone believed him dead, he recovered from his wounds and he is still very much alive and presently in Paris. And also on your 'most wanted' list. You know him as Morpheus."

"The professional assassin?" said Piccard.

"He was a hired assassin," Merlin said, "but he is no longer. I make no apologies for Modred, nor do I excuse his behavior or what he has done with his life. Perhaps I am to blame for that. Nor does Modred himself make any excuses for how he has lived his life. When you realize that he is a powerful adept in his own right, and has had over two thousand years in which to amass his resources and perfect his craft, then perhaps you'll understand why the I.T.C. has never been able to apprehend him. And even if you did, you would never be able to hold him. The only way you could stop Modred would be to kill him. An immortal *can* be killed, if the wound is immediately fatal, but after you have heard me out, I think you will agree that no matter what he has done in the past, Modred must now remain alive. And free."

"If I might interrupt a moment," said Piccard, somewhat dazed at all these revelations, "you keep mentioning immortality. How is that humanly possible?"

"It is not *humanly* possible," Merlin replied. "It is possible only because neither Morganna nor Modred were ever completely human. They were born half-breeds, as was I."

"Wait a moment," said Renaud. "You mean to tell us that there are actually inhuman creatures among us? Members of some alien race?"

"Not alien," said Jacqueline. "They were here long before we were. And they look a great deal like us. But they are not human."

"They were called the Old Ones," Merlin said. "An immortal race of magic users that dates back to the dawn of time. When primitive humans first appeared, they were already far more evolved than they were, with a well-developed civilization of their own. The myths of Atlantis and the lost continent of Mu are derived from them. They subjugated primitive humans and used them in their thaumaturgic rituals, killing them to obtain their life energy to empower their spells. Necromancy, in its earliest form. It is far older than the white magic that we practice now. The bloody rites of the ancient Egyptians, the sacrifices of the Aztecs, the Mayans and the Druids; the ritual killings of the Cult of Kali; all had their beginnings in the necromantic rites of the Old Ones. They became part of human folklore and mythology, the inspiration for the gods of the Greeks and Romans, the source of creation myths and the basis for the legends of vampires, shapechangers and other supernatural beings. The Arabic tribes knew them as the Djinn. The Native American tribes called them Kachina and gave them other names, such as Gitchee Manitou. And the Celts called them, simply, the Old Ones."

"What happened to them?" Raven asked. "If they're still alive, why don't we know about them?"

"Because very few of them have survived," said Merlin. "At some time before recorded history began, there was a cataclysmic war between them, on the scale of one of your world wars. It came about when humans started to evolve and many of the Old Ones ceased to look upon them as animals, but as intelligent beings like themselves. Many of them came to feel that it was wrong to take human life for its thaumaturgic potential and they began to practice a new and more humane form of magic, one that did not kill the source of the spell's energy, but allowed for recovery. That was the beginning of white magic, so named for the Council of the White, the ruling body of the Old Ones, comprised of the most powerful sorcerers among them. But there remained among them those who did not share their concern for the developing humans, who did not wish to surrender the power that could be gained more quickly and easily through necromancy. These were called the Dark Ones and they rebelled against the authority of the Council of the White, which led to a devastating war. Its memory survives in human legends as the Ragnarok, the Gotterdamerung—the Twilight of the Gods.''

They were all utterly still, hanging on Merlin's every word with awestruck expressions on their faces. For the first time, they were hearing the explanation to myths and questions that had puzzled humanity for centuries.

''In the end,'' said Merlin, ''the Council of the White defeated the Dark Ones and there were only a few survivors left. The war had completely decimated the immortals. But the surviving Dark Ones still would not surrender to the Council's will, so they were entombed alive in a subterranean chamber deep beneath the Euphrates Valley. And to insure that the Dark Ones would remain imprisoned for all time, the surviving members of the Council gave up their lives to empower the greatest spell they ever cast. The spell of the Living Triangle.

> 'Three stones, three keys to lock the spell,
> Three jewels to guard the Gates of Hell.
> Three to bind them, three in one,
> Three to hide them from the sun.

Three to hold them, three to keep,
Three to watch the sleepless sleep.'

And with the casting of the spell," continued Merlin, "they infused their life energies into three enchanted runestones—a ruby, a sapphire and an emerald. All save one of them. And that sole survivor of the Council placed the runestones in a small chest over the Dark Ones' tomb, as keys to lock the spell that would prevent them from escaping. That last member of the Council was my father, Gorlois. Like many of the Old Ones before him, he took a human for a wife. My mother. Morganna was also his daughter, by another human female. And throughout the years, those humans who possessed unusual abilities, such as extrasensory perception, and those who are capable of magic use today, such as yourselves, owe their talents to having had an Old One for an ancestor. But over the years, the strain became diluted until immortality was no longer passed on. And for thousands of years, the runestones kept the Dark Ones prisoner in their secret tomb. Until recently, when the runestones were discovered and removed."

"The Annendale Expedition!" said Piccard. "The dig sponsored by the American corporation and Shiek Rashid Al'Hassan!"

"Precisely," Merlin said. "And once again, I am partially to blame. When I awoke and brought back the discipline of thaumaturgy, the spread of magic throughout the world roused the Dark Ones from their slumber. They reached out against the power of the runestones, and though they could not escape, they drew upon the life energy released by the evil acts of mortal men and slowly, they grew stronger. And when Al'Hassan, who was the first of my students to achieve the rank of archmage, discovered the thaumaturgical trace emanations stemming from the site of their tomb, he cosponsored an archeothaumaturgic dig, hoping to unearth ancient magical artifacts from prehistoric times. Instead, he became possessed by the power of the Dark Ones and they brought him to their hidden chamber. He removed the chest containing the runestones, thereby taking the key out of the lock and making it possible for the Dark Ones to escape as soon as they had grown strong enough. And for that to happen, Al'Hassan needed to cast a spell that would bring about the release of a tremendous amount of life energy, channeled directly to the Dark Ones.''

"The cataclysms that occurred several years ago!" said Raven. "The tidal wave in Buenos Aires! The rain of fire in Moscow! The blackout and mass hysteria in New York and the earthquakes in Peking, Hawaii and the United Semitic Republics!"

"Exactly," Merlin said. "It was Al'Hassan's spell to release the Dark Ones. And he succeeded. We tried to stop him. Morganna died in the attempt, slain by Al'Hassan. I died when I lost my battle to contain the Dark Ones and my body fell into their pit as they came streaming forth. Yet even as the Dark Ones were being freed, the power of the Living Triangle struck back through its avatars, killing many of the Dark Ones. But an undetermined number of them managed to make good their escape, and now they are loose upon the world. And the power of the Living Triangle, working through the runestones, is the only thing on earth that is capable of stopping them.''

"I recall a case involving three enchanted runestones," Raven said. "Faye . . . or Morgan . . . was assigned to that case. They were stolen from a New York gallery by two young thieves, but the charges were mysteriously dropped."

"That's right," said Piccard. "And we've been trying to locate those two thieves ever since, to bring them in for questioning. Their names were—"

"Wyrdrune and Kira," Merlin said. "You will recall that I spoke of the avatars of the spell of the Living Triangle. They have become those avatars. The runestones chose them.''

"They *chose* them?" said Renaud. "Inanimate gems?"

"They are not inanimate," said Merlin. "They are the repositories of the astral spirits of the Council of the White. And they each have bonded themselves to the three avatars.''

"Then who is the third?" asked Piccard.

"Modred, of course," said Merlin. "Each of them is descended from Gorlois, the last surviving member of the Council. Modred because he was Morganna's son. Wyrdrune and Kira because they are descended from her sisters, Elaine and Morgause. Wyrdrune was one of my pupils. A somewhat undisciplined young warlock who, when the power of the three runestones is combined, has powers even greater than mine. Kira is not an adept at all, yet under the combined presence of the runestones, she too can exercise incalculable power. And as for Modred, he is the strongest of the three. He was the one who defeated Al'Hassan."

Merlin turned to face Renaud. "Perhaps now you'll understand why Chief Inspector Blood and Captain Farrell were not entirely forthcoming with you. If knowledge of this became public, there would be mass hysteria. Every adept would be under suspicion of being an inhuman necromancer. The public would panic and strike out against magic users in their fear. And that would only serve to increase the Dark Ones' power. In Whitechapel, we tracked down one of the Dark Ones and destroyed him before he could come into his full power. In Los Angeles, we found two more and it was in the battle we had with them that your fellow agent, Thanatos, was killed. And now we have tracked several more to Paris. Tonight, Jacqueline encountered one of their acolytes, a man named Jacques Pascal, a human who had been possessed by them and sent out to kill, so that they could absorb the life energies of his victims. It was undoubtedly Pascal who was responsible for the murders of Joelle Muset and Gabrielle Longet. But this new murder you've told us about clearly indicates that the Dark Ones have at least one other acolyte, possibly more. And the manner of the murder would suggest that they have made a shapechanger. Or what you would call a werewolf."

"*Mon Dieu*!" said Renaud. "A werewolf! Such a thing is possible?"

" For the Dark Ones, almost anything is possible," said Merlin.

"Why on earth didn't you come to *us*?" asked Raven. "How could you keep such a thing secret from the I.T.C.? We could have helped you!"

"And you could have hindered us, as well," said Jacqueline. "How could you expect to go up against the Dark Ones when you could never even manage to apprehend someone like me, who is only a witch? Besides, Modred never trusted you. Al'Hassan, one of the directors of your own board, was in the service of the Dark Ones!"

"Those are not the only reasons," Merlin said. "I hope you will excuse Jacqueline's natural antipathy toward the I.T.C., but the fact remains that there is no way the agency could be mobilized to help us against the Dark Ones. Your bureaucracy has become large and unwieldy. There would be no way to insure that the information would not leak out to the public. We cannot work against the Dark Ones through organizations, only through trusted individuals. People like Michael Blood, Rebecca Farrell, Ben Slater and Sebastian Makepeace. And now you."

Raven nodded. "I see," she said. "You're right, of course. I can't dispute your logic. To alert the entire agency would entail far too great an element of risk. And if the Dark Ones are everything you say they are, it's possible that they could have already infiltrated us. Which would mean that we can't even trust our own people. I'm almost afraid to ask this question, but how do you know you can trust us? Isn't it possible that one or more of us could be in the power of the Dark Ones?"

Merlin smiled. "You're underestimating your old teacher, my dear," he said. "I know each of my students better than even their parents know them. If I had reason not to trust you, I'd see it in your thoughts. As for the possibility of your being in the service of the Dark Ones, if that were the case, then the stone set in this ring would have been glowing with a brightness that would almost blind you."

They all stared at the ring on Billy's hand.

"You mean that is a runestone?" said Piccard. "I thought you said that there were only three of them?"

"Three that are part of the Living Triangle," Merlin said. "This one is a fourth, not part of the spell, but equally as powerful in its own right. It holds the astral spirit of my father, Gorlois. And if any of you were in the service of the Dark Ones, I have no doubt that Gorlois would have manifested himself and killed you on the spot. And even if I wanted to, there would have been nothing I could do to stop him."

Renaud stared at the ring and swallowed nervously. Billy reached across the table and picked up the switchblade knife. He pressed the release button and the blade snikked out. He held it up in front of Renaud.

"Still think I'm too young for one o' these?" he said with a grin.

Chapter
SEVEN

They stood in the darkness of the sewer underneath the street, the eerie silence broken only by the sounds of water dripping and lapping up against the channel walls.

"What happened to Billy and Jacqueline?" asked Kira.

"The cops showed up just as I was coming down," said Wyrdrune, "and Merlin moved the sewer access cover back into place."

"We've got to go back," said Kira.

"No," said Modred. "Merlin did that to buy us time. Both he and Jacqueline know what they're doing. If the police took them into custody, Merlin can get them out anytime he chooses. Right now, it's more important that we find Pascal."

"We'll never find anything in all this darkness," Wyrdrune said.

He raised his hands and his lips moved as he silently spoke a spell. A soft green aura appeared around his hands as he held them apart at about chest level, palms facing each other, fingers spread. Then the aura crackled and fine, jagged bolts of thaumaturgic energy shot out from his fingertips, meeting in the space between his hands and forming a spinning globe of greenish ball lightning about the size of a man's head. It lit up the area around them.

"There, that oughta do it," Wyrdrune said, putting down his hands.

Suddenly, the bright green ball of light began to pulsate rapidly. Its spinning action increased and it shot away from Wrydrune, darting straight toward Kira.

She cried out in alarm and ducked. It passed inches over her head, struck the tunnel wall, bounced off, and came whooshing straight back at them like a miniature fighter plane on a strafing run.

"Look out!" yelled Kira.

They ducked and the ball passed just over their heads, took off away from them on a zigzagging course across the width of the tunnel, hung for a moment in midair, hovering like an angry bee, then came swooping back at them again. Kira and Wyrdrune each threw themselves to one side, but Modred remained standing where he was. As the crackling ball came hurtling straight at his face, he held up his hand, palm out, and it came to a dead stop in the air, hovering in front of him, pulsating and spinning around, shooting off angry sparks. Slowly, Modred raised his other hand over the brightly glowing globe, as if he were palming a basketball. He brought his hand down over the ball and lowered it until it floated at chest level. Modred slowly moved his hands around it, like a potter smoothing clay, and the glow gradually became steady as the beaming globe ceased to pulsate and shoot off sparks.

Kira and Wyrdrune both stood up. Wyrdrune had a sheepish expression on his face.

"Sorry about that," he said.

Kira shook her head. "Tell me something, warlock," she

said, "how on earth did you ever survive thaumaturgy school?"

"I . . . I guess I got it wrong somehow," said Wyrdrune awkwardly.

"You merely rushed your spell," said Modred. "Magic requires patience. Here." He pushed his hands out away from him, like passing a basketball, and tossed the glowing ball to Wyrdrune.

"Hey!" Wyrdrune cried, quickly bringing up his hands and awkwardly bobbling the globe.

"*Relax*," said Modred. "Control it."

Wyrdrune finally got it floating steadily, like a giant firefly, slightly above his head and several feet in front of him.

"That's better," Modred said.

"Try not to drop it in the water," Kira said wryly.

Wyrdrune grimaced at her.

"You see Pascal's body anywhere?" she said.

They looked around. They were standing on a stone walkway, slightly above the channel where the sewer water flowed through the tunnel.

"No sign of him," said Wyrdrune.

"He couldn't have gone far," said Kira. "Not with three bullets in his chest."

"Not necessarily," said Modred. "Unless any of the wounds were immediately fatal, there's a good chance that the Dark Ones could have kept him going. Do you see any sign of blood?"

"Bring the light down lower, warlock," Kira said. "And for God's sake, pay attention to what you're doing!"

"You think it's easy keeping ball lightning under control, you try it," Wyrdrune said. Slowly, he brought the glowing ball of electrical energy down to just above floor level.

"There," said Modred, pointing out the blood trail. "He's still alive and moving. Come on. He can't be very far ahead of us."

They moved off down the tunnel, the globe lighting the way for them. The sound of water dripping echoed through the tunnel.

"Damn, it stinks down here," said Wyrdrune.

"It's a sewer, what did you expect?" said Kira. "It still smells a damn sight better than Fulton Street."

In the distance, they heard the chittering of rats.

Wyrdrune shuddered. "Damn," he said. "I knew there would be rats down here. Some of them are probably as big as a house."

"Hold it a minute," Modred said, as they came to a branching-off point. He bent down, then pointed to a tunnel to their left. "He went this way."

The globe of lightning moved around the corner and down the left-hand tunnel. They followed close behind.

"Watch yourselves," said Modred. "If he knows we're following him, he might try to hide and jump us."

"With three bullets in his chest?" said Kira.

"You saw what happened at the club," said Modred. "If the necromancer's astral spirit takes possession of him, he won't even feel the pain. You could cut off both his legs and he'd keep on coming, even if he had to crawl."

"What could he do against the three of us?" asked Wyrdrune. "We have the power of the Living Triangle."

"Which might not avail us if he has the advantage of surprise," Modred replied. "Don't get cocky, son. Even a mage can die."

"I can't believe it," Kira said as they moved down the tunnel. "How the hell can he keep on going when he's losing so much blood?"

"The Dark Ones can keep him moving 'til he drops," said Modred. "But you're right. At this rate, he can't possibly last long."

They came to the end of the blood trail where another branching-off point occurred. The stone walkway continued on ahead of them, but there was no more blood sign. It stopped at the edge of the walkway. Across from them, on the other side of the channel, there was a smaller tunnel in the opposite wall, leading off into the darkness.

"He went into the water and down that opposite tunnel," Modred said.

"Great," said Wyrdrune. "We've lost him."

"Not yet we haven't," Modred said.

"You're not suggesting we go after him in *there*?" said Wyrdrune.

"What's the matter, warlock?" Kira said. "Afraid of getting your feet wet?"

She jumped down into the channel with a splash. The water came up to her thighs. She sloshed across toward the opposite tunnel. Modred went in after her.

"There's got to be about a zillion germs in there," said Wyrdrune with a disgusted grimace.

"Come on, warlock," Kira said. "Don't be such a baby. Get the lead out."

"Oh, jeez," said Wyrdrune. He went into the water. The bright green globe was hovering across the channel, at the entrance to the tunnel. "I'm probably getting infected by a dozen varieties of voracious bacteria," said Wyrdrune as he sloshed across with a pained expression on his face. "My goddamn balls will probably shrivel up and drop off."

"What makes you think you've got any?" Kira said with a grin. "Loosen up, for God's sake. A little dirty water isn't going to kill you."

"Try taking a dip in the Hudson River," Wyrdrune said.

"The Hudson's been running clean for the past fifty years," said Kira.

"Good. Then you swim in it."

Kira rolled her eyes.

They stepped up into the branch tunnel entrance, which was slightly higher than the bottom of the channel. The water was only to their knees now. This tunnel was much smaller and narrower, with the roof only inches above their heads.

"If this keeps up, we'll soon be crawling through this muck," said Wyrdrune.

"Stop talking so much," Modred said softly. "Sound carries through these tunnels. Be still and listen."

They stood silently for a moment, listening intently. Some distance ahead of them down the tunnel, they could hear the dim sounds of splashing.

"It's him," said Modred. "Come on. Stay on your guard. And keep quiet. If we can hear him, it means that he can also hear us."

"Then we're not likely to sneak up on him, are we?" Wyrdrune said.

Modred merely glared at him.

"All right, I'll shut up," said Wrydrune.

"You're almost as bad as your damned broom," said Modred.

Wrydrune took a deep breath and exhaled heavily, but said nothing. They followed the sounds ahead of them, the glowing ball lighting their way.

I suppose he thinks Pascal can't see this light show moving down the tunnel behind him, Wyrdrune thought, though he kept it to himself. We could be blowing bugles down here, for all the good it's going to do him. He's not going to get away. He's dying, for God's sake, his last drops of blood mingling with the sewage. We'll probably come up on him floating facedown in this shit. And meanwhile, Jacqueline and Billy are probably having hot coffee down at the police station with Renaud. If I'd only waited a couple of seconds longer, he thought, I could be with them in a nice, cozy interrogation room or jail cell instead of wading through this garbage.

They came to the end of the tunnel. It was a short branch passageway, connecting two much larger tunnels. It opened out onto another wide channel, with another walkway on the opposite side. They could no longer hear the sounds of splashing, only of dripping and lapping water.

"He must have crossed here and come out on the other side," said Modred.

"Yeah, but then which way did he go?" asked Wyrdrune, glancing down both ends of the long tunnel.

"Well, we're not going to find out by standing here," said Kira. "Let's go, warlock. No more hanging behind. You first, this time." And she gave him a slight shove.

"Hey!" said Wyrdrune as he stumbled forward out of the branch tunnel, losing his balance.

His right foot went down into the channel . . . and kept on going. This channel was much deeper and the water was up to his chest. He fell forward and then went down into the water, over his head. The illuminating globe, no longer under his control, dropped down into the water and was extinguished in a hiss of steam. Wyrdrune came up in darkness, sputtering and spitting, the slimy water streaming from him.

"Oh, Jesus Christ!" he said. He spat repeatedly. "I think I swallowed some." He coughed and gagged. "God, I'm going to be sick!"

"Shut up!" said Modred.

"Drop dead!" Wyrdrune retorted hotly. "How you'd like to swallow a mouthful of filthy, stinking, disgusting—"

"*Will you shut the hell up, damn you!*" Modred said. "There's something wrong! *Be still!*"

The tone of his voice silenced Wrydrune at once. He stood perfectly still in the chest-high water. And then he felt it.

"Oh, shit," he said hoarsely. *"There's something in here with me!"*

Modred quickly held up his hands and red fire crackled from his fingertips, forming into a flaming, bright red ball of energy that he tossed out ahead of him. It quickly rose up toward the roof of the tunnel, illuminating everything around them.

"*Ho-ly shiiit!*" cried Wyrdrune.

Right in front of him, water streaming from its slick brown-furred body as it rose up out of the channel, was a gigantic rat, the size of an elephant. It bared its fangs and snarled, its chittering sound magnified a hundred times into a deafening roar that filled the tunnel.

Wyrdrune plunged into the slimy water and started stroking like an Olympic swimmer going for the gold. As the gargantuan rodent lunged after him, Kira and Modred flung out their arms and searing bolts of thaumaturgic energy shot out from their fingertips, exploding as they struck the rat's huge body. It screamed with agony and turned toward them, gobs of saliva dripping from its fangs, but they continued the barrage. The beast bellowed as it became wreathed in an incandescent aura of thaumaturgic energy and began to burn. Clouds of steam rose up from the water as the deafening roar of its dying throes echoed through the tunnel and then it collapsed in upon itself and vanished in billowing clouds of steam and roiling water.

Modred teleported himself and Kira to the walkway on the opposite side of the channel.

"Wyrdrune!" he shouted.

There was no response.

"Warlock!" Kira cried, glancing at Modred with alarm. "Warlock, where the hell *are* you?"

Wyrdrune rose up out of the sewage, water streaming from his hair. He was covered with filth and slime. He looked like a drowned cat.

"A rat as big as a house," he said. "Jesus, I *had* to say it, didn't I?"

Modred stretched his arms out toward him and Wyrdrune came floating up out of the channel, water streaming off him as he rose into the air. With his outstretched arms, Modred guided him over to the walkway where they stood and gently set him down.

"Thanks," Wyrdrune said sourly. "Why the hell didn't you do that in the first place?"

"Are you all right?" asked Kira with concern.

"Yeah, no thanks to you. Jesus, look at me!"

"Count your blessings, warlock," she said. "You came that close to being rat bait."

"I warned you," Modred said. "Never underestimate the Dark Ones."

Wyrdrune shivered. "God! I *hate* rats!"

Modred was looking at the floor of the walkway around them. "Over here," he said, pointing to a pool of water and a wet trail that led away from them, down the tunnel. "That's the way he went."

Modred and Kira quickly moved off in the direction that Pascal had taken, the flaming red ball moving ahead of them and Wyrdrune following miserably behind. About two hundred yards farther down the tunnel, they came upon Pascal.

He was lying stretched out on his stomach, his legs splayed out behind him, his fingers scrabbling at the walkway in front of him, as if he was trying to drag himself along, but he had nothing left. His expensive clothes were sopping wet and covered with blood and slime. He turned weakly and glanced at them, fear in his bulging eyes, his face white as a sheet. His lips were blue with cyanosis, his skin was stretched tight over his bones, his eyes were glazed and he looked as if he had been completely drained of blood.

"Leila!" he croaked weakly. "Leila, help me!"

"Where are they?" Modred asked him.

"Leila, *please*!"

"She's abandoned you to die," said Modred. "Don't be a fool, man. We can at least save your soul from being damned. Tell us where they are!"

"Leila . . ."

"Talk to me, Pascal!" said Modred. *"Where are the Dark Ones?"*

"Save . . . me. . . ."

"Pascal!"

He slumped down and lay still.

"It's too late," said Kira, looking down at him. "He's gone."

"*Damn* it!" Modred swore, turning away furiously.

"All for nothing," Wyrdrune said.

"No, not for nothing," Kira said. "At least we know he's dead. That's one less killer on the streets of Paris." She glanced at Modred. "*Could* we have done that?" she asked.

Modred glanced at her with a frown. "Done what?"

"Saved his soul from being damned," she said. "I didn't know the runestones had that power."

"They don't," said Modred.

"But you said—"

"Souls neither go to Paradise nor are they damned to Hell," said Modred. "They simply cease to exist."

"You lied?" she said. "You lied to a dying man?"

"No," said Modred. "I lied to a *dead* man. Look."

He pointed at the body. Kira turned to look at it and gasped. In death, Pascal had reverted to his true form. The corpse of an eighty-year-old man lay shriveled on the walkway at their feet.

"He died the moment he gave himself over to the Dark Ones," Modred said.

"He may have had no choice," said Kira quietly as she looked down at him. "You left him thinking that his soul would be forever damned. You didn't have to do that. No matter what he might have done, he was still a human being. You owed him at least that consideration."

"Grow up," said Modred. "I owed him nothing. Come on. Let's get the hell out of here."

He turned and started walking back down the tunnel.

Kira stared after him. "There was a time when I thought I loved him," she said softly.

Wyrdrune looked at her. "I thought so, too," he said quietly, so that only she could hear.

She shook her head. "God, he's so cold," she said. "It frightens me. In some ways, he's really no different from the Dark Ones."

"There's one very important difference," Wyrdrune said. "He's on our side."

Colette Dubois had the face of an angel and the body of a harlot. Her hair was long and fine and so blond that it was almost white. Her eyes were a striking dark blue, flecked with tiny bits of gold. Her face was heart-shaped, with a slightly pointed chin, a turned-up nose and a mouth that was shaped in a perpetual, full-lipped pout. Her complexion was flawless and, at twenty-three, she looked no more than seventeen. Her breasts were large and firm, slightly upturned, and her waist was so small that a man could almost encircle it with his hands. Her legs were long and shaped to sheer perfection. With that face and that body, she looked like a combination of innocent young girl and strumpet, the sort of fantasy most men only dream about. They stared at her every-where she went. She attracted them the way a magnet draws iron filings. With her stunning looks and soft, vulnerable, breathy voice, she could easily have had any man she chose. Only she hated men.

She had learned to hate them early, when she was only fourteen and her father had seduced her. And it had been just that, a calculated, methodical seduction, progressing slowly in stages over a period of time, as soon as she had started to mature, which she had done quite early. The fatherly affection had gradually progressed from paternal hugs and kisses to caresses, then more intimate kisses, and finally to the act itself. It was, without a doubt, abuse and molestation, yet in another sense, it was not entirely one-sided. Right from the beginning, Colette had known exactly what was going on and, in her own manipulative way, she had encouraged it. Not because she liked it, but because it gave her a sense of power.

Unknown to her father, she had lost her virginity at the age of twelve, to a boy who was five years older. At the age of eleven, she had witnessed her older sister, who was four-teen, making love with her boyfriend in her bedroom when their parents were away. On previous occasions, she had heard the sounds they made from her own bedroom and cu-rious to see what was going on, she had hidden in her sister's closet and observed the action undiscovered. An unusually precocious girl, she had known what they were doing, though she had no real understanding of the physical sensations and emotions that accompanied the act. What struck her most were the reactions of her sister's boyfriend. She had always thought of boys as being stronger and superior, but although it had been clear to her that they both obviously enjoyed what they were doing, it was equally as clear that her sister was the one in control. And afterward, at the climactic moment, her sister's boyfriend had seemed like a completely different person. He trembled and made small, whimpering noises and clung to her like a child clings to its mother. And her sister had held him and made soft, cooing sounds while he lay on top of her, breathing heavily, and he seemed so . . . weak. That, more than anything else, had fascinated her.

She found herself wondering if she could make a boy so weak and she soon had an opportunity to find out, with the very boy she had observed with her sister. In a very calculated way, acting as she had seen her sister act, she had seduced him and found that she could, indeed, make him as weak as her sister seemed to make him. And though the act itself was vaguely pleasurable to her, the idea of controlling him like that was absolutely intoxicating. And she wanted to do it again, with someone else, to see if she could reproduce that same feeling of control. And although she didn't know it, or could not have fully understood it if she did, Colette had been destined for that course from birth. There was something wrong with her. Deep down inside, something vital and important had been missing from the very start. She was a budding sociopath, with no sense of right or wrong and an overwhelming, pathological compulsion to control and manipulate others. And by the time her father noticed her in a new way and started acting out his own sick compulsions, Colette had already had at least a dozen lovers and the idea of controlling her father in the same way, the most powerful man in her life, was exhilarating to her. She had allowed him to fulfill his twisted needs and then she made him pay for it. By the time she was sixteen, he was her abject slave. She had utter contempt for him. A year later, ridden with guilt and remorse he could not bear, he committed suicide. And although she was not entirely responsible, Colette believed that it was she who drove him to it and that filled her with even more contempt for his weakness. And she transferred that contempt to every man she ever knew.

It might have been possible to feel sympathy or pity for Colette if it were not for the fact that she was an empty shell, utterly immoral and totally remorseless. The only pleasure that she got from life was from manipulating and controlling others. It was an all-encompassing, pathological need. She had an irresistible desire to make people jump through hoops, especially men, and she was driven to reduce them to pliable nonentities. For which she hated them. By the age of eighteen, she had stopped having sex with men. She no longer took any pleasure in it and experience had taught her that it wasn't necessary to achieve the desired effect. The implied promise of it was all that was required. For physical relationships, she much preferred the company of women. They were not as weak as men, but she manipulated them as well. It was the only thing that gave her any satisfaction.

She had a job dancing nude in a small saloon located in the Latin Quarter. It was not one of the fancier establishments, such as the Cafe Noir, with elaborate stage shows and chorus girls dancing in choreographed routines. Colette did not like sharing the stage with anyone. She wanted to have all the attention for herself, so she danced in a club that had several small stages set about the room, with chairs placed around them so that men could sit around the perimeter of the stage with their drinks and cigarettes and stare up at her as she danced, moving through a succession of seductive poses. They would give her tips and for a bit more money, she would give them a "table dance" away from the stage, in one of the darkened corners of the club. The whole thing was a sexual tease, with no real contact occurring between her and the patrons of the club. She might touch them slightly, with a stroking motion on the upper arm, a light caress upon the cheek or run her fingers through their hair, but they could not touch her and the club employed large bouncers to make sure no one got out of line. It was yet another way she could control them and she was paid for it, as well. But though she smiled at them and gave them smoldering looks as she performed, she felt nothing. And though the club had a strict policy against going out with customers, she often did just that, especially with men who had money to spend.

She got so that she could identify them almost immediately. It was easy. They were always the ones who tipped more generously, as if to show off, and often asked for the more expensive table dances, during which they could have the opportunity to tell her how much they wanted her. She would lead them on, telling them that she was not allowed to date the customers, but saying it in such a way that led them to believe that she could be talked into it.

She kept them coming back to the club, again and again, investing more of their time and money, until she was sure she had them well and truly hooked. Then she would finally consent to see them outside the club, but always in a public place, always ''just for coffee,'' playing the cautious innocent who just happened to dance naked in a bar because it was the only way she could make enough money to help support her ailing mother. In truth, she had no idea of her mother's state of health or that of anybody in her family. She had not seen or spoken with them since her father's suicide, when she had confronted her mother with the reason for it and thoroughly burned all her bridges.

After the first few dates, she would have them so firmly in the palm of her hand that they would start telling her the most intimate details about their lives. They were almost always married and they almost always cheated on their wives, which meant that they would probably cheat elsewhere, too, such as in their business, and little by little, leading them along, gradually allowing them slight liberties —a kiss here, a touch there, always with the implied promise that more would be eventually forthcoming—she made inroads into their private lives, like a cancer slowly spreading through a person's system. She would get them to spend money on her to show off how successful and powerful they were, reacting with a feigned childish delight to every gift and telling them they ''shouldn't have,'' and she would get them to reveal more and more about themselves, to show her how honest and sensitive they were, until one day they would wake up and realize that she was in a position to totally destroy them. And then the game would begin in earnest.

Colette was not really interested in blackmail. She was interested in using what she learned to make them do things, like a chess master moving pieces on a board. She found it more difficult to do with women, who were not as easy to manipulate as men, but she enjoyed the challenge. At any given time, she had at least half a dozen people on the string, playing with them like a puppeteer. The more complex her machinations, the better she enjoyed it. She was always very careful in the selection of her pawns. It would not do to pick someone whom she could inadvertently push too far, someone who could strike back and hurt her. A true sociopath, the only pain that she was capable of feeling was her own. The only person she was capable of feeling sorry for was herself. It would have been easy to think of her as being evil, except that she quite literally did not know the difference between what was good and what was evil. She was, like most sociopaths, almost an alien being, able to mimic human behavior, but it was all a sham, a performance. She did what was expected of her in any given social situation, but she didn't really feel much. She could, however, feel fear.

She felt it as she was walking home one night after dancing at the club. She was tired and her feet hurt and she was anxious to get back to her apartment and slip into a nice, warm bath. It was late, almost three o'clock in the morning, and the streets were practically deserted once she left the Latin Quarter. Her high heels made clip-clopping sounds on the pavement as she walked with a quick, purposeful stride.

Because she often had to leave the club at a late hour, she carried a small pistol in her purse and, like everything else that she had ever done, she had practiced with it diligently, like an automaton, until she knew just how to use it with optimum results. Because it was a small-caliber weapon, so that it could be easily concealed, she knew that it worked best up close, where she could go for a head shot. She had practiced drawing the pistol from her purse and firing it quickly so that she could make such a shot nine times out of ten and, because of that, she felt reasonably secure walking through the street at night. But on this night, she did not feel secure at all.

It had rained earlier that evening and the streets were slick and lambent, the moisture on them reflecting the glow of the streetlights. It was a cool night and a pleasant breeze was blowing. She was almost halfway home when she suddenly felt the hairs rising on the back of her neck and experienced the inexplicable sensation that she was being followed.

It was one of those instinctual, almost subliminal sensations. She hadn't seen or heard anything, but it was the sort of reaction people sometimes get when they have the sudden feeling that someone is staring at them from across a crowded room. They turn and, sure enough, someone is staring. Colette stopped suddenly and turned around, but she didn't see a thing in the street behind her. She stood perfectly still, her hand on her purse, gazing intently into the shadows. Was that a movement? She wasn't sure. She swallowed nervously and continued walking, slightly increasing her pace.

She felt it again.

She glanced over her shoulder and, this time, she was almost certain she had seen a movement, just a quick glimpse out of the corner of her eye. She started walking faster. And then she heard it. The unmistakable sound of footsteps, trying to match her own pace, but not quite succeeding. *Clip-clip, clop-clop, clip-clip, clop-clop*—just slightly out of synch. She quickly stopped and turned.

Nothing.

This time, she was certain that it wasn't only her imagination. She was definitely being followed. Stalked. Her stomach muscles tightened up. Don't run, she told herself. If you start to run, he'll know he's got you. He'll know he's in control.

Suddenly, it occurred to her that he might be intending to follow her all the way to her apartment, so that he would know where she lived. Perhaps it was one of the customers from the club, one of those sly voyeur types who would try to find out where she lived, so that he could watch her from concealment, perhaps slip cryptic notes under her door or send her gifts anonymously. He would try to find out her telephone number so that he could call her and say nothing when she answered. It was a form of manipulation and that was something she could understand. She had encountered those types once or twice before. They were generally small, cowardly little men trying to live out a fantasy of power. She knew how to handle them. On the other hand, it could be a mugger or a rapist. She knew how to handle those, as well. That was why she had the gun. Either way, she had no intention of allowing her stalker to find out where she lived.

She turned into the next alleyway and walked down it a little ways then flattened herself with her back against the wall, so that she could easily see the entrance to the alley. She slipped her hand into her purse and took out the pistol. For a few moments, nothing happened. There was no sound of approaching footsteps, no sign of anyone following her. An then a huge dog came padding silently into the alley. It stopped a short way inside and growled. And as she watched it in the glow from the street lamp on the sidewalk, Colette suddenly realized that it was not a dog at all, but a large wolf. A wolf on the streets of Paris! No, it was impossible. It *had* to be a dog. But she felt the cold fist of fear squeezing her insides. Her small pistol suddenly seemed terribly inadequate.

The animal could smell her. It bared its teeth in a snarl and growled again. Slowly, it moved farther into the alley, stalking her. She held up the gun and tried to keep her hand from shaking.

"Michel!"

The voice came from close by, just around the corner of the building. A woman's voice.

"Michel, where are you?"

The beast stopped where it was and turned its head, whimpering slightly. A woman was silhouetted in the light as she came to stand at the entrance to the alley.

"There you are!" she said. "Michel, what are you doing in there? What is it? Are you chasing cats again?"

Colette let out an audible sigh of relief. She put down the gun.

"Who's there?" the woman said.

The animal began to growl again.

"It's okay," Colette said, stepping out away from the wall. "I . . . I was afraid of your dog. I thought it was going to attack me."

The animal growled again. "It's all right, Michel," the woman said. "Sit."

The beast whined slightly and sat down in its haunches, its tongue lolling.

"I'm sorry if he frightened you," the woman said. "But he won't hurt anyone unless I tell him to."

"He must make you feel safe, walking the streets at night," Colette said. "What kind of dog is that?"

"He's not a dog," the woman said. "He's a wolf."

Colette had been just about to reach out to pet him, but she immediately backed away. "A wolf! Really? You have a wolf for a pet?"

"No need to be afraid," the woman said. "He does anything I tell him." She smiled. "Sometimes he's almost human."

Colette was fascinated that this woman could actually have a trained wolf. To actually control a wild beast like that. . . .

"Did you raise him from a pup?" she said.

"Baby wolves are called cubs," the woman said. "But no, he was almost fully grown when I found him."

"Found him?" Colette said.

The woman laughed. "It's a long story," she said.

"I'd like to hear it," said Colette, looking at the woman.

She was really very beautiful. Even more beautiful than she was. She had long, flaming red hair, high cheekbones and copper-colored skin. Her eyes were gorgeous, a striking shade of metallic green. She wore a long dark cloak, open in the front, a black blouse, skin-tight black leather pants and high-heeled boots. Colette found herself powerfully attracted to her. Their eyes met and they gazed at each other silently for a long moment.

"Would you like to have a drink together?" Colette said. "My apartment isn't far from here. You can bring your wolf and tell me how you found him. What does he eat?"

"Anything I tell him to," the woman said with a smile. "Would you like to pet him?"

"Is it all right?"

"Go on. He won't hurt you."

Slowly, Colette stretched out her hand and stroked the beast's fur. It licked her hand.

"Hello, boy," she said. "You gave me quite a scare, but we're going to be friends, aren't we?" She glanced up at the woman. "My name's Colette."

"Mine's Leila."

Chapter
EIGHT

They had the routine down to a fine art. The first step was picking out their victim. That was the simplest part. Tourists were easy to spot. Sometimes, they went after tourists who traveled in pairs, or even in small groups of three and four, but the ones who were by themselves made the best marks. Suddenly, the unsuspecting tourist would find himself surrounded by a group of small, bedraggled children, shouting and cajoling, tugging at his clothes, grabbing at his hands and getting in his way as they begged for coins. One of them would thrust something at the unsuspecting victim, a folded up newspaper was most often used, and while the disoriented mark's attention was thus distracted, nimble fingers would dart underneath the paper and pluck out his wallet. The wallet would immediately be passed to one of the other children, usually the smallest or the swiftest runner, and by the time the victim realized that his pocket had been picked, the one with the wallet was long gone. The police could do nothing in a situation such as this and many tourists found their pockets lightened in this manner by the gangs of gypsy children, against which the authorities were practically helpless.

The old man who walked across the square with his gold-headed cane looked foreign and, better still, he looked prosperous. His clothes were well tailored and his coat looked expensive. The cane he carried didn't give them any pause. He did not look very threatening and most people would never think of striking out at a pathetic-looking bunch of children. They surged toward him, surrounding him, crying out and begging and tugging at his clothes. To be on the safe side, two of them fastened on to the hand holding the cane. Marcel, the oldest at fourteen, thrust a paper at him while Karl, an accomplished pickpocket at eleven, ducked beneath it as he made to grab his wallet. Then, suddenly, everything went wrong.

Karl felt a strong hand clamped around his wrist and Marcel stared as the old man's eyes fixed firmly upon his and began to glow with a green fire. He dropped the paper as he stiffened, his eyes glazed and unfocused. Karl tried to jerk away, but an instant later, he also felt the burning gaze upon him and, like Marcel, he stopped resisting. The chatter of the other children fell silent as they, too, fell under the spell and became silent, standing with slack jaws and unfocused stares, like a bunch of dirty little statues.

The old man smiled as he looked around at them. "Filthy little beggars, aren't you?" he said, his voice belying his aged appearance. "But you'll all do. Yes, I think you'll do quite nicely."

He turned and started walking toward a nearby alleyway. And, like baby ducks following their mother, the children all trooped after him. Inside the alley, the "old man" turned and faced them, only he was no longer an old man. He stood before them, dressed in a long, hooded black robe, his coppery-hued features framed by flame red hair. He held his arms out wide, as if to hug them, and the children all clustered together.

"Come," he said with a smile. "Come and meet your other playmates. We have new games to show you."

There was a brief flash of bright green light, and the alleyway was empty.

It was almost morning by the time they got back to the hotel. Their limo driver, who had fallen asleep waiting for them, stared at them with chagrin when he saw the state they were in, especially Wyrdrune, who was wet from head to toe from his immersion in the stinking sewer water. The reaction of the hotel staff was not much different, but since the Ritz was, after all, a world-class hotel and they were staying in one of its most expensive suites, after their initial shocked reaction, they immediately became solicitous, asking if they'd had some sort of accident and if there was anything they could do to be of help. Modred thanked them politely and explained that there had, indeed, been an unfortunate accident, that someone had left a sewer grating open and Wyrdrune had fallen through it, but miraculously escaped serious injury and they had gotten wet helping him out. It was, perhaps, an improbable-sounding story, but the hotel staff asked no questions. They merely inquired if a doctor was required or if they should call anyone to report the incident. Modred thanked them once again and declined, saying that after such a harrowing experience, all they wanted was to go upstairs and shower, have their clothes thrown out, then go to sleep. But the moment they walked through the door, they saw that they had company. Jacqueline and Billy had returned. Raven and Piccard were with them.

"Good God, what happened?" Jacqueline asked on seeing them.

"That can wait," said Modred, looking at the two strangers standing with her. He frowned slightly as he gazed at them. "Adepts," he said.

"These people are agents of the I.T.C.," Jacqueline said.

"I had surmised that," Modred said tensely, keeping his eyes on them. "Before we begin our explanations, perhaps you'd better give us yours."

"It's all right," said Merlin. "Allow me to present agents Raven and Piccard. Raven was once one of my students. They know everything."

"Do they, indeed?" said Modred softly. "I think that may have been a very serious mistake. I hope you can convince me otherwise, or there's a good chance that neither of them will leave this room alive."

"Your threats don't impress me, Morpheus," Piccard said. "It *is* Morpheus, is it not?"

"His name is Modred," Jacqueline said.

"Whatever he calls himself, we've been looking for him for a very long time," Piccard said.

"Well, it appears you've found me," Modred said. "What are you going to do about it?"

"Stop it!" said Raven. "You've both got your feathers ruffled like a pair of fighting roosters. We didn't come here for a confrontation or to place anyone under arrest."

"We didn't come here to be threatened, either," said Piccard.

"Enough," said Merlin. "Modred, these people can be trusted. The decision to tell them everything was mine. It's my responsibility."

"It was not your choice to make," said Modred. "You presume a great deal, Ambrosius. But then you always did."

"Talk, talk, talk," the broom said, shuffling into the room with its red nightcap perched atop its broomstick. "Doesn't *anyone* believe in sleeping anymore? Honestly, it's enough to make your bristles fall out. You're all making me crazy!" It stopped suddenly in front of Wyrdrune. "*Gevalt!* What happened to you? Just look at you! And that smell! *Feh!* You smell like a public toilet!"

"Close," said Kira.

"I'll never understand how the hell you can smell anything without a nose," said Wyrdrune.

"A stench like that, believe me, you don't *need* a nose to smell," the broom said. "And you two aren't much better," it said to Modred and Kira. "What on earth have you been doing? No, better yet, don't tell me, I'm sure it was disgusting. Look at you! What kind of way is this to entertain your guests? Go take your clothes off and get into a shower, for God's sake. I'm going to have to open all the windows.''

''In a minute, Broom,'' said Wyrdrune. ''First we have to—''

''In a minute, nothing,'' said the broom, pushing him toward the bathroom with its spindly arms. ''You get out of those stinking, sopping clothes right now before you catch your death of cold! I'll see if room service can send up some steaming chicken broth. Come on now, get.''

''Broom, for cryin' out loud—''

''And don't give me any of your backtalk,'' said the broom, cutting him off. ''You march right into that bathroom, Mister Wizard, and get out of those wet clothes. I promised your mother I'd take care of you, God rest her soul, and I'm not going to put up with any nonsense, so off you go.''

The others couldn't help themselves. They burst out laughing as the broom shoved a protesting Wyrdrune into the bathroom and the tension broke.

''I've never seen anything like that in my entire life,'' said Raven. ''It's positively charming! Is it your familiar?''

''No,'' said Modred, amused in spite of himself. ''It's his.''

''And it bosses him around like that?'' Piccard said, grinning. ''What sort of spell did he use to animate it?''

''That's part of the problem,'' Modred replied. ''He doesn't remember. He couldn't reproduce it if he tried.''

''Oh, dear,'' said Raven. ''For a wizard, that's not very responsible, is it?''

''That's just the point,'' said Merlin. ''He's not a wizard. He's only a warlock, as Kira is so fond of reminding him. He never stood for certification. He was kicked out of school before he could complete his studies.''

''So that's why we've never been able to find any record of him,'' said Piccard. ''We naturally assumed that it must have taken a wizard to spirit those gems out of a roomful of sorcerers. To think it was accomplished by a mere student!''

''Not quite a *mere* student,'' Merlin said. ''Wyrdrune was

the most talented natural adept I've taught since Al'Hassan. The problem in Wyrdrune's case has always been that he has no discipline. He was forever overreaching himself, like an infant trying to walk before it's learned to crawl. The broom is a perfect example. I haven't the faintest idea what sort of spell he used, but knowing him, he undoubtedly attempted something very complicated and involved, with all sorts of strange embellishments and no real understanding of what in God's name he was doing. You see the result. He animated it to help his ailing mother around the house while he was away at school and it somehow became impressed with her personality. *I* can't even figure out how it manages to speak, much less reason, but its sophistication should give you some idea of Wyrdrune's natural abilities."

"And yet he was expelled from thaumaturgy school?" Piccard said. "What on earth did he do?"

"He burned down a concert hall in Boston," Kira said.

"Seriously?" asked Raven.

"He didn't mean to," Merlin explained. "He was trying to earn some extra money and he took a part-time job as a special effects adept with a band that wasn't too particular about whether or not he was actually certified, especially since he was willing to work cheaply. He cast a fire spell for one of their effects and it got out of his control."

"As I recall, a fire was used as a diversion in the theft of the runestones," said Piccard.

"He tries to learn from his mistakes," said Kira wryly. "He's got the fire spell down pat now. It's his teleportation that's a little shaky."

Raven raised her eyebrows. "He's only a warlock and he can teleport?" she said.

"Well, sort of," Kira replied. "He's like a shaky student pilot-adept. His takeoffs are okay, but his landings need a little work. To some extent, the runestones augment his natural power," she added, "as they do with me. Genetically, I suppose I have the talent to become an adept, but I've never studied thaumaturgy. Still, I am capable of hurling bolts of thaumaturgic energy, but not just anytime I want. It's not really my doing. It's the runestone.'' She stripped off her black leather glove and opened her hand.

Raven and Piccard both came closer, to look at it. "Fascinating," said Piccard. "I have a thousand questions and I am not sure where to start."

"Why don't we begin by letting them get out of their wet clothes?" said Raven. "I'll call room service and order some more coffee."

A short while later, they were all sitting around the coffee table in the main room of the suite. Wyrdrune, all washed up, was wearing a terry cloth robe. Kira had changed into a cotton caftan and was sitting barefoot with her feet tucked under her on the couch. Modred had put on one of his silk brocade dressings gowns, a pair of slacks and slippers.

"For the sake of honesty," Piccard said, "perhaps we should begin by making sure we understand each other." He glanced at Modred. "I'm sure that neither of us is very comfortable with the prospect of working together. I cannot ignore the fact that you are a wanted criminal and I believe I speak for my partner, as well. There can be no clean slates between us, nor would you believe me if I suggested otherwise. However, due to the unique circumstances of the current situation, I believe that we must have a sort of truce. That, in and of itself, makes Raven and me lawbreakers, but it is a question of priorities. Merlin has convinced us that the Dark Ones pose a far greater threat than you do. I understand that you have given up your former, uh, 'occupation,' though that still does not absolve you of past crimes. However, that is a question that must, of necessity, be postponed indefinitely. We also understand that the nature of this situation is such that we cannot communicate what we have learned to our superiors. When it comes to that, I have to agree with Merlin. The knowledge of the Dark Ones' existence must be kept secret from the general public in order to prevent a widespread panic and we cannot vouch for the entire agency. So that leaves us all involved in a situation that, while it may be moral, is nevertheless clandestine and decidedly illegal. I suppose we shall have to live with that as best we can, but we will not be able to support you in your efforts to defeat the Dark Ones if there is not an element of trust between us. So I will tell you frankly that the moment you betray that trust, all bets are off. And the moment the threat of the Dark Ones is eliminated, I'm coming after you.''

"A fine and noble little speech," said Modred with a wry smile. "All right, Piccard. I can accept those terms, so long as you understand that it must work both ways. The moment either you or Raven betray our trust, *I'll* be coming after *you*."

"Fine," said Raven with a grimace. "If we're all done flexing our muscles now, perhaps we can get down to the matter at hand."

Briefly, Modred told them about the events of that night, of how Pascal had fled down to the sewers and of how he died without revealing anything except the name of the Dark One whom he served, which was of little use to them at the moment. Then Raven told them about the latest murder, that of the prostitute who was found with her throat torn open, claw marks on her body and mutilated with the telltale thaumaturgic runes.

"For the time being," she finished, "we can run interference for Renaud. We can report that we are still pursuing our investigation, functioning in an advisory capacity to the police. That way, anyone else in the agency will be officially kept out of the case and it will remain in Renaud's jurisdiction, so long as we're in charge."

"What about Max Siegal?" Kira asked.

"He has already been released," said Raven. "Needless to say, he will be told that it was due to lack of hard evidence and to the fact that a similar crime was committed while he was in custody. The attorney that Jacqueline retained for him will make the customary outraged noises to the media, the police department will apologize profusely and there will be talk of a lawsuit for false arrest, but it will all be purely for show and the purpose of Siegal's exoneration in the public eye. Nothing will come of it."

Kira nodded. "That seems like the best way to handle it," she said.

"The question is, where do we go from here?" Piccard said. "One of the acolytes is dead, but another remains on the loose and there can be others still. For all we know, the Dark Ones could be amassing an entire army of acolytes to murder for them."

"That there will be others, I have no doubt," said Modred, "but dozens, not hundreds or thousands. Not an entire army, by any means."

"What's to prevent them?" asked Piccard.

"The laws of thaumaturgic energy," said Wyrdrune. "The more people they have under their control, the more power they'd have to expend and the Dark Ones are trying to build up their power, not deplete it."

"But the more acolytes they have under their control, committing murders for them, the more life energy they can absorb," Piccard said. "Isn't that true?"

"To some extent, it is," said Modred. "However, to use a rather peculiar, though perhaps not entirely inappropriate analogy, that would be a lot like the process of investing. To use money as the analogy for thaumaturgic power, imagine that you invest funds in a small business in order to increase your capital. It takes a certain initial expenditure to infuse capital into that business so that you might recoup on your investment and make a profit. If the business then becomes very successful and you consistently bank the profits, eventually, you will accumulate a fortune. However, if instead of banking the profits, you decide to reinvest them back into the business in order to increase its size, or, more appropriately in this case, invest the profits in another business and continue to follow that practice, then eventually you will have a large number of businesses in operation, but in terms of the money that you have ready to hand, you won't be much better off than when you started."

"Only you would be worth a great deal more on paper," said Piccard. "To follow your analogy, wouldn't the Dark

Ones benefit from such a situation? At some point, they could decide to stop reinvesting in new acolytes, at which time they could then draw on all of that potential profit, as you put it. And in the meantime, we'd be kept busy trying to track down a large number of killers.''

"Except that isn't the way the Dark Ones think," said Merlin. "If they did, in fact, think that way, they would have had no objection to white magic. But they were greedy for the quick accumulation of power that necromancy gave them, instead of the steady, but considerably slower methods offered by white magic. They went to war rather than give up necromancy. And when they escaped from their confinement, instead of uniting together to fight the runestones, they scattered throughout the world, seeking sanctuary in the hope that others among them would be the first to fall while they built up their strength in safety. Remember how they used Al'Hassan. They will try to do the same thing here. They will function through a small number of acolytes, hoping to increase their power as quickly as possible so that they might then attempt the sort of spell that would bring about the deaths of large numbers of people all at once, thereby releasing a massive amount of life energy that they could absorb. And if that gave them the power to defeat the runestones, they could then absorb that energy as well and become preeminent among the others of their kind.''

"But what's to stop them from leaving Paris and starting over someplace else now that they know you're on to them?'' asked Raven.

"Absolutely nothing,'' Wyrdrune said. "Only they won't do that.''

"Why not? she asked.

"Because they're greedy,'' Wyrdrune replied. "To use Modred's terms, they have an investment to protect. They've used up thaumaturgic energy in order to possess their acolytes and keep them under control. If they left now, they'd lose whatever they had gained by starting over someplace else. They'll cut and run only as a last resort.''

"But you don't know that for sure,'' Piccard said.

"No, we don't," Wyrdrune admitted, "but they've followed the same pattern each time we've encountered them. They'll continue trying to accumulate as much power as they can in the hope that it will enable them to defeat us. Keep one thing in mind—we're more than just a threat to them. We're also the carrot on a stick. If they can kill us and destroy the runestones, it would give them an incredible amount of power, because then they'd be able to absorb the life energies of the Council of the White and after that, nothing on earth could stop them."

"And if they could manage to kill even one of us," Modred added, "it would effectively break the spell of the Living Triangle. Then the two survivors would be only as strong as the spirits of the individual runestones they possess, and that would make them far more vulnerable. The Dark Ones know we represent a threat to them, but their greed for power won't let them run. There is too much at stake. They'll play the game out to the very end."

"What happens if they win?" asked Raven.

For a moment, they all sat in silence until, finally, Merlin spoke. "Then it would usher in the Third Thaumaturgic Age," he said. "The Dark Age. The Age of Necromancy."

"Only none of us would have to worry," Wyrdrune said, "because in that event, we wouldn't be alive to see it."

"Is the power of the runestones the only thing that can destroy the Dark Ones?" Raven asked.

"Fortunately, no," said Wyrdrune. "In London, Billy killed one with his knife. An immortal *can* be killed, but it has to be an immediately fatal wound. If the necromancer has the strength and the time to use a spell to heal himself, he can easily survive a wound that would kill an ordinary man."

"And immortals also have natural, regenerative powers that are far greater than any human's," Merlin said. "Which means that you cannot hope to incapacitate them, at least not for long. Trying to arrest them is simply out of the question. Any attempt to do so would result in death for the arresting officers and even if they could successfully be captured, there is no way that you could ever hope to hold them. You must remember, above all, that we are not dealing with a human enemy. The *only* way to stop them is to kill them.''

''Well, at least they can be killed by conventional means. That's something hopeful, anyway,'' Piccard said.

''So far, they've struck at night,'' said Raven. ''We can have the Paris police covering the streets, working in teams. Renaud can head the task force. We can tell them that they're dealing with a dangerous psychopath and give them orders to shoot first and ask questions later, but that still presents some problems. They're not trained to shoot perpetrators on sight, thank God, but in this case, that could work against them. And there's always the possibility that innocent people might be killed.''

''Innocent people *are* being killed,'' said Kira.

''But we can't have them killed by the police,'' said Piccard. ''Raven's right. There has to be a hostile act before the police can shoot. There isn't any way around that. But without the advantage of surprise, a necromancer could easily get the advantage over them.''

''Perhaps,'' said Merlin, ''but we still have one thing working in our favor. It's not enough for the Dark Ones to simply send out their acolytes to kill. In order to acquire the life energy of a victim, they must be present to cast a spell that would allow them to absorb it. That's the reason for the mutilations, the thaumaturgic runes carved or burned into the victims' bodies. Originally, the process was part of an elaborate sacrificial ritual. Obviously, they have discarded most of the ritualistic aspects of the killings in order to save time, but it still takes at least a few moments to effect the process. The victim cannot simply be killed outright. The runes must be carved into the body while the victim is still living and the spell must be cast. That could give the police the time they need if they happen upon a killing in progress.''

''But what about the shapechanger?'' Raven asked. ''The acolyte they've turned into a werewolf? How can we brief the police about that without admitting that thaumaturgy is involved, which would immediately take it out of their jurisdiction?''

''Yes, I can see where that would be a problem,'' Merlin said, frowning.

''Why not tell them that evidence suggests the murders might be the work of some kind of satanic cult?'' said Wyrdrune. ''That would explain the runes, without admitting the possibility of necromancy, and it would also explain why there could be more than one killer. And since we already know that one of the victims had her throat torn out and there were claw marks on her body, the police could be told that at least one of the killers apparently has a trained attack dog that should be shot on sight.''

''Yes, that could work,'' Piccard said, nodding, ''but what do we tell them when the so-called attack dog reverts to mortal form after it's been killed?''

''Well, we can cross that bridge when we get to it,'' said Wyrdrune. ''You could always 'belatedly realize' that thaumaturgy was involved after all, that one of the members of the cult was an advanced-level adept, perhaps their leader, but since he would be dead at that point, there would be no reason for the I.T.C. to officially step in to round up his non-adept followers. Would it be that difficult to arrange some sort of cover-up?''

''No, probably not,'' Piccard replied. He nodded. ''It sounds workable. What do you think?'' he asked his partner.

Raven nodded. ''I think it's an excellent suggestion,'' she said. ''We could say that we're investigating a satanic cult that does not actually use thaumaturgy, but only employs thaumaturgic trappings in its killings. But to be certain, we'd have to remain on the scene to assist in the investigation. And in the meantime, increased police presence on the streets at night would make it more difficult for the killers to claim their victims. It could force the Dark Ones out into the open. It's a good plan. We certainly don't have any better alternatives at the moment.''

''Just remember that the Dark Ones need a few moments

to work undisturbed in order to absorb the life energies of their victims," Wyrdrune said. "That's why the killings usually take place at night, in secluded places and dark corners. Tell the police to watch the alleys. They like dark places."

"Dark places," Modred said thoughtfully. "Like the Paris sewers."

The others all looked at him intently.

"The sewers," Piccard said. "Of course! They run throughout the entire city. A perfect way for the killers to move about unobserved."

"Pascal fled down into the sewers after Jacqueline shot him," Modred said. "At first, I thought he merely took the first convenient avenue of escape, but the more I think about it, the more it seems as if he was heading for a specific destination. When we finally came upon him, he was calling the name 'Leila' with his dying breath. Apparently, at least one of the Dark Ones here in Paris is a female. And Pascal wasn't merely trying to escape. He wasn't simply running away from us. He was running *to* her."

"You think the Dark Ones are hiding in the sewer system?" Merlin said, frowning. "It hardly seems like a very hospitable place to seek shelter."

"He's right," said Raven. "They're basically old, decrepit tunnels with sewage running through them. They would certainly afford the killers a way of moving about the city unobserved, coming up through access shafts, but I can't imagine how anyone would actually stay down there for any length of time. Some derelicts, perhaps, who don't mind sleeping on the cold and damp stone walkways, but why would the Dark Ones want to establish a headquarters down there?"

"You don't think it's possible?" said Modred.

Raven shrugged. "Anything is possible, but of all the places in the city they could pick to hide in, why would they want to choose the sewers?"

"They've been underground for centuries," said Modred. "Wyrdrune's right. They have an affinity for dark places. In Los Angeles, one of the acolytes sought shelter in a hidden chamber excavated beneath a mission and the Dark Ones themselves hid in the service tunnels beneath an amusement park. In London, one of them had established his headquarters in the passageways of an ancient dungeon beneath a castle, inhabiting chambers connected by a maze of underground passageways—''

"A maze of underground passageways," Piccard said, interrupting him suddenly. *"The Catacombs!"*

"The Catacombs?" said Wyrdrune.

"A vast network of underground corridors and chambers beneath the city, dating back centuries," Piccard said. "They grew out of old, abandoned Roman quarries and were used during the Revolution as a storage place for those slain in the Reign of Terror and for bones disinterred from overcrowded cemeteries. Until recently, a small, mapped-out section of the Catacombs near the Place Denfert-Rochereau was used as a tourist attraction. They were closed when the city's engineers declared them unsafe and the entrance to them was sealed, but the corridors still exist beneath large sections of the city and its outskirts, most of them completely unexplored. No one has set foot in them for centuries."

Modred leaned forward, alertly. "Is it possible that access to them could be gained through the sewer system?" he asked Piccard.

"I shouldn't think so," Piccard replied. "The sewers only date back to the nineteenth century and, to my knowledge, they were never connected with the Catacombs. If the excavation for the sewer system ever revealed any of the passageways, they were long since eliminated by the construction of the sewer tunnels."

"Then it *is* possible the sewers could have been constructed in places where a portion of the Catacombs had been," said Modred. "Which would mean that some of the old corridors could run behind the sewer walls."

"Yes, I suppose it's possible," said Piccard.

"Is there any plan of the corridors underneath the city?" Wyrdrune asked.

Piccard shook his head. "There is a plan of the city's sewer system, but no plan of the Catacombs is known to exist. Quite probably, no such plan ever existed. I don't even know of any existing entrance to the Catacombs, since the one used for conducting guided tours was sealed years ago, and we could not get in through there in any case. There was extensive excavation and new construction in that district. I have no idea how we could even get down there, much less explore the hidden corridors."

"Through the sewers," Modred said. "There has to be a way to get into the Catacombs by way of one of the sewer tunnels. Pascal was trying to get back to his dark mistress. And that giant rat we encountered was meant not so much to kill us as to delay us, so that we could not follow Pascal to the access point from the sewers to the Catacombs!"

"But we don't know for certain that they're down there," Raven said.

"They're down there," Modred insisted. "It would be the perfect place for them. A hiding place sealed off from the city above it, with access to a system of tunnels through which they could gain access to any part of Paris. It fits. They could hide down there for years and never be discovered."

"But even if we could find the point where access to the Catacombs could be gained from the sewers, how could we ever hope to explore the Catacombs themselves?" Piccard asked. "It could take years."

"For you, perhaps," said Modred, "but not for us. Once we were down there, the runestones would show us the way. They would lead us to the Dark Ones."

"But what if you're wrong?" asked Raven. "What if they're not down there? You could get lost inside those corridors and never find your way out again."

"The runestones would lead us out," said Modred.

"Only what if the tunnels should collapse while you're down there?" asked Piccard. "The recent construction above the corridors could well have weakened them. No one has been in the Catacombs for years. For centuries. Your passage through them could well be enough to trigger off a cave-in. You would be buried alive."

"It's a chance we'll simply have to take," said Modred. "We're going to have to go back down into the sewers and find the place Pascal was heading for. Somewhere down there, there has to be an entrance to the Catacombs and we must find it."

Wyrdrune sighed. "I knew he was going to say that. I just got finished washing all that slime off me and now we're going back down there again. Broom gets to go out and enjoy the Paris nightlife while I get to tour the sewers. Some fun this trip is turning out to be."

"You want us to go with you?" asked Piccard.

"No," said Modred. "There's no reason for you to take that risk. You'd be of more value coordinating the police task force with Renaud. The acolytes must be stopped before the Dark Ones can gain enough power to attempt a spell that would bring about mass murder. Get as many people on the streets as you can. Get a map of the city's sewer system, mark off all the access shafts and have patrols keeping an eye on them. Above all, you must stress to the members of the task force the possibility that at least one of the killers *could* be an adept and they must exercise extreme caution. Have them keep in touch with each other and with the task force headquarters at regular intervals. At the first report of anything suspicious, you must teleport to that location at once. And be prepared for anything."

"But what about you three?" asked Raven. "You'll be down there completely on your own. There's no way that we'll be able to keep in touch with you. Isn't there anything else that we can do to help?"

"Yeah," said Wyrdrune sourly. "You think you could come up with a few wet suits?"

Chapter
NINE

Colette awoke late in the day to a brand-new world, full of possibilities she had never dreamed of in her wildest imagination. She reached across the bed and touched the spot beside her where the sheets were slightly damp and rumpled and there was an indentation in the pillow, as if to reassure herself that it wasn't just a dream. Then she sat up in bed and saw Michel, curled up on the floor with his head on his forepaws. He raised his head and those feral, yellow eyes looked at her with a knowing gaze. He belonged to her now. And she belonged to him. They were kindred spirits. Predators. And together, they both belonged to Leila.

It had been the most incredible night of Colette's life. As usual, it had started off with her being in control. They arrived at her apartment and she helped Leila off with her cloak, then poured them both some wine from a freshly opened bottle of Reisling. They sat together on the couch, making small talk, all the while having a conversation with their eyes and bodies that had nothing to do with what was being said out loud. Colette had done most of the talking. Leila seemed fascinated when she found out what Colette did for a living and she wanted to know what it was like, how it felt to dance naked on a stage in front of men, what she did and how she orchestrated their reactions. She seemed to understand it all instinctively, the sense of power that it gave her, the assurance of being in control, and she wanted to hear all of the details. She asked her which moves the customers found sexiest and Colette wound up putting on some music, changing into one of her revealing dancing outfits and giving her a demonstration, slowly stripping down by stages in time to the music, all the while wondering what Leila looked like with her clothes off. The eye contact between them was electric.

Leila watched her with a smile as she demonstrated the moves she used up on the stage, clapping her hands and laughing with delight at her most blatant and effective poses, giggling throatily when Colette stood with her back to her, as she did with the male patrons at the club, and then bent over to look at her between her legs, slowly running her fingers up her calves and the inside of her thighs. She flirted with Leila the way she did with the patrons in the club, giving her smoldering "come hither" looks and gently running her fingers through her hair, with her erect nipples mere inches from her face. And when Colette took Leila's hand and guided it to the the cleft between her breasts, Leila had not resisted, as Colette had known she wouldn't, and when she led her to the bedroom, Leila had followed silently, allowing her to take control, standing still, her eyes half shut while Colette slowly undressed her and eased her down onto the bed.

She had marveled at Leila's golden, copper-hued skin, at her silky, bright red hair, at the firm tautness of her lissome body, more beautiful even than her own, and at some point while they were making love, she suddenly became aware of the wolf standing at the foot of the bed, its forepaws up on the footboard, watching them intently with its unblinking yellow eyes.

Then, as Colette gasped with disbelief, the wolf sprang up onto the bed and suddenly it was a wolf no longer, but a beautiful, slim and muscular young boy with an expression just as feral as the beast's had been. And Colette, too stunned to react, watched as the two of them coupled with a shocking, fierce brutality, as if they were attacking one another, and then they turned to her and she discovered what it was like to be completely out of control. It was at the same time both terrifying and exciting. Throughout it all, Michel had not said a single word and when it was over, he climbed down out of the bed, curled up on the floor and Colette watched the transformation with a mixture of horror and fascination as he once more became a wolf and went to sleep. And she had felt Leila's lips softly brush her ear and heard her whisper, "He's yours, now. And you are *mine*."

And then Leila had gently turned Colette's face toward hers and kissed her deeply, her hand cupping the back of Colette's head, pressing her close, and Colette suddenly felt herself receding, as if she were falling, spinning crazily down into some bottomless abyss. She felt herself filled with Leila's presence, like cold fire seeping through her bones, forming burning ice crystals deep inside her mind.

Vivid images came flooding into her, filling her with sights, sounds and sensations unlike anything she'd ever experienced before. The tableau of Leila's life enveloped her, becoming part of her experience as if she had lived it all herself.

She stood dressed in flowing robes atop a Mayan pyramid, a heavy, feathered golden crown upon her head, gold rings with precious stones upon her fingers, enchanted amulets around her neck, a dark, obsidian dagger with a golden hilt clutched in her hand as she gazed down at the chanting multitudes below. And then her gaze shifted to the altar she stood over, with the sacrificial victim bound to heavy rings set deep into the stone, a sheen of sweat gleaming brightly on his body, muscles tense and knotted, eyes staring up at her in fear as she slowly brought the knife down and incised the sacred symbols deep into his flesh, intoning the ancient life-absorbing spell that would fill her with his power, then raising the obsidian dagger high in both hands and plunging it down into his heaving chest. . . .

Centuries of death and bloodletting passed before her, visions of incredible carnage and incalculable power. Spells of astral flight and transformation unfolded in her mind as she hurled her spirit out across vast distances and stalked the jungle in the form of a sleek jaguar, hunting and running down her prey, feeling the warm, sweet taste of blood coursing down her throat. She fell and fell, down through the eons, buffeted by the rushing winds of time, and as she cried out and felt her demon lover slip away from her, she felt rather than heard the whispered promise that all this would now be hers, an eternity of unimagined power, a limitless vista of fulfillment, hers for the taking, hers to share with Leila and to hold forever in the darkness of her soul. And she awoke alone to the harsh glare of daylight streaming through her bedroom window, the enticing smell of Leila on the rumpled sheets and the wolf staring up at her with its knowing, yellow eyes.

"Michel," she said, "come here."

The wolf stood up on human legs and walked over to the bed, his lean and youthful body pale in the morning light, his boyish skin soft and almost hairless, his teeth flashing in a predatory grin, his eyes still with that knowing look. A look that knew no weakness. A look that recognized a fellow beast in human form.

She took his hand and pulled him down onto the bed.

"I still say the risk is now too great." The voice was deep and mellifluent. It spoke softly, but still reverberated slightly in the subterranean stone chamber. "The avatars are here and we have already lost one of our acolytes. What is the point in taking unnecessary chances? The time has come for us to move on."

"I will decide when the times comes for us to leave," said Leila. "*If* that time should come."

"You have grown far too reckless, Leila."

"And you have grown far too cautious, Azreal. I have already found a replacement for Pascal, one who will not suffer from the pangs of conscience he was given to. One who will be even more bloodthirsty than Michel. Colette will serve us well and bring us all the power we require to move on to the next stage of our plan."

"Perhaps," said the other necromancer, holding up his goblet for one of the young runaway girls to fill. "But perhaps Azreal is right. We risk much by staying here."

"And we stand to lose even more by leaving, Balen," Leila replied. She stood and gestured at their surroundings. The underground chamber of the Catacombs had been transformed with opulent furnishings and Persian carpets, with couches and cushions on the floor and ornately carved tables from which their ensorcelled street urchins served them. Burning braziers provided the illumination and filled the chamber with the scent of incense that masked the musty smell.

"Is this all you really want?" she said. "To hide down here among the bones, quaking in a hole like a pair of frightened rabbits, with your empty-eyed consorts to wait on you hand and foot and provide you with meaningless diversion?"

"And what of your diversions?" Azreal asked her. "After so many years of being imprisoned formless, nothing but spirits without substance, is it so wrong to indulge in the pleasures of the flesh? Pleasures for which you, I might add, seem to have an equal appetite."

"I do not ask that you practice self-denial," Leila said. "But everything I do is with an end in mind. Have we spent so many centuries entombed beneath the earth that it has become our natural habitat? That we are afraid to walk out in the sun, to claim the power that is ours by right of our superiority to these pathetic beings? Do you not hunger for something more than *this*?" She glanced around the chamber. "It galls me that we must live like this when we could have a palace for our own, with multitudes to serve us instead of these few wretched children."

"We must bide our time, Leila," Balen said. "We must wait until we have grown strong enough to insure that the runestones cannot defeat us."

"How *long* must we wait?" asked Leila. "You say wait. Azreal says move on. I say the time for us to act is *now*. The opportunity is here. The power of the runestones is within our grasp, if we are only bold enough to take it! And once the misbegotten spawn of Gorlois is slain and we have absorbed their energy, there will be nothing left to stop us! There are three of them and three of us! One triangle against another, the White against the Dark! And the initiative is ours to take!"

"Exactly," Balen said. "And the time is ours to choose, as well. We must take care to choose it wisely."

"And if we leave now," added Azreal, "it could be months or even years before they could find us once again. Our powers would grow even stronger, so that when we met them for the final conflict—"

"But what if we were *not* the ones to meet them for the final conflict?" Leila asked. "What if some of the others found the courage that you lack and seized their power for themselves? No, I will not be cheated of it! I will not run when the power of the runestones could be ours!"

"It is a power that could mean our death," said Balen. "Some of the others have already fallen to them. I do not intend to join their number. Not after so many years of waiting for this chance."

"And yet if we don't take it, it is a chance that might not come again," said Leila. "You forget that I alone among us have already faced them and I survived to tell the tale. The avatars are not as fearsome as you think. They are not true immortals, but merely humans, descended from a bastard stock."

"Humans to whom the spirits of the Council of the White have become bonded," Balen said. "And that makes them much more than 'merely' human."

"Yet they can be destroyed," said Leila.

"As *we* can be destroyed," said Azreal. "I say that we should leave and make a new start elsewhere. Let the others try their luck against the runetones while we hoard and increase our power until we can meet them on more even terms."

"We *are* on even terms," said Leila. "We are on more than even terms already! We can use our acolytes to serve us while their white magic prevents them from using others as we do. They care about the foolish humans, while their lives mean nothing to us. That can be used against them."

"When the time is right," said Balen.

"I say it is right now," Leila replied.

"And I say it is not," said Azreal.

She gave him a cold and steady stare. "Would you try your power against mine, Azreal?" she said softly. "Perhaps the both of you would care to test your strength against me. If more power is what you want, mine would more than double yours. If you have the strength to take it."

Azreal stared at her defiantly for a moment, then finally turned and looked away.

"Enough, Leila," Balen said. "This is not the way. If we fall to fighting amongst ourselves, we only serve the interests of our enemies. You are the strongest of the three of us. Neither Azreal nor I dispute that. But you are not yet strong enough to take on the runestones by yourself. The three of us together stand a far better chance. Azreal and I only want to be certain that we have a good chance of succeeding. We have waited for so long, what harm would it do to wait a little while longer?"

"The longer we remain here, and the longer we delay, the more we play into their hands," said Leila. "How long do you think it will take for them to realize where we are? And once they have deduced that, how long do you think it will take for them to find us? We have waited long enough. The time for us to strike is now, while the advantage is still ours."

"And if we fail?" said Balen.

"I have already escaped from them once, when they pursued Pascal," said Leila. "If need be, I can escape from them again. But I will not run without a fight, not when we have so much to gain."

"Then you have already decided to move on to the final stage," said Azreal. "What of our plan to gain an acolyte among the agents of the Bureau or the I.T.C.?"

"Pascal would have given us that opportunity," she replied, "but Pascal is dead and now that we know the avatars are here, we can afford to waste no time on that. If an opportunity arises, we will take it, but we must move quickly if we are to move at all."

"Then we had best discuss our plans," said Balen. "We must make certain that there is no room for error."

"There will be none," Leila said. "Our acolytes will set the plan in motion and we will channel the power that we gain through them into a spell that will release all the life energy we need. Remember that in order to draw on the full power of the Living Triangle, the avatars must be together to effect the spell. Separately, they can be much more easily defeated."

"Then they would be fools to attempt taking us on separately," said Azreal.

Leila smiled. "True, but they will have no choice," she said. "Remember that they care about the humans and they trust them. And it is the humans who will bring about their downfall."

Max Siegal's studio was crowded with well-wishers who had come to help him celebrate his release from jail. The crowd was liberally sprinkled with the inevitable party crashers, but Max didn't really mind. He was just glad to be out of jail. In spite of the reassurances of his attorneys, he had been convinced the case against him looked so bad that he would be brought to trial and found guilty. When Renaud came to tell him that all the charges had been dropped and he was being released, he had scarcely been able to believe it.

During the time that he had been in jail, the murderer of the Rue Morgue had struck again, leaving no doubt that it was the work of the same man who had killed Joelle Muset and Gabrielle Longet. Renaud had apologized to him on behalf of the police department, asking him to try and understand how they could have drawn the conclusions that they did, given the circumstantial evidence. The detective had gone to great pains to convey the sincerity of his apology. Max had refrained from taking out his anger and frustration on the police inspector, expressing his outrage by displaying the famous Siegal temper. Instead, he simply shook hands with Renaud and told him there were no hard feelings.

The story was carried in all the papers and on TV, as well. All his friends had come to help him celebrate and they saw a new Max Siegal, a man who walked around with a glass of mineral water in his hand instead of brandy or a whiskey, a man who seemed much more relaxed. He had announced that he would never paint a nude again, but would devote his talents to impressionism, following in the steps of the old masters he admired.

"But Max," Francois Benet said, "what of your public? You have tried exploring new directions before with no success. The galleries always want the nudes. They are what you are famous for."

"At the moment, I am famous for having been a suspect in a sensational series of murders," Max replied to his old mentor. "And even though the charges have been dropped, there will always be that taint of suspicion, at least until the real killer has been found. That will cause all the galleries to raise their prices. Never fear, Francois. Right now, they will buy anything I paint."

"Hello, Max," said Jacqueline with a smile.

"Jacqueline!" said Max. "You came!" He threw his arms around her in a hug. "Francois," said Max, "allow me to introduce my very dearest friend, the one who stood by me throughout this entire ordeal and was instrumental in my release, Mademoiselle Jacqueline Monet."

"Charmed, mademoiselle," Francois said, bending over her hand and brushing it slightly with his lips. "I have heard much about you, but perhaps we can speak later. Right now, I'm sure that you and Max have a great deal to discuss."

He graciously excused himself.

"I thought you weren't going to come," said Max, holding her hands and gazing at her affectionately.

She smiled. "How could I not come?" she said. "I would have come to see you sooner, but I have been informally assisting the police in investigating this case and I simply couldn't get away."

"I know," said Max. "Renaud told me. He said that you were trying to convince him of my innocence right from the beginning."

"If he had only listened sooner—"

Max put his fingers up to her lips. "Let's not talk about that now," he said. "Renaud is a good man. He was only trying to do his job and the circumstantial evidence made things look very bad for me, indeed. It was my own fault. I never should have gone back to see Suzanne Muset. It was a stupid thing to do."

"Yes, but it was just like you to try and square things with her," said Jacqueline.

"And now I have to square them with you," said Max. "How can I ever repay you for all you've done?"

"Friends don't have to repay one another, Max," she said.

"Well, at least we can finally have a chance to spend some time together," Max said.

Jacqueline sighed. "I'm sorry, Max. I'm afraid I can't stay."

"What do you mean? Why can't you stay?"

"I only stopped in to see how you were doing. When this is over, then maybe we can spend some time together, but—"

"When this is over? I don't understand. The charges against me have been dropped. I thought that it was all . . . wait a minute. It's this murder case, isn't it? Renaud said something about you helping the police in their investigation. You mean to tell me that you're still involved?"

"Yes, Max, that's what it is. And we're getting close to the real killer. In fact, I really should be leaving."

"But why?" asked Max. "Haven't you already done enough? Jacqueline, this could be very dangerous. Whoever the killer is, he's a sadistic, brutal psycopath. Why should you risk getting involved? Let the police handle it."

She touched his cheek. "Max, if I'd done that from the start, you'd still be in jail."

He sighed. "I suppose you're right. But I can't help being worried."

"I can take care of myself, Max. Relax. I won't be in any danger. Renaud would never allow it. I'm simply assisting them with contacts and information, that's all. But you're right about the killer. And he must be stopped before he can claim anymore innocent victims. You understand that, don't you?''

Max nodded. "Yes, I understand. But it's been so long since I've had a chance to see you. We haven't even had a chance to talk."

"There will be time for that," she said. "But right now, I really have to leave. Go on. Your friends are waiting for you."

She leaned forward and gave him a soft kiss on the lips.

"Let me go with you," he said. "Maybe I can help."

"No, Max," she said. "This has to do with a part of my life that you really know nothing about. And believe me, you'd be better off not knowing. We have always understood that about each other, haven't we? You have your own life and I have mine. The time we spend together is for us, but the time we spend away from one another is a separate thing and there are a lot of reasons why it should remain that way."

"You've never told me what those reasons are," he said.

"You've never insisted on hearing them before."

"Well, I'm insisting now."

"And I can't tell you."

"Can't? Or won't?"

"Both," she said. "We have always respected one another's privacy before, Max. Don't start becoming possessive now. It would never work. When this is over, we can talk and maybe I'll think about telling you my reasons, but not now. In the meantime, you have a party in your honor to attend. And I have work to do."

She kissed him again and left.

He stared after her for a long moment, torn between respecting her wishes and wanting to follow her, to insist that she come back and drop this crazy idea of assisting the police in their investigation. Suddenly, he had the inexplicable feeling that if he didn't go after her and bring her back, he might not be seeing her again.

"Max, darling!" A woman came up to him and put her arms around him, giving him a kiss. She started to say something to him, but he quickly disengaged himself and hurried toward the door. He bolted through it and started running down the stairs, but on the way down, he encountered Stefan Rienzi coming up.

Rienzi grabbed him as he tried to get by and spun him around on the landing, throwing him up against the wall. His eyes were wild.

"Where *is* she?" he shouted, holding Max by his shirtfront. "What have you done with her?"

At first, Max didn't recognize him. "What? Let me go! Who—"

"Murderer! What have you done with Suzanne?"

Recognition dawned. "Rienzi!"

Rienzi slammed him back against the wall. *"You bastard! What have you done with her?"*

"I don't know what you're talking about," said Max. "Let me go, I have to—"

Rienzi drove his fist hard into Max's stomach and Max doubled over, the wind knocked out of him. Rienzi hit him again, twice more, then shoved him down onto the floor of the landing. Max fell, fighting for breath. Rienzi reached into his jacket pocket, took out a small pistol and aimed it at Max.

"You and your rich friends!" he said, his voice trembling with emotion. "You think you can do anything you please! You even think you're above the law!"

"Rienzi, don't. . . ." Max gasped.

"Go on! *Beg! Beg* for your life like your victims must have begged for theirs! You lousy son of a bitch! You killed her, didn't you? The moment they let you out of jail, you went back to finish what you started!"

"Rienzi, please, listen to me. . . . I didn't—"

"You're not going to get away with it this time!" shouted Rienzi. "I don't care how much money you and your rich friends have! It isn't going to save you! I don't care what happens to me, I—"

Upstairs, on the landing above them, a woman screamed. "He's got a gun!"

Someone behind her shouted, "Help! Call the police!"

Rienzi brought his hand up and left off a wild shot at the

people on the floor above them, who had heard the commotion and come out to see what was going on. There was shouting and screaming and a rush to get back out of the way. Rienzi fired again.

"Get back!" he shouted. "Get back, all of you!"

Max struck out with his feet and knocked Rienzi down. As Rienzi fell, Max threw himself on top of him. They struggled for the gun. It went off once again, the shot striking the wall, and then the gun fell from Rienzi's grasp as he fought against the larger, heavier man, his desperation lending him strength. He rolled over on top of Max and got his hands around his throat. He started squeezing. There was the sound of footsteps coming quickly down the stairs, and then Francois and several other men were pulling Rienzi off him. Two of them held the struggling young writer while Francois punched him in the stomach, once, twice, three times. Rienzi sagged down and then Max found his voice and cried out, "Don't! Stop it! Leave him alone!"

Someone helped him to his feet and held him up, supporting him as he coughed and drew deep, rasping breaths, holding his throat where Rienzi had tried to choke him.

"Max!" said Francois. "Are you all right? What happened? Who *is* this man?"

"Somebody call the police!"

"They've already been called. They're on their way."

"Max. . . ."

"I'm all right," said Max, rubbing his throat. Rienzi was on the floor, holding his stomach as several of the men stood over him.

"Has anybody seen the gun?" asked Francois.

"It's right here," said one of Max's young artist friends, handing him the weapon. "He dropped it."

"You shouldn't have touched it," someone else said. "The fingerprints—"

"To hell with the fingerprints," said someone else. "We all saw what he did! He tried to kill Max!"

"Watch him! Don't let him get up!"

"Where the hell are the police?"

Max made his way over to where Rienzi sat slumped against the wall. The man was crying.

"Rienzi," Max said, crouching down beside him. "Rienzi, listen to me. . . ."

He tried to take the writer's arm, but Rienzi shook him off. "Don't touch me! Murderer! I'll kill you for what you've done! I swear, I'll kill you!"

"You all heard that!" someone said. "You're all witnesses! You all heard what he said!"

"Be quiet!" said Max. "Rienzi, please, listen to me. Please. I didn't kill Joelle. And I didn't kill Gabrielle, either. I swear to God, I haven't killed anyone. I was in jail when the last murder occurred. I *couldn't* have done it. That's why the police released me."

"You paid them off!" Rienzi said. "You and your rich friends and your high-priced lawyers—"

"Nobody was paid off, Stefan," Max said, finally remembering the man's first name. "Please, let me explain. The night Joelle was killed, I was right here, in my studio, drunk. She was here, that's true. I was going to paint her, but she expected something else. She started coming on to me. I've had affairs with some of my models, I admit it, but I don't have sex with underage girls. I rejected her advances and we argued. Actually, we didn't even argue, she mainly shouted at me and I just sat there, waiting 'til she ran out of steam. And then she left and I got angry and smashed the painting over the easel and proceeded to get drunk. And the next morning, the police came to arrest me and that was the first I heard of Joelle's murder."

"You expect me to believe that?" said Rienzi bitterly.

"It's the truth," said Max. "So help me God."

"What about what happened with Suzanne? I was there! I *saw* you with the knife!"

"That was a stupid mistake," said Max. "After I was released on bail, I went back there because I wanted to explain what happened to Suzanne, but the moment she saw me, she became hysterical. She grabbed a knife from the kitchen. It was one of your own knives. She lunged at me and I managed to get the knife away from her and that's when you came in. Ask her if you don't believe me."

"I *can't* ask her!" said Rienzi. "She's gone! You came back and *took* her!"

"No," said Max. "No, I didn't. I swear it. When did you discover she was missing?"

"Sometime this evening," Rienzi said. "I was moving some of our things into our new apartment and when I came back, she was gone and I found *this* tacked to the door."

He took a slip of folded paper from his pocket. Several thaumaturgic runes were drawn upon it in what appeared to be blood. They were the same runes that had been carved into the bodies of the murder victims.

"You shouldn't have touched it," said Francois. "You should have left it where it was for the police to examine."

"What good would the police do? There's the killer!" He pointed at Max. "And they've released him twice!"

"I've been right here since this afternoon," said Max.

"You're lying!"

"He's not lying," said Francois. "Some of us were here with him, getting ready for the party. We had lunch together and Max has been here since shortly after noon."

"They're your friends," said Rienzi, though he seemed to be weakening in his conviction. "They're covering for you."

"Do you really think we'd all protect a murderer?" said Francois. "Do you really believe that the police would have released him and dropped all charges if they were not completely convinced of his innocence?"

"I . . . I don't know what to think," Rienzi said, looking confused.

At that moment, the police arrived. Two uniformed officers came up the stairs and stopped when they saw the group gathered on the landing.

"What's going on here?" one of them demanded.

"Nothing, Officer," said Max. "We were having a party and there's been a slight altercation, nothing serious."

"We've had a report of shooting at this address," said the other policeman.

"I'm afraid there's been a mistake," said Max. "There's been no shooting. Just a small argument, that's all."

Francois carefully positioned himself to cover the bullet hole in the wall.

"You know how it is," Max continued apologetically. "A few drinks, tempers flare, a couple of blows are exchanged. Really, that's all it was. It seems one of my guests became alarmed and called the police. Evidently, there was some exaggeration. I'm really very sorry about it."

The policemen glanced around at them with disgust. "We have better things to do than to waste our time with this sort of thing," one of them said. "We ought to cite you for creating a disturbance."

"Yes, you're absolutely right," said Max contritely. "It was all entirely my fault."

"Well, let's try to keep things under control, shall we?" said Officer Michaud. "We have better things to do than respond to false alarms."

"Of course," said Max. "Please accept my apologies. And thank you for being so understanding."

"Merely doing our job, monsieur," Michaud said, touching the visor of his cap. "Let's move it back inside and try to keep some order, shall we?"

"Certainly, Officer," said Max. "And thank you once again."

Michaud nodded and as they left, they all went back inside.

"We should have told them about that young woman's disappearance," said Francois.

"I didn't want to risk them finding out about the gun," Max said. "There was no reason for this man to be arrested. He was distraught and clearly not responsible."

Rienzi looked at Max with anguish.

"You stood up for me," he said. "And I was going to kill you."

"Forget it," Max said. "Come on, have a drink. It will help steady your nerves. We'll call Renaud and tell him what's happened, then you and I will go back to the Rue Morgue and search through the entire neighborhood."

"I'm coming with you," said Francois.

"Me, too," said one of the other artists.

"Count me in," said another.

Rienzi glanced around at them all. "I . . . I don't know what to say," he said, his voice breaking. "I almost made a terrible, terrible mistake."

"We all make mistakes," said Max, clapping the man on the shoulder. "I've made more than my share. We'll call Inspector Renaud and then we'll go look for Suzanne."

"We won't find her alive," Rienzi said in a hollow voice. "She's lying dead somewhere, I know it."

"We don't know that yet," said Max.

He stared at the piece of paper with the runes on it, being careful to handle it only by its edges, though he knew his fingerprints were already on it. That would probably mean trouble.

"Why would the killer have left this behind?" he asked. "Joelle was killed in her apartment. The same thing with Gabrielle. Why would he have taken Suzanne away when he could easily have killed her then and there?"

"Who knows what a maniac might do?" Francois said.

Max frowned. "First Joelle, then Gabrielle, and now Suzanne. All in the Rue Morgue, all in the same building. *Why?*"

"You think perhaps the killer is someone who also lives there?" said Francois.

"No," said Rienzi, shaking his head. "That's not possible. The only other people who live there are two elderly women and the proprietor of the shop on the first floor. He's almost seventy years old and has to walk with aid of a cane."

"Perhaps it's someone in the neighborhood," Francois said. "We can ask around, surely one of the neighbors must have seen or heard something. They might not tell the police because they're afraid to get involved."

"I think we should go over there and have a look around," said one of the journalists, smelling a story.

"We should call the police first," said someone else.

"Charles, you call them," Max said. "Ask for Inspector Renaud. Tell him what's happened. I'm going over there."

"I don't think that would be wise, Max," Charles replied. "You've already had more than your share of trouble. Stay out of it. Leave this to the police."

"I can't, Charles," Max said, shaking his head. "I have a personal stake in this. Whoever this man is, I've spent time in jail because of him and I was almost shot. I've had enough. I can't simply stay here and do nothing."

"Don't be a fool, Max. Stay out of it. You're making a mistake."

"No, Charles," Max said grimly. He took out his handkerchief, wrapped the piece of paper in it and handed it to Charles. "The killer's the one who's made the mistake. He's out there somewhere and I'm going to find him if I have to search every single street and alleyway in Paris."

Chapter TEN

Renaud hung up the phone and swore softly.

"What is it?" asked Piccard.

"Max Siegal again," he said in a weary voice. "The damn fool seems determined to get himself in trouble. That was Charles Martine, a prominent businessman and art collector who also happens to be a personal friend of the commissioner. He was calling from a party at Max Siegal's studio. Suzanne Muset, the first victim's older sister, has apparently been kidnapped from her apartment in the Rue Morgue. A piece of paper was left on the apartment door, covered with those same thaumaturgic runes written in blood. Her boyfriend, Stefan Rienzi, evidently believed that Siegal was responsible and went to his studio to confront him. It seems there was

an altercation, but Siegal and his friends convinced him that
he had nothing to do with it, only now they've gone back to
the apartment to investigate and search the neighborhood for
any sign of the missing girl. And Martine says they have a
gun. He said they were in a surly mood and, worse yet, some
journalists were with them. I'd better send some people over
there before they get themselves in trouble.''

"Didn't Jacqueline go over there?" asked Raven.

"Yes, but she hasn't returned," Renaud said. "I hope she
had sense enough not to go with them." He sighed. "That's
all we need now, a bunch of angry vigilantes roaming the
streets, accompanied by reporters, no less. We'd better nip
this in the bud right now, before somebody gets hurt. My
men out there are edgy. All we need is for some innocent
bystander to get shot and this whole thing will blow up in
our faces.''

"I think I'll commandeer a unit and get over there," Piccard said, getting up and putting down his container of coffee.
"What's the address?"

Renaud gave it to him. "I'll have another unit meet you
there," he said. "I'd appreciate if you could avoid placing
any of them under arrest, but I want those people off the
streets.''

"I'll take care of it," Piccard said, leaving.

"Jacqueline struck me as having better sense than to get
involved in something like that," Raven said.

"Frankly, I wouldn't put it past her," said Renaud. "She
never has been one of our more law-abiding citizens," he
added with a grimace. "This whole thing has me extremely
nervous. I haven't slept in two days and I'm so keyed up,
I'm not even tired.''

He looked around at the command post they had set up for
the task force. The room was a bustle of activity as com-
munication clerks kept in constant touch with the officers of
the task force on the street.

"Anytime you have civilians involved in something like
this," he said, "the odds of something going wrong are

dramatically increased. I wish there could have been some way to avoid it.''

"I know how you must feel," said Raven, sipping her coffee. She, too, had gone without sleep for two days. "Unfortunately, there's really nothing we can do about it. I'm still trying to get used to the idea that we're faced with an inhuman enemy, immortal necromancers who are more powerful than any adept alive. And the worst thing about it is that we don't even know how many of them are out there.''

"For me, the worst thing is the waiting," said Renaud. He drummed his fingers on the desk, then glanced at his watch. "They should be going down into the sewers about now. Do you have to do anything to get ready?''

Raven shook her head. "All I need to do is sit here and be receptive," she said. "I don't need to go into a trance or anything like that. It doesn't work that way. Merlin will simply contact me when he's ready.''

"Police work by telepathy," said Renaud, shaking his head. "Wouldn't it have been simpler for him to just carry a radio set?''

Raven shook her head. "I doubt we'd be able to get a clear signal from down there," she said. "Besides, under the circumstances, the last thing we'd need is anyone monitoring our conversation. It's far safer this way. Besides, it isn't actually telepathy, but a form of astral projection.''

"What's the difference?" Renaud asked.

"The principle is essentially the same," said Raven, "but it won't be mind-to-mind contact so much as spirit-to-spirit.''

"Sounds very metaphysical," Renaud said.

"It is, actually. You've heard stories about people separated by great distances who suddenly had the inexplicable feeling that something traumatic had happened to a relative? A mother suddenly feels certain that something's happened to her son and then finds out the next day that he'd had an accident and was in the hospital. A daughter dreams that her father comes to say good-bye, then finds out the next day that he had died that night. That's a form of astral projection.

The theory is that it's an ability inherent in everyone, but especially so in people who possess thaumaturgic potential, or as we now know, people descended from the interbreeding of humans and Old Ones thousands of years ago. A very advanced adept has the capability to do it at will, but it requires a great deal of energy and concentration.''

"So you mean he projects his spirit out of his body in order to contact someone else?" Renaud said.

Raven nodded. "Under normal circumstances, it's a spell-assisted process. The adept picks a safe and quiet place and concentrates, projecting his astral self outward—similar to meditation, only much more powerful and focused. He doesn't actually leave his body, although in rare instances that's possible—as Merlin did when his physical self died—but a portion of his consciousness is liberated to travel out along the astral plane. Have you ever had a dream where you felt that you were floating up above your body, looking down at yourself?"

"Yes, once or twice," Renaud admitted.

"You were subconsciously performing a mild form of astral projection in your sleep," said Raven. "It's not uncommon. That's a particular experience that a lot of people have, though they don't really understand it for what it is. It is, in a sense, your spiritual level of awareness flexing its muscles."

"I can grasp the concept," said Renaud, "but what I don't understand is how Merlin can manage to do this while his physical self is actually moving about beneath the streets of Paris with the others. If the process requires such a great deal of concentration, how can he function on both the spiritual level *and* the physical level, if I'm phrasing it properly, doing two different things at the same time."

"You mean like walking and chewing gum?" said Raven with a grin. "Actually, I'm being facetious. You're quite correct. Under ordinary circumstances, that would not be possible. An extremely powerful and talented adept could split his awareness to a certain degree, such as functioning through his projected astral self while at the same time remaining aware of his or her own physical surroundings, but to split awareness on the level that we're talking about wouldn't be possible if it weren't for the fact that Merlin is, in a manner of speaking, two completely different people. He has his own discreet personality, but he is a spiritual entity sharing consciousness with another individual. Billy. And while Merlin can concentrate on projecting his spirit on the astral plane, Billy can actually take care of making their body function on the physical level. Or, to use my joking analogy, Merlin does the walking while Billy chews the gum.''

Renaud shook his head. ''It's simply mind-boggling,'' he said. ''Most of the time, I think of him as Merlin, even though when I look at him, I see a scrappy young teenager. And then Billy starts speaking and I have to completely readjust my frame of reference. It's confusing enough for me, I can't imagine what it must be like for them.''

''I know what you mean,'' said Raven. ''Merlin's personality is so strong, you tend to forget that you're talking to a boy. Though in a sense, you're not. You're really talking to both of them. Just as when you're talking to Wryrdrune, Kira and Modred, you're also communicating with the spirits of the runestones, though they don't choose to express themselves the way that Merlin does. Perhaps they can't. I honestly don't know. It's a level of thaumaturgy I've never encountered before.''

''This whole case is like nothing I've ever encountered before,'' said Renaud with a sigh. ''The very idea of the Dark Ones frightens the hell out of me.''

''It should,'' said Raven.

''What happens if the runestones can't defeat them?'' Renaud asked.

''Don't even think about it,'' Raven said.

At that moment, Jacqueline returned. ''Has there been any contact yet?'' she said.

''Not yet,'' Renaud replied, ''but your friend, Siegal, is becoming something of a headache. I should have kept him in jail, for his own good.''

"What do you mean?" Jacqueline said with a frown. "I just came from there. He was having a party. I spoke to him."

"Yes, and apparently, right after you left, Stefan Rienzi showed up," said Renaud. He briefly told her about Martine's call. "And now it seems they've gone out there to see if they can find Suzanne," he finished. "And Martine said that at least one of them had a gun."

Jacqueline sighed. "Damn," she said. "I'd better get back over there."

"No, you stay right here, where I can keep an eye on you," Renaud said. "I've already dispatched a unit and Piccard is on his way there, as well. Let's not add to the confusion."

Raven suddenly sat up. "He's making contact," she said. "They're going down."

They had decided to wait till nightfall to go down into the sewers. Renaud had arranged for wet suits to be delivered to their suite, as well as some flashlights and weapons which he had unofficially obtained for them, so that they could save their thaumaturgic energies for when they really needed them. Modred preferred to carry his own spellwarded 10-mm semiautomatic in a shoulder rig, while Wyrdrune and Billy each had police-issue 9-mm semiautomatics with lightweight polymer frames and laser sights procured from the special tactical force. They all had spare magazines in belt pouches. Kira would carry a short, pump-action police riotgun with a pistol grip and lightweight stock, with the same small laser sight mounted on the barrel rib. Piccard had offered them the use of some machine pistols, but Modred had balked at using fully automatic weapons. The last thing they needed in the close confines of the sewers was bullets ricocheting all over the place.

"Be sure to let us know where you're going to come up," Renaud had said before he left to get back to the task force headquarters. "I'll have my officers out in force, watching every alleyway and sewer entrance. We wouldn't want to have any accidents."

"Ambrosius will remain in touch with Raven," said Modred. "Just make sure your people don't indulge in any heroics. Have them radio in for backup the moment anything happens. Tell them not to take any chances. We don't want any loss of life if we can help it."

"They've been fully briefed," Renaud had said. "They're edgy, because they're not quite sure what to expect, but they'll follow instructions. They've been told that we're going up against some sort of murder cult that may or may not involve adepts, so they won't do anything foolish. I'd still feel better if you'd let me send some men down with you."

"If we run into the Dark Ones, they'd only wind up getting in the way," said Wyrdrune. "It's more important to have them out patrolling the streets, so we can try to keep the Dark Ones from claiming any more victims and increasing their strength. If they're down there, we'll find them. And with any luck, we'll be able to finish it down there, and not up in the streets where people might get hurt."

"Good luck," Renaud had said.

"Thanks," Kira said. "You, too."

They still had a few more hours before it grew dark, so they took the opportunity to catch some much-needed sleep. When they awoke, it was to discover that Sebastian Makepeace had arrived. Not wanting to disturb them, he had set his carpetbag down by the closet and had room service send up a tremendous meal to nourish his six-foot-six-inch, three-hundred-pound frame. There was enough food to feed four very hungry people and wine for at least half a dozen.

Flamboyantly dressed, as usual, in a loud, checkered coat, brown velvet trousers, gold-buckled shoes and silk shirt with a flowing Flemish neckcloth, his long white hair topped by a black beret set at a jaunty angle, he was sitting at the table, playing cards with four of the hotel's animated vacuum cleaners.

"Sebastian! Good. You made it just in time," Modred said.

"Ah, the sleepers awake!" Makepeace boomed, a large Jamaican cigar clamped between his teeth. The vacuum cleaners made whirring noises as they held their cards. "We're playing for attachments," Makepeace explained. "A modified form of strip poker, I suppose. You might say I'm taking the cleaners to the cleaners, though what I'm going to do with an assortment of brushes and carpet beaters is beyond me. I suppose I might be able to ransom them back to the hotel cleaning staff." He glanced around at the machines. "Or are *you* the hotel cleaning staff?"

"Same old Makepeace," said Wyrdrune wryly. "World's biggest and weirdest fairy."

"And I'm pleased as punch to see you, too, Melvin," Makepeace said. He took the cigar out of his mouth and sniffed the air. "Do I detect a peculiar odor?" he said.

"Must be that rope you're smoking," Wyrdrune said sourly.

"No, it's a decidedly biological odor," Makepeace said, "faint, but rather pungent. And it seems to be coming from you." He frowned. "You didn't wet your bed, did you?"

"No, I didn't wet my bed," Wyrdrune replied in an irritated tone.

"He took a dip in the sewer," Kira said with a chuckle. "You should've used more soap."

"I used plenty of soap," Wyrdrune retorted, "but Sebastian's got a nose like a bloodhound."

"Please," said Makepeace in an offended tone. "The physical senses of faeries are far superior to those of mere domestic animals."

"Apparently, so are their appetites," said Merlin, glancing at the remains of the meal.

"Greetings, Ambrosius," Makepeace said cheerfully. "You're looking well. Have you gone through puberty yet?"

"'Allo, yourself, you bloody great whale," Billy replied. "'Ave ya busted any chairs lately?"

"Only in a rather animated discussion in an East Village taproom, my boy," Makepeace said. "A minor disagreement over the virtues of domestic versus imported beer. The other party was foolish enough to maintain that the mineral water laughingly referred to as 'light beer' was superior to—''

"Gin," one of the vaccum cleaners said in a metallic voice, laying down its cards.

"What do you mean, gin, you infernal contraption?'' Makepeace said. "We're playing *poker*!''

The vaccum cleaner whirred and clicked.

"Full house.''

"Full house, my Aunt Martha's buttocks! How do you get a full house with two threes, a deuce and a pair of jacks? You've got two pair!''

Click, whirr.

"Two pair.''

"Straight flush," said Makepeace, laying down his cards. "That'll cost you your hose and your drape cleaning attachment. Oh, never mind, here, take it all back. You need it more than I do. Go on, game's over, go suck up a hairball or something.''

The canisters picked up their attachments and clanked and whirred out of the room.

"I've been attempting to deduce what you're planning to do with all this rather bizarre paraphernalia," Makepeace said, pointing to the equipment laid out on the couch. "It's been something of a challenge. Wet suits, flashlights and firearms with laser sighting systems. You're either planning to assault a barge upon the Seine or you're going after some sort of mutant, killer snipe.''

"We're going down into the sewers to confront the Dark Ones and their acolytes," said Modred. "And you've arrived just in time to come along.''

"Into the *sewers*?" Makepeace said, aghast. "My dear boy, I'll have you know that these are three-hundred-dollar, crushed velvet trousers. I have absolutely no intention of ruining them by wading through French sewage, to say nothing of my silk socks and Cabretta leather shoes. Can't you convince them to come up and have it out like gentlemen in a somewhat more congenial location?''

"I'm afraid not," Wyrdrune said. "And we have only four

wet suits, sized for us. Besides, there isn't enough rubber in all of Paris to make one up for you. Looks like you'll have to get your feet wet."

Makepeace pushed his chair back from the table and stood, indignantly drawing himself up to his full height, which was considerable. "Well, if you think I'm going to ruin my clothes by sloshing about like Jean Valjean through the Parisian plumbing, you're very much mistaken."

"We need your help, Sebastian," Modred said. "This is serious."

"Ruining a pair of five-hundred-dollar shoes is serious," said Makepeace. He sighed. "Oh, well, if I must go wading through rat-infested sewage, I suppose style must, of necessity, make some concessions to practicality." He threw his hands up in the air and said, "Voilà!"

In an instant, his flamboyant clothes were gone and he stood attired from head to toe in a one-piece, black-trimmed, white rubber suit with a close-fitting hood and matching boots.

Wyrdrune snorted. "You look like a damn dirigible."

"Keep it up, Melvin," Makepeace said, "and I'll perform my impression of the Hindenburg disaster."

"That was a hydrogen-filled blimp, wasn't it?" said Wyrdrune, suiting up with the others. "I always had you figured for hot air. Anyway, try not to explode until we've taken care of the Dark Ones."

"How would like fire ants in your wet suit?" Makepeace said.

"That's the least of my worries," Wyrdrune said. "I'm still trying to figure out what they're going to think when we go through the lobby dressed this way."

"This hotel has catered to American tourists for centuries," said Modred. "By now, I doubt that anything would surprise them."

Half an hour later, they stood in the alley over the sewer entrance where Pascal had fled when he was shot. It was growing dark. Wyrdrune levitated the lid, moving it back out of the way to expose the ladder leading down.

"Are you ready?" Modred asked Billy.

"Right," said Billy. "Ole' Merlin's tellin' Raven that we're goin' in."

Wyrdrune grimaced. "I wish there was some other way of doing this," he said.

"There isn't," Kira said. "Go on. You first."

"Thanks," he said wryly, and started to lower himself down through the opening. He paused. "Hey, Sebastian. Think you'll fit through here? We might have a problem if you get yourself stuck."

"I have no intention of crawling down a hole like some sort of woodchuck," Makepeace said indignantly. "I'll meet you down there."

He made a flourishing gesture with his arm and vanished, teleporting down below. Once they all reached the bottom, they snapped on their flashlights to conserve their thaumaturgic energy and checked their weapons.

"All right," said Modred. "We'll retrace the route we took before, when we were following Pascal. Let's keep together. If I'm not wrong, somewhere down here is an entrance to the Catacombs. If we get close, the runestones will let us know, but keep in mind that the Dark Ones will be able to sense our presence just as we'll be able to sense theirs, so there's not much chance of our gaining the advantage of surprise. Keep the talking down and stay alert. All right, let's go."

Piccard missed Max Siegal by only a few moments. The police unit Renaud had dispatched to the scene was already waiting for him by the time that he arrived in the second unit and they had secured the premises.

"Piccard, I.T.C.," he said, showing his I.D. to the officers on the scene. "What have we got here? Have you seen Siegal?"

"They've already been and gone," the uniformed officer told him. "We took a quick look upstairs in Rienzi's apartment. We couldn't tell much. There seems to have been a struggle on the premises, but there was no sign of blood.

Merely a few pieces of furniture knocked over, several items broken, as if they'd been thrown . . . could have been a domestic argument for all we know."

"Did you question the neighbors?" asked Piccard.

"The neighbors are all elderly. No one saw or heard anything," the officer replied. He consulted his notepad. "Siegal and Rienzi, accompanied by several men, showed up about ten or fifteen minutes ago. There was a young woman with them. She had apparently been waiting at the apartment when they arrived. We have only a first name for her, Colette. According to the neighbors, who were briefly questioned by Siegal and his friends before they left, the young woman was a dancer who claimed to be a friend of the missing girl. She's described as being blond, leggy and extremely attractive. The neighbors said she was in a very agitated state over the disappearance of Suzanne Muset. Two of the people with Siegal and Rienzi identified themselves as reporters. One of them might have been with the *Tribune*. As I said, the neighbors weren't particularly helpful. We secured the scene and waited for you to arrive, as per Inspector Renaud's instructions. Other than that, I'm afraid we haven't got much."

"All right," Piccard said. "I'm going to go take a look upstairs. Which apartment is it?"

"Three-B," the officer said.

Piccard nodded. "I'll take charge of this," he said. "I want you and your partner to cruise the neighborhood and see if you can locate Siegal and the others. I want them detained. Use restraint, but if they resist, place them under arrests."

"On what charge?"

"Interfering with a homicide investigation," said Piccard. "There's reason to believe that at least one of them may have a gun, so exercise caution. I don't expect they'll give you any trouble, but you can never tell. If you find them, search them carefully, relieve them of any weapons they may have and call in. I want those people off the streets."

"Yes, sir. We'll get right on it."

As the officer and his partner got back into their unit and

pulled away, Piccard went upstairs with the two policemen he had arrived with. When they got to the apartment, he told them to wait outside and went in by himself.

There was no sign of entry having been forced. He stood inside the entryway and looked around the small apartment. A lamp had been knocked over. The coffee table was at a peculiar angle, as if someone had knocked into it and shoved it aside. There were some broken bits and pieces on the floor, ceramics of some sort that had been thrown and shattered. The carpet was rumpled, but other than that, the officer was right. There was not much that could be ascertained by a quick glance at the scene. Piccard closed his eyes and concentrated, stretching out his hands, palms out. Almost at once, he staggered and threw his arm out to steady himself against the wall. The thaumaturgic trace emanations were so strong, he was overcome by dizziness and he shook his head to clear it. He had never encountered anything so powerful before. He quickly left the apartment.

"I want this place sealed," he said. "No one goes in without my personal authorization, is that clear?"

"Yes, sir."

"You stay here and see to it," he said to one of the officers. He turned to the second one. "You come with me."

They hurried back downstairs and to the patrol unit. Piccard picked up the handset and radioed in. He was patched through to Renaud.

"Piccard here," he said. "I'm at the scene on the Rue Morgue."

"Did you find Siegal and the others?" Renaud asked.

"No, we just missed them. They couldn't have gone far. I've sent one of the units out to cruise the neighborhood and look for them, with orders to detain them and call in the moment they are found. Do you know anything about a young woman named Colette, last name unknown, a dancer, apparently an acquaintance of Suzanne Muset?"

"No, the name means nothing to me," said Renaud. "Why?"

"It seems she was waiting at the apartment when Siegal

and the others arrived. Apparently, she's with them now. They questioned the neighbors, then left. I'm not sure if it means anything or not. However, I took a look at the apartment and made a quick scan. Definite presence, stronger than anything I've ever encountered before. It almost made me black out. I'm still a little dizzy."

"What do you make of it?" Renaud asked.

"I can only guess," Piccard said, "but I'd say it seems highly probable that the victim was literally spirited away. I'm inclined to think that the disarray in the apartment was merely a blind. Given such power, she couldn't have had a chance to struggle or resist in any way. Has Raven had any contact yet?"

"Yes, she's in contact now," Renaud said, careful not to be specific over the police band. "Are you heading back in?"

"Not yet. I'm going to look around, see if I can pick up anything else. There's something bothering me about all this, something I can't quite put my finger on. We've had two murders and now an apparent kidnapping, all in the same building. There has to be a reason."

"Are there any sewer access points near you?" asked Renaud.

"Of course!" Piccard said. "I'll check."

"Get back to me as soon as you can," Renaud said.

"Right," said Piccard. "Out."

He replaced the handset and got out of the unit. "Stay here," he told the officer. "Sound the horn if they call us back."

He walked around outside the building. There was a small antique shop on the first floor, run by the old man who lived above it. Another building abutted it on the left, but on the right there was a narrow alleyway. Piccard entered it. There was a side entrance to the antique shop. The door was bolted. Just beyond it was a metal dumpster. The alley ended in a cul de sac, with wooden crates stacked up against the back wall. He closed his eyes again and extended his awareness. Once more, the sensation hit him so strongly that his head reeled. Slowly, he walked down the alley until he came to the point where the emanations were the strongest. He looked down.

"Voilà," he said softly. He was standing above a sewer access cover. It was open. As he bent down over it, something caught his eye. He reached out and picked up a torn scrap of white material. He hurried back to the patrol car.

"Give me your flashlight," he said to the officer. He radioed in again.

"Renaud? Piccard here. You were right. Definite trace emanations, leading directly to a sewer entrance in the alleyway beside the building. The grate was open and I found a torn scrap of cloth caught on the opening of the access shaft. It looks like a piece of a woman's blouse. Tell Raven I'm going down."

"You want some backup?"

"No, I'm going in alone. I'm leaving the unit stationed outside, at the entrance to the alley. If you don't hear from me in half an hour, tell Raven to inform the others."

"Be careful, Piccard."

"I fully intend to be. Over and out."

He hung up the handset, instructed the officer to remain with his unit outside the alley and let no one in, under any circumstances. Then he took the flashlight, checked his sidearm, and went down into the access shaft.

As he got off the ladder, he snapped on the flashlight and played the beam around him. He was in one of the smaller tunnels running underneath the street, standing on a narrow concrete walkway that was buckled and veined with cracks. Sewage water ran sluggishly in the channel to his right and the tunnel wall opposite him had a large fissure running the length of it. It looked about ready to collapse. It had been years since any real maintenance was done on the ancient sewer tunnels and large sections of them were structurally unsound. If the city didn't find the money to start fixing up the tunnels, they were bound to start collapsing before long. He swallowed nervously and hoped the tunnel would not collapse while he was down there. The crack looked very wide and water was seeping through it.

Once again, he felt the powerful trace emanations of thaumaturgic energy, almost as if it were a trail left for him to follow. He didn't even have to concentrate very hard to sense it. It was all around him. The entire tunnel seemed to be throbbing with it. He momentarily debated going back up and calling in, having Raven direct the others to this section of the tunnel system, but he decided to look around a little more, just to be sure. He followed the damaged concrete walkway to a point about thirty or forty yards down, where a large branch pipe joined the tunnel. He followed the trace emanations inside. They seemed even stronger now.

He bent down low, crouching over with the roof of the pipe just above his head. Scummy water eddied around his calves. He shined the flashlight beam ahead of him. He could see the far end of the branch pipe, where it connected with another tunnel about twenty-five yards ahead. He moved along the pipe and stepped out into the other tunnel, into a sewer channel that was about knee-deep. It was a junction point, where several branch tunnels met. He played his flashlight beam around the entire area. There was structural damage here, as well. A portion of the tunnel's ceiling had collapsed and there was rubble piled up in the channel. The wall beside him was veined with fissures. Water dripped. He recoiled with disgust as the slick brown bodies of several rats wriggled past him through the slime. And then he heard it. A soft whimpering. The sound of someone crying.

He moved the flashlight beam in the direction of the sound and saw a spot where a large section of the tunnel wall had collapsed, leaving a pile of debris sticking up out of the water and beyond it, a dark opening, like the entrance to a cave. And huddled inside that opening, curled up into a little ball, was a young girl.

"Suzanne?" he said.

Caught in the beam of the flashlight, she cowered before him, trembling, staring at him with wide, frightened eyes. Her hands were held up to her mouth. Her clothes were torn and dirty and her hair was wet and limp. Her bare legs were streaked with filth. Rats scurried around her on the pile of rubble.

"Is your name Suzanne?" Piccard said, moving toward her and holding out his hand. "It's all right, don't be afraid. It's all right. I've come to help you."

She scuttled back, away from him, farther back into the darkness of opening in the collapsed wall. He splashed through the water, coming closer, shining the beam ahead of him.

"Don't run away!" he said. "No one's going to hurt you. You're safe now. It's all right. Come, let me take you out of here."

He started to climb up after her, shining his flashlight beam into the opening in the wall. He couldn't see her anymore, but he could still hear her quiet, frightened sobbing.

"Come out, mademoiselle," he said. "Come, it's all right. I only want to help you. I—"

He froze as his flashlight beam caught a pair of lambent, yellow eyes. He heard a deep, animal growl and suddenly something came hurtling out of the opening, straight at him. He cried out as the beast struck him in the chest, bearing him back down into the water, and he felt its teeth tearing at his throat. The flashlight spun away into the darkness.

They were somewhere beneath the Rue de Rivoli when their runestones started glowing dimly. The tunnels here were in a greater state of disrepair than in the other sections they had passed through and often they had to make their way around the debris of partially collapsed walls and ceilings.

"This whole thing looks like it could come down at any moment," Wyrdrune said nervously. "If we have to start firing shots down here, we're liable to start a cave-in."

"Have they had any contact from Piccard?" Modred asked Billy

"No," said Billy. "It's over 'alf an 'our since 'e went down an' they 'aven't 'eard a thing. Renaud wants to know if 'e should send some men down after 'im."

"Tell him no," said Modred. "If something's happened to Piccard, the police won't be able to help him." He stopped, trying to read the faded signs marking the streets above the tunnels. "The Rue St. Roch," he said, barely making out the lettering. "You realize where we're heading, don't you? We're within blocks of where the first murders occurred, in the Rue Morgue."

Kira glanced at the runestone in her palm. It was glowing brighter. "We're getting close," she said. "Piccard must have gone down somewhere not far from here."

"The fool should have stayed out of it," said Modred, as they moved forward cautiously. "The entrance to the Catacombs has to be somewhere beneath the Rue Morgue."

"I trust it's drier in there," Makepeace said.

"You think they know we're coming?" Kira asked.

"I'm almost sure of it," said Modred. "But they haven't done anything yet. *Why?*"

"I'm not complaining," Wyrdrune replied uneasily.

"They must be planning something," Modred said. He glanced at Billy. "Renaud's had no word of Siegal and the others?"

"No sign of 'em," said Billy after a moment in which Merlin silently relayed the message. "They've got units cruisin' the entire area. It's as if they've simply disappeared."

"Great," said Wyrdrune. "I've got a real bad feeling about this." The runestone in his forehead was glowing brightly. "Something's going to happen any time now. I just know it."

Modred stopped. "Through here," he said, pointing at a branch tunnel. "Can you feel it?"

Kira nodded. "It's getting very strong," she said.

They looked at the branch pipe. There was only room for them to go through one at a time.

"They could get us in there and bring the whole thing down over our heads," said Wyrdrune. He gazed down the length of the branch pipe. "How do you feel about just teleporting through to the other side?" he asked.

"We could," said Modred, "but I'm not sure we ought

to waste our energy when we're this close. That may be exactly what they want us to do."

"They're just waiting for us, aren't they?" Kira said. "They're not even going to try to run."

"They're going to make a fight of it," said Modred. "They want the life force of the runestones. They know that if they can destroy us, nothing on earth can stop them."

"Cheerful thought," said Makepeace, eyeing the branch pipe nervously. He swallowed hard. "Well, who goes first?"

"I will," said Modred. He unholstered his pistol and racked the slide, chambering a round. He thumbed off the safety. "Watch yourselves," he said.

"We still don't know how many of them there are," said Kira.

"Well, there's only one way we're going to find out," said Modred. He bent down and entered the pipe.

Chapter
ELEVEN

The two young prostitutes they had encountered on the corner of the Rue St. Roch and the Avenue de L'Opera said they had seen a man dressed in a dark cloak with a woman answering Suzanne's description. The woman seemed to be drunk, they'd said. The man was half walking, half carrying her, supporting her with her arm around his shoulders. They'd passed by, heading down the Rue Gaillon, and gone into a brownstone near the plaza.

Rienzi had grabbed one of them by the arm, insisting that they point the building out to them. Alarmed, the girl had tried to jerk away, but Rienzi would not let go.

"Show us!" he demanded. "Show us which building!"

"Please," Max said to them. "The girl's been kidnapped. Won't you please show us where they went?"

He reached into his pocket and pulled out his wallet. He took out some bills and handed them over.

"Just point out which building they went into, that's all we ask," he said.

"Perhaps we ought to summon the police," Francois said.

"But who knows what will happen to her by the time they arrive?" Colette said in an anguished voice. "Oh, I never should have let her stay there! I should have made her move in with me after what happened to her sister and poor Gabrielle."

Rienzi and the others believed that she had worked with Suzanne at the club. When they arrived back at the apartment, they had found Colette waiting for them, in a state of high anxiety. Suzanne had called her earlier, she said, sounding very frightened. She had stepped out for a few moments, to pick up some cigarettes, and she was certain that someone had followed her back home. After all that happened, with Stefan gone, she was afraid to be alone. Colette told them that she had said she would come over right away, only when she had arrived, there was no answer at the apartment. She had tried the door and found it open. She had seen the inside of the apartment, the lamp knocked over, things lying broken on the floor, the rug bunched up as if there had been a struggle. She had just been about to go call the police when the others had arrived.

They had questioned the neighbors, but no one had seen or heard anything. They had then gone out to search the streets, but they had no luck with anyone they met until they encountered the two young prostitutes. Their description of Suzanne and what she had been wearing left no doubt in Rienzi's mind. He insisted that it had to be her. After Max had paid them, they went down the block with them and pointed out the building they had seen the dark-cloaked man go into with Suzanne.

"Perhaps Francois is right," said one of the others. "Maybe one of us should go call the police. The man who took her may be armed."

"We are armed, as well," Rienzi said, brandishing the gun that Max had given back to him. "We cannot take the chance of waiting. He may kill Suzanne."

And, as if on cue, they heard a frenzied scream come from an open window up above them.

"Up there, on the fourth floor!" Francois shouted, pointing at the window.

"You stay behind us," Max said to Colette, as they ran inside the building. With Rienzi in the lead, they took the stairs two and three at a time until they got to the fourth floor.

They heard the scream again.

"Down here!" Rienzi said, running down the corridor to his left. Colette stayed behind the rest of them. She knew exactly where they were going. They were heading toward her own apartment.

Several of the neighbors poked their heads out of their doors, but when they saw Rienzi rushing past with a gun held in his hand, they quickly shut their doors again and bolted them. Rienzi reached the door of Colette's apartment and kicked it in. They rushed inside.

It was dark.

"I can't see!"

"Someone get the lights!"

The door slammed shut behind them.

"Who closed the door?"

"Turn on the lights!"

Suddenly, torches blazed up on the walls around them.

Max and the others found themselves standing in the center of a large chamber with walls of solid rock. At regular intervals throughout the chamber, there were niches carved into the walls, stacked high with human bones. Rats scurried across the floor. Burning braziers placed around the edges of the chamber gave off a pungent, strong aroma of sickly sweet incense.

"What the hell . . . ?" said Max, looking all around him.

The others stood stunned, glancing around at their surroundings with incomprehension.

"What happened?" said one of the reporters. "Where the devil *are* we?"

"In the Catacombs, gentlemen," said Colette from behind them. They turned to see her standing with the two young prostitutes, smiling at them.

"What is this?" said Rienzi, pointing his pistol at Colette. "How did we get here? What have you done with Suzanne?"

"She's right here," said a woman's voice from the other side of the chamber. They turned and saw the Dark Ones standing behind them, dressed in long, black, hooded robes. Suzanne stood between Azreal and Balen, a vacant expression on her face. Her eyes looked glazed.

Rienzi started forward. "Suzanne!"

She did not respond.

He aimed his pistol at the three. "What have you done to her? Let her go!"

Leila swept her arm out and Rienzi cried out as the gun went flying from his grasp. They all found themselves suddenly rooted to the spot, unable to move a muscle.

"I thought you would be bringing the police," Leila said to Colette.

"These men came first," Colette replied. "They found me waiting there. I had no choice. I had to bring them."

"No matter," Leila said. "They should do just as well." She frowned and shut her eyes briefly. "We shall soon be having company," she said after a moment. She glanced at Colette. "You and the others know what to do," she said. "Go now."

"They're getting closer, Leila," Azreal said nervously. "I can feel their presence."

"Calm yourself, Azreal," she said. "Things are still proceeding according to plan. This is only a minor inconvenience, one that is easily remedied."

She made a pass with her hand and Max and the others were suddenly attired in police uniforms.

"You see?" she said.

"We're wasting time," said Balen.

"Patience," she said. "First we must bait our trap."

She stared hard at Max and the others and they felt an icy coldness seeping through them as she imposed her will on theirs. Max felt himself receding, falling away. He fought the sensation, but there was nothing he could do. Her will became his own as she possessed him. And, like the others, he knew what he had to do.

Officers Moreau and Bernajoux were slowly cruising down the street in their patrol car. Bernajoux, a lower-grade adept who studied thaumaturgy nights at the Sorbonne, was handling the driving chores, keeping the cruiser moving with his levitation and impulsion spell while Moreau flashed the searchlight into each dark alley that they passed.

"I still say there's more to this than we've been told," said Bernajoux as he guided the vehicle along. "There's been no word in the streets of any Satan cult."

"That doesn't mean there isn't one," Moreau said, peering into the alleys that they passed, shining the searchlight to illuminate the shadows.

"I'm telling you, Renaud's keeping something back from us," said Bernajoux. "The murder victims all had thaumaturgic runes carved into their bodies and now there are two agents of the I.T.C. working with the task force in a so-called advisory capacity. Doesn't that tell you anything?"

"It tells me that they think an adept might be involved, but there is as yet no proof," Moreau said. "What are you doing, searching for conspiracies?"

"I just don't like not knowing what we may be getting into," Bernajoux replied. The vehicle lurched slightly.

"Stop worrying so much and concentrate on your driving," Moreau said irritably.

"It just makes me nervous, thinking that we might be going up against a criminal adept," said Bernajoux. "We're simply not trained to handle that sort of thing."

"What's to handle?" said Moreau. "Our instructions were

clear. If we see anything suspicious, we call in. And if we spot anyone trying to murder someone on the street, we stop them, pure and simple. If they resist, then bullets will stop an adept as well as any other man. But I don't think we're looking for an adept at all. If people like that turn to crime, they don't turn to murder. Corporate crime is more their style. If you ask me, we're looking for some psycopath who's trying to make it look as if an adept or a Satan cult is responsible. It's probably someone who has it in for adepts for some strange reason. A serial killer who likes reading about himself in the newspapers and—wait. Stop the car!''

''You see something?''

''Back up, quickly! In that alley there. . . .''

Bernajoux reversed the vehicle. Moreau beamed the searchlight down into the alleyway. There were several figures back in the alley. They seemed to be bending over something.

''Hold it right there!'' Moreau said over the loudspeaker.

''Should I call in?'' asked Bernajoux, but Moreau was already getting out of the car. ''Moreau! Wait!''

Moreau had his weapon out in one hand, his flashlight in the other. He was entering the alleyway.

''God damn it,'' said Bernajoux. He quickly reached for the handset. ''Unit thirty-one, calling HQ; Unit thirty-one, calling HQ, come in!''

As Moreau approached the figures, he saw that there were two of them. Young prostitutes, no more than teenagers. They were bending over a body. In the beam of his flashlight, he could see that it was the body of a man. His shirt had been torn open and one of the girls was holding a knife. He aimed his gun at them.

''Drop the knife! Don't move!''

''*Come in, Unit thirty-one.*''

''Unit thirty-one here. We have an assault in progress at—''

Suddenly, Bernajoux heard Moreau fire two shots, and then he heard his partner scream.

"Merde!" Bernajoux was out of the car in a flash, drawing his weapon as he ran down the alley.

"Unit thirty-one, come in! Unit thirty-one, what is your location?"

Moreau was down. He was still screaming. In the darkness, Bernajoux could barely make out a figure crouching over him. Bernajoux grabbed the flashlight off his belt and snapped it on. A young girl looked up at him, illuminated in the flashlight's beam. The expression on her face was bestial. There was blood dripping from her snarling mouth. And she had fangs.

Bernajoux fired, but she threw herself to one side and he missed. He fired again, and then he saw the second one launching herself at him, screaming as she leaped through the air, higher than it seemed any human could possibly jump. He caught a glimpse of dripping fangs and clawed fingers and he fired again as she came down on him. He was borne to the ground. He felt sharp claws sinking into his shoulders and he pressed the gun against her chest and fired three more times. She jerked against him and lay still. He rolled her off him, but then the second one was on him. He caught a brief glimpse of a gleaming knife blade and then he felt the heat of it sinking to the hilt into his chest. It rose again and fell, and rose again and fell, and the gun fell from Bernajoux's limp hand as the knife kept plunging down, again and again and again. . . .

The reports started coming in from all over the city. They were coming up out of the sewers in groups of two and three and four, bedraggled, filthy street urchins, falling on anyone who happened by. The dispatchers at the task force headquarters were jammed with incoming calls. Three people slain in the Boulevard St. Martin. Two more citizens murdered in the Rue Jacob. It was as if, suddenly, some inexplicable madness had struck the homeless runaways of Paris, all at the same time, turning them into rabid, homicidal beasts. The officers of Unit 23 shot down two of them near the Quai

D'Orsay. Their report seemed unbelievable. What they had described encountering weren't children, but feral creatures that seemed only half human. Like werewolves, the stunned officers had said. And they were coming up out of the sewers and killing anyone who happened to get in their way. Two men killed in the Rue de Madrid. A woman slain in the Rue St. Antoine, three of the killers shot down by police in the Champs Elysees. And still the calls kept coming in.

"My God, how many of them *are* there?" said Renaud, unable to handle all the calls that were coming in. He got on the radio and issued orders to all units to shoot on sight and not to attempt arrest. "Tell them what's happening!" he shouted to Raven. "Tell them they're coming out all over the city! Get them back! We've got to *do* something!"

Raven sat with her eyes shut, her body rigid, her fingers clamped on the edge of the desk.

"Raven!" Renaud shouted. He took her by the shoulders and shook her. *"Raven, for God's sake!"*

She opened her eyes. "There's nothing to be done, Renaud," she said calmly. "It's all up to your men. It's a diversion."

"A diversion! People are dying out there!"

"The only chance we have now is for them to stop the Dark Ones," Raven said. "This is it. Brace yourself. Whatever happens, we'll know in the next few moments."

They stepped out of the branch pipe into the next tunnel. It was a junction point, where several other tunnels met in a large, circular area. In the beams of their flashlights, they could see that portions of the ceiling had collapsed and the walls were veined with fissures. Rubble lay piled up in the sewer channels and across from them, an entire section of the wall had fallen in, revealing a darkness beyond.

"This is it," said Modred. "That has to be the way into the Catacombs!"

As they slowly waded through the water toward the opposite side, Billy suddenly spoke up.

"It's Raven," he said. "She says there's acolytes comin'

up all over the city, through the sewer grates. They're killin' everyone in sight. There's a bloody war goin' on up there!''

"They're trying to draw us off," said Modred.

"We've got to do something," Kira said.

"We are doing something!" Modred snapped back. "Can't you feel it? Can't you feel how close they are?"

"What the . . . Jesus Christ!" said Wyrdrune, springing back as something in the water floated up against him.

"What is it?" Kira said, spinning around.

There was a body floating in the water.

"It's Piccard," said Wyrdrune. "His throat's been torn out."

"Look out!" said Modred. He shined his light across the tunnel. Kira turned quickly, the red beam of her laser sight lancing out. A red dot appeared on the chest of one of the men moving toward them.

"Don't shoot! Police!"

Several uniformed officers were moving toward them.

"What the hell are you doing down here?" demanded Modred.

"We were sent down to assist," said Francois as they moved closer. "What's happened here?"

"It's agent Piccard," said Wyrdrune. "He's dead."

"Dead?" said Francois, moving closer with the others. "How?"

"His throat's been torn out," Makepeace said.

"You men had better get out of here, right now," said Modred.

"We came to help," said Max as they kept moving closer.

"There's nothing you can do," said Modred. "Get out of here!"

"Now just hold on a minute," said Francois. "We've got our orders. We were given specific instructions to—"

"Renaud!" said Raven. "Have you sent any men down into the sewers?"

"What? No, of course not."

"You didn't send any men down after Piccard?"

"No. Why, what's—''

"Merlin! Renaud gave no orders for anyone to go down into the sewers! Look—''

"—*out*!'' shouted Billy. The laser sight put a red dot on Francois's shoulder and Billy fired. Francois fell back into the water as the others lunged forward.

Billy heard a growl behind him and turned just in time to see a huge black wolf come springing down at him from a mound of debris. He fired and missed as the beast struck him and they fell back into the water.

"I've lost contact!'' Raven said.

Renaud had no time for her. He was at the switchboard, busy issuing orders as calls continued to come in from patrol units all over the city.

Modred brought his gun up, but Rienzi was too close. As Modred fired, he knocked his gun aside and bore him down into the water, fingers that had become claws reaching for his throat. They were shapechanging, their faces sprouting hair, their snarling mouths revealing fangs. Red laser beams crisscrossed the tunnel as Kira's shotgun roared and one of the men went down, but they had gotten too close and Max leaped upon her, driving her down beneath the water. Make-peace took a deep breath and exhaled, blowing two of the creatures backward with hurricane force. Wyrdrune got two shots off, wounding one of them before two more bore him down and he found himself thrashing in the scummy water, trying to dislodge the beasts as they forced his head under.

"*Now*,'' said Leila with a smile.

"Raven,'' Jacqueline said, grabbing the sorceress's hand. "Raven, you've got to get me down there! Please!''

"I . . . I've lost contact. I don't know what's happening. . . .''

"They're in trouble, Raven! Concentrate! Get through to Merlin! *Try!*"

Raven stood up. "Take my hand," she said.

Renaud was oblivious to them as he shouted orders to the dispatchers, sending back-up units to sites where reports of assaults were coming in. Sirens screamed across the city as units converged on areas where the acolytes were spotted and the police were shooting them down as they charged in blood-crazed frenzy.

"Raven!" he shouted. "Raven, what the hell's happening down there?"

He turned.

"Raven?"

But Raven and Jacqueline had disappeared.

The wolf snapped at Billy's throat as they thrashed in the water, then squealed with pain as Billy drove his knife deep into its shoulder. It raked his chest with its claws, then leaped away, plunging through the water and leaping up onto the rubble. It jumped across to the walkway and ran with a limp into one of the branch pipes.

"Oh, no, you don't," snarled Billy, sloshing through the water after it.

"*Billy, don't—*" said Merlin's voice inside his mind.

"Lay off, old man!" shouted Billy. "'E's mine!"

"*Billy, not now! Raven's trying to get through. . . .*"

But Billy was already scrambling up onto the pile of rubble, leaping down onto the walkway and plunging through the branch pipe after Michel. Merlin, in astral contact with the sorceress, could do nothing to stop him as he sped down the tunnel, his short height allowing him to run full speed without having to bend over. He came out the other side in time to see Michel, in human form, splashing through the sewer channel. He made a flying dive and brought him down.

Michel, his naked skin slick with the slimy water, slipped out of his grasp and they fought in the knee-deep water, struggling for the knife. Michel was wounded in the shoulder, but he was larger and his desperate fury gave him strength.

As they struggled, his features started to transform. An animal growl rumbled up from deep in his throat and hair started sprouting from his face. His ears extended and developed furry tufts, claws sprouted from his fingers and his bared teeth lengthened into fangs. He drove a hairy knee into Billy's groin and twisted the knife out of his grasp as Billy grunted and doubled over with pain. With a snarl, he drove the knife with all his might at Billy's midsection . . . and suddenly there was a blinding flash of white light from the fire opal stone in Billy's ring and the knife blade glanced off solid steel.

Michel backed off, stunned, as the doubled-over form of Billy was suddenly replaced by a large and powerful knight in full armor. Gorlois slowly straightened up, towering over him, and Michel stared fearfully at the dull green light that came from behind the slit in the steel helmet's visor.

"No. . . ." said Michel, shaking his head. "No, please . . . don't. . . ."

He threw the knife, but the blade struck the visor with a clang and glanced off. Michel turned and fled.

Gorlois slowly drew his broadsword as Michel splashed panic-stricken through the water. He drew back his arm and hurled the blade. It whistled through the air and struck the werewolf in the back, penetrating through his chest. Michel fell facedown into the water, the weight of the sword rolling him over to float on his back, the bloody sword point protruding from his chest like a small mast. In death, he slowly reverted back to human form, his sightless eyes staring up at the roof of the tunnel.

Modred drove his fist into Rienzi's face and he fell back into the water. Modred had lost both his flashlight and his weapon, as had Wyrdrune and Kira. Makepeace held out his arms, sweeping them outward in an arc, and a glowing arch appeared beneath the roof of the tunnel, illuminating the entire area. And then he saw them, standing in the huge fissure in the wall that led into the Catacombs. Three figures cloaked in dark robes.

"Modred, look out!" he shouted.

Leila hurled a powerful bolt of thaumaturgic energy and it struck Modred in the chest, picking him up and hurling him all the way across the tunnel. He struck the wall with tremendous force and collapsed onto the walkway. Pain exploded in his head and he teetered on the edge of consciousness.

"No! God damn it, no!"

The runestone in his chest blazed and he felt its revitalizing power coursing through him.

At the same moment, the emerald in Wyrdrune's forehead flashed and a beam of force shot out from it, striking the men holding him down and throwing them back into the water. Balen extended his arms, fingers splayed wide apart, energy crackling around them. An amorphous red mass formed in the air and flew toward Wyrdrune like an airborne ameoba, undulating and expanding as it hurtled at him. It washed over him and Wyrdrune cried out as he was wreathed in a crackling crimson aura that lifted him up out of the water and held him struggling in midair as he screamed with pain, feeling the life force of the Dark One inundating him, trying to drain him of his soul. Makepeace inhaled deeply and the aura was sucked away from Wyrdrune, releasing him to fall with a splash into the water. Then Makepeace exhaled, blowing the undulating red cloud back toward the necromancers. Balen threw up his hand quickly and a spout of water shot up from the channel, extinguishing the pulsating cloud before it could reach him.

Kira thrashed beneath the water as Max held her down, his powerful hands squeezing her throat. She raised her hand up out of the water and the runestone flashed. A bright blue flash of energy exploded in Max's eyes and he cried out, releasing her and bringing his hands up to his face. She came up, coughing, gasping for breath, and was struck in the chest by a powerful beam of force as Azreal directed all his energy at her, throwing her back into the water.

As Modred struggled to his feet, Leila stretched her arms out to finish him off, but in that moment, Raven and Jacqueline appeared, standing on the walkway across the tunnel.

Jacqueline held her gun out in both hands and fired four rapid shots at Balen. They struck him in the chest and threw him back into the darkness of the fissure. Raven held out her arms and sent a bolt of energy at Leila. It struck her and she staggered, then turned toward Raven with a snarl and hurled a ball of fire straight back at her. It struck the sorceress and burst, wreathing her in flame. Raven screamed and fell into the sewer channel. Clouds of steam billowed up as she struck the water.

"*Kira!*" Modred shouted. He tore open his wet suit and a crimson beam shot out from his gleaming ruby runestone, striking Kira's upraised palm. Another beam shot out from her sapphire runestone and lanced across the tunnel, striking the glowing emerald in Wyrdrune's forehead. A third beam blazed forth from the emerald runestone, shooting back to Modred and their energies were united in the Living Triangle as the flashing pyramid of power was formed, rising over them and filling the entire tunnel with a blinding light that strobed with crackling bolts of green and red and blue.

"*No!*" shouted Leila, springing to her feet and pushing Azreal forward as she scrambled back into the entrance to the Catacombs.

Azreal screamed as the energy of the Living Triangle enveloped him. His cloak burst into flame and his screams echoed through the tunnel as the flesh melted from his bones.

Throughout the city, the Dark Ones' acolytes dropped in their tracks as Leila desperately summoned up a final spell. Her form shifted and her features seemed to flow as she dropped down to all fours and became transformed into a sleek and sinewy jaguar. With a powerful leap, she took off running down the corridor as a rumbling echoed through the subterranean chamber and the ceiling of the tunnel behind her fell in. The walls crumbled, sealing the passageway behind her.

"Max!" said Jacqueline, splashing through the water toward him. "Max, are you all right?"

"Jacqueline?" he said.

"It's me, Max," she said. "It's all right. You're safe. It's over now."

"Jacqueline . . ." he said, groping for her blindly. "What happened? I can't see!"

There was a rumbling all around them.

"Look out!" shouted Wyrdrune. "It's all coming down!"

The walls and ceiling of the tunnel started to collapse. Debris rained down into the water around them as the ceiling buckled and fell in on them. Kira dragged Raven up out of the water and pulled her back toward the shelter of a branch pipe. Wyrdrune scrambled to Jacqueline's side and together, supporting Max between them, they hurried toward one of the connecting tunnels, Makepeace forming a protective shield of force around them. Modred covered his head with his hands as concrete rained down upon him, splashing into the sewer channel and filling the tunnel with a cloud of dust. Moments later, it was over. A large part of the ceiling had fallen in and several of the tunnel walls had collapsed completely, leaving them in darkness filled with swirling concrete dust.

"Kira!" Wyrdrune shouted.

"I'm all right," she called back from inside the branch pipe where she crouched over the sorceress. "But Raven's hurt. She's been badly burned. Where's Modred?"

"I'm right here," he said, struggling to push his way out of a pile of debris. His arms and face were cut and bleeding, and his chest was burned and blistered where Leila's bolt of energy had struck. Parts of the rubber wet suit had melted into his skin. He groaned with pain and stumbled to his feet. He shut his eyes and drew a ragged breath, but he could already feel the runestone healing him.

"Hold on," Makepeace called out to them. "I'll give us some light."

He held out his hands, fingers spread wide, and tiny, sparkling particles formed in the air, floated out into the center of the tunnel and hovered like a swarm of multicolored fireflies, illuminating the area around them. Rienzi and several of the men who'd come with Max stood around, dazed, not knowing what had happened or how they'd got there.

Modred limped through the turbid water to where the others were. He paused by the bullet-riddled body of Balen, lying crumpled and broken beneath a mound of concrete and collapsed steel beams. The body of the necromancer was rapidly decomposing, turning to dust right before his eyes. Nothing remained of Azreal.

"Did we get them all?" asked Wyrdrune.

Modred gazed at the debris sealing off the entrance to the Catacombs. "No," he said. "The third one got away. Perhaps she was buried in the cave-in."

"Where's Billy?" Wyrdrune asked.

"He went after the werewolf," Kira said. "Down that pipe over there . . ." She turned and her voice trailed off as she saw that the entrance to the pipe was buried behind a pile of fallen debris. "Oh, no . . ." she said.

Suddenly, the mound of rubble burst outward with tremendous force and an armored knight stepped out into the tunnel. He straightened up and Rienzi's jaw dropped open as he saw the huge figure standing only several feet away from him. He squeezed his eyes shut and opened them again, but the knight was gone and Billy stood in his place.

"Gor'blimey, what a mess," he said, looking around. "D'we win?"

Sergeant Legault stood inside an alleyway with three other officers, staring down at the bodies of Colette and three scruffy teenagers, two boys and a girl. Behind them, paramedics were busy patching up a young man while two other officers were trying to calm his hysterical girlfriend. The young man's nose was broken and his eyes were puffed and swollen. His lip was cut and his ear was bleeding. He had been badly beaten and his shirt had been torn open. The blood from the wounds in his chest and stomach had soaked his clothes and left sticky red trails on his skin.

The two young people had left a nearby nightclub and were walking back to their apartment when they were suddenly set upon by four inhuman-looking creatures who came leaping at them out of the shadows and dragged them back into the alley. A passing unit had responded to their frenzied screams and as the officers rushed into the alley, the attackers had turned from their intended victims and launched themselves at the policemen, who had emptied their weapons into them.

"I don't understand," one of the officers said to Legault as he stared down at the bodies. "They weren't human! They were . . . *monsters*! I saw with my own eyes!"

As the paramedics placed the wounded young man on a stretcher and loaded him into the ambulance, helping his girlfriend in after him, the officer speaking with Legault shook his head in utter bafflement.

"We did not shoot children!" he insisted. "You must believe me, Sergeant!"

"I believe you," said Legault.

"It's a nightmare. You should have seen them. They were not like this. They were. . . ." His voice trailed off.

Legault merely nodded.

"It *was* necromancy, wasn't it?" one of the other officers said. "It had to be. There's no other explanation."

Legault said nothing.

"The media is going to have a field day with this," the third officer said. "Some kind of satanic murder cult, transformed by necromancy, suddenly coming up out of the sewers and attacking everyone in sight. And who knows how many more of them might be hiding down there?"

"I don't think that there are anymore," Legaualt said. "And if there were, then they have probably reverted back to normal, like the others we have captured."

"What I don't understand is why," the first policeman said. "*Why* did they do it? What was the point? There had to be a reason!"

"When you're dealing with insanity," Legault said, "there's not always a reason. At least not one that we could understand. In any case, it makes no difference. It's out of our hands now. The I.T.C. will be wrapping up the case." He took a deep breath and exhaled heavily. "And if you ask me, they're more than welcome to it. I've had enough for one night. And for many, many sleepless nights to come.''

He turned and started walking slowly back to the patrol car.

Epilogue

It was morning and they all sat in their hotel suite with Renaud, waiting for the limousine that would take them to the airport. Their bags were packed and sitting by the door and, though they hadn't had a chance to see very much of Paris except what lay beneath the city streets, they were all anxious to get home.

"I've spoken with the doctors at the hospital," Renaud said, "and they assure me that Raven will recover. Her burns were quite severe, but with the aid of rest and thaumaturgic treatments, she should be fit enough to return to duty within six to eight months.

"I'm relieved to hear that," Kira said. "For a while there, I wasn't sure she'd make it."

"She's strong and she's a fighter," said Renaud. "She'll make it."

"What about Max Siegal and the others?" Wyrdrune asked.

"Three of them did not survive," Renaud said. "We found their bodies buried in the collapsed tunnel. The street above it buckled for almost a block and the entire area has had to be closed off until repairs can be effected. If nothing else, at least this will ensure that the city finally gets around to repairing the dilapidated sewer system. It's been long overdue. As for the Catacombs, they're sealed off once again. If there are any other entrances, they will be discovered in the process of the inspection for the repair work and they will be sealed off, as well. I expect we may find some more bodies down there before we're through. As for Siegal, Rienzi and the others who survived, well, they were very lucky. The ones you wounded in your struggle will recover. None of them remember anything about what happened. And perhaps that's all for the best.''

"What about Max's eyes?" asked Kira with concern. "Will he be able to see again?"

"Eventually," Renaud said. "But it will take some time. Fortunately, the damage wasn't permanent. The doctors say that his vision will return over a period of months, slowly and in stages. First, he will be able to perceive some light, then shadowy images, and in time, with treatment, his vision should be restored to normal. But it will be a long time before he will be able to paint again.''

"I'm sorry," Kira said with a rueful grimace. "I wish it didn't have to happen.''

"Ironically, he doesn't really seem to mind that much," Renaud said. "I've spoken with Jacqueline. She's remaining with him, to take care of him until his vision is restored. She said that once he found out that the damage wasn't permanent, he was, obviously, enormously relieved, but he believes that he can benefit from the experience. He says that it will give him time to think, to look inward. He says that he can see colors in his mind and he will paint in mental images, without the aid of brush or canvas. And, in the meantime, he said that this experience—which will officially be described as an accident—will increase the value of his work, not that he needs to worry about money. And it will also give him more time to spend with Jacqueline, which seems to be the most important thing to him right now.''

"I'm sure it's important to Jacqueline, as well," said

Modred. "Perhaps more important than she knows right now, but she will find that out soon enough. She's done more than her share. Her life could use a change."

"I agree," said Renaud. "Let us just hope it is a change for the better, away from her previous activities. I would be extremely happy never to have to hear her name again in my official capacity."

"So how is the official disposition of the case going to read?" asked Wyrdrune.

"Due to Raven's condition, Sergeant Legault and I will be assisting in the preparation of the I.T.C. report," Renaud replied. "As a matter of fact, I should be getting back to headquarters to meet with the agents who've been assigned to the disposition of the case. There is no way, regrettably, to avoid the mention of necromancy. Too many people have died in too unmistakable a manner and the media will be hounding us for details. But officially, the report will read that the killings were perpetrated by a satanic murder cult which hid under the streets of Paris and met somewhere in the Catacombs. The renegade adept who organized and led them has not been found and it is presumed that he perished in the cave-in. Perhaps we will eventually discover a body that is suitably unidentifiable and, by process of elimination, we will establish that it must have been the missing adept. Of the Dark Ones there will, of course, be no official mention. Only Legault and I have knowledge of that information and we will keep it to ourselves. And there will be no mention of yourselves, either. The battle beneath the streets of Paris took place between the cult and agents Raven and Piccard. Raven was seriously injured and Piccard lost his life in the line of duty. You were never involved."

"We appreciate that," said Wyrdrune.

"And I will appreciate being kept informed of how I can get in touch with you again. Strictly unofficially, of course. I doubt that I shall ever sleep easily after all this. Please don't misunderstand, but nothing would please me more than to never have to contact you again."

"I quite understand," said Modred. "But even if we do

not have to return to Paris, there may come a time when we may have to contact you, either for information or to have someone vouch for us."

"You may count on my full cooperation, to the best extent of my ability," Renaud said. "What worries me the most is that missing necromancer. What if she didn't perish in the cave-in?"

"Then, undoubtedly, our paths will cross again," said Modred. "If not in France, then somewhere else. If she survived, I strongly doubt she will remain in Paris. She will flee somewhere else, to gather new acolytes around her, perhaps to seek out others of her kind. And, sooner or later, we will meet Leila again."

"I do not envy you your task," Renaud said. "Well, I'd best be getting back." He stood and offered his hand to each of them. As he took Modred's hand, he smiled wryly. "Who would have thought that I would ever be shaking hands with Morpheus himself, and wishing him a *bon voyage*?"

Modred smiled. "Morpheus is dead," he said. "And Modred gratefully accepts your hand in friendship."

The phone rang and Makepeace picked it up. "The limo has arrived," he said.

Kira sighed. "I always wondered if I'd ever get to Paris," she said. "Somehow, this was not what I expected. I didn't even get to see the Eiffel Tower."

"Believe me, you didn't miss much," said the broom, coming into the room carrying a pile of boxes in its arms. "A bunch of girders and an elevator. Big deal. But at least the view wasn't half bad."

"Good God, Broom, what *is* all that stuff?" asked Wyrdrune.

"I just bought a few things," said the broom.

"What things?" Kira glanced at the labels on the boxes. "Broom, these are all designer originals!"

"Designer originals!" said Wyrdrune. "That stuff must have cost a fortune! Who are they for?"

"They're for me," the broom said.

"For *you*?" said Wyrdrune with disbelief. "But Broom, you don't wear clothes!"

"*Nu*? So I'll hang them in the closet and look at them every now and then," the broom said defensively. "What was I supposed to do, come back from Paris without a thing to wear?"

Kira giggled.

Wyrdrune put his hand up to his eyes and groaned. "I don't believe it," he said. "We come to Paris and the broom sees all the sights and goes on a shopping spree while we wind up in the sewer."

"So what can I tell you?" the broom said, with a shrug. "*C'est la vie* boychik. *C'est la vie.*"